FADE
TO DEAD

THE FIRST BOOK IN THE JESSICA WIDEACRE SERIES

FADE TO DEAD

TARA MOORE

URBANE
Publications

urbanepublications.com

First published in Great Britain in 2016 by Urbane Publications Ltd
Suite 3, Brown Europe House, 33/34 Gleaming Wood Drive, Chatham, Kent ME5 8RZ
Copyright © Tara Moore, 2016

The moral right of Tara Moore to be identified as the author of this work has been
asserted in accordance with the Copyright, Designs and Patents Act of 1988.

A CIP catalogue record for this book is available from the British Library.

ISBN 978-1-910692-77-6
EPUB 978-1-910692-78-3
KINDLE 978-1-910692-79-0

Design and Typeset by Julie Martin
Cover by The Invisible Man

urbanepublications.com

FSC

The publisher supports the Forest Stewardship Council® (FSC®), the leading international forest-certification organisation.
This book is made from acid-free paper from an FSC®-certified provider. FSC is the only
forest-certification scheme supported by the leading environmental organisations, including Greenpeace.

For my mother and father.
Always my inspiration.

ACKNOWLEDGEMENTS

"Walking with a friend in the dark is better than walking alone in the light." So said Helen Keller, and, indeed, I walked with many friends 'in the dark' as I worked on this, my first thriller. Since to list them all would mean writing another book, I will simply say thank you to all those who encouraged, supported and propped me up with wine and good advice along the way. I would, however, like to single out just a few who were particularly unstinting with their time: my husband, David Moore and my brother-in-law, Kevin Moore; my two sons, Tarek and Emmet; friends, Kate Hamlyn, Val Sullivan, Mary and Eric Bartholomew and Diane Simpson. Thanks also to my terrific editor, Sean Costello, and to Matthew Smith at Urbane Publications, with whom I hope to have a very long and fruitful relationship (in the writing sense). Final thanks go to the lovely readers who are my motivation for getting up to write each day.

The girl was pretty, but way too skinny for his own tastes. Now him, he preferred them curvy: big tits, big arses, a Jessica Rabbit handful. She was young too, barely legal, just the way the boss liked them. He picked his teeth with a broken thumbnail and squinted across from the opposite side of the street. One week he'd been watching her now, huddled in her usual spot on London Bridge, a piece of old cardboard all that stood between her and the freezing pavement. A bitter, sleet-bearing wind blew up along the Thames. Ignored by the commuter herd stampeding home from the City, he saw her shiver and cross her stick-like arms for warmth. Only once did he see someone drop a coin into the plastic beaker beside her, then quicken their step as though ashamed of the charitable impulse. Moments later, a careless foot sent the cup reeling. The solitary coin inside rolled across the pavement, over the edge and into the gurgling drain below. The girl broke then, dropped her head into her hands. Casually, he crossed the street.

CHAPTER ONE

DI Jessica Wideacre drew in a deep breath and steadied herself with a mental count from one to five. After sixteen years in the force she'd seen countless bodies, visited countless murder sites, but nothing inured her to the horror when the victim was a child or, as in this case, little more than a child. She hoped it never would.

"Who found her?" Her voice was strong, all signs of emotion professionally reined in.

"A man out walking his dog. Isn't it always?" DS Hennessy, a sickly cast to his ruddy countenance, shrugged himself deeper into his heavy parka and scrunched his face up against the needles of rain slanting in from the east. "Hardy beggars. Nights like this, Bonzo could shit himself inside out, for all I care."

The sergeant was a corpulent man, leading Jessica to suspect poor Bonzo spent more than his fair share of time in a state of great discomfort. She tossed a soggy red curl out of her eye and went to kneel beside the body. Saturated by several days' worth of rain, the grass squelched beneath her, soaking the knees of her trousers. She leaned in for a closer examination, and cloudy brown eyes gazed sightlessly back.

Hennessy bristled as she reached across to close the young girl's eyelids. Hennessy was do-it-by-the-book old school. She flashed him an unapologetic glare. "She's somebody's daughter." Given recent weather conditions, she doubted much in the way of evidence would have been preserved anyway.

Percussive, the rain continued to lash down, dancing across the small, naked body. The girl's dirty-blonde hair fanned out around her head in an arc, weighted round the edges by carefully placed stones. If her killer turned out to be The Director, then Jessica knew hair extensions would have been added to satisfy some sick urge in the creepy bastard. It was part of his m.o. to give his victims a makeover before putting a sickening end to their young lives.

"Poor kid." Her voice was low. "Looks like our man, all right. Far as I can see, she's been strangled, but not before he had his fun with her." Anger fuelled her impatience. "Where the hell are forensics?"

"A call's gone out to Shackleton. She should be here any minute." The sergeant jerked his head to where a middle-aged man, a golden Labrador in tow, stood talking to a young WPC. "Want a word with the dog-walker?"

The man looked strained, nervous. Jessica watched him rake his fingers through his thinning hair over and over again, reprising what was probably a childhood ritual of comfort. She rose to her feet and strolled across. He looked as though he might have been crying, though it was difficult to tell with the rain coming down in torrents. She hoped he had. The girl deserved crying over.

He had nothing to add to his story. Millie had run away into a thicket. He'd called and whistled for her but, in the end, he'd had to go looking. His voice cracked. He wished to God he hadn't. "How will I ever sleep again?" he asked Jessica piteously. "How will I ever get her face out of my mind? Oh, God! Oh God! Oh God!"

He wouldn't, Jessica thought. The memory would stay with him, would haunt him till the day he died. Her eyes would haunt him. In vain he'd wish he could turn back the clock; that, to paraphrase Hennessy, he'd stayed indoors and left Millie to shit herself inside out. She patted his sleeve – there, there. Small comfort, but all she could offer. For many years, her own dreams had become the meeting place of the dead. You learned to live with it, or not. There were some she knew who had not. Times like now, she envied them. Stop the world, I want to get off.

"You've got his statement?" she asked the WPC, who nodded and patted her notebook. "Good, then take him home. We'll have him in tomorrow to go through it in more detail but, right now …" Her voice trailed off.

As the WPC drove away with the shaken man staring wanly from the back seat, Laura Shackleton's 4 x 4 slewed almost sideways into its place. Jessica jumped backwards as the wheels spurted up mud. For a woman standing little more than five foot tall and weighing in sopping wet at around eight stone, it was an unlikely vehicle. Jessica smothered a grin as the door opened and Laura Shackleton swung out of it, dropping several inches to the ground. Her petite, child-like stature tended to bring out the protective instinct in big strong men. The urge passed swiftly when they realised that, beneath the Dresden figurine appearance, the forensic pathologist's balls were way bigger than theirs. Jessica and her had history. They'd got off on the wrong foot, but time had forged both tolerance and respect, and now they rubbed along well enough together. Kept it professional. Jessica passed her a set of protective clothing as Laura came straight to the point.

"The Director? Bastard been busy again?" She began to shrug herself into the paper overalls, rolling up the sleeves several times. Ditto the legs, which she tucked into Spiderman welly boots, probably obtained from the children's department at M & S. She leaned down and pulled a couple of plastic shoe-protectors over the bottoms.

"At a guess, "Jessica said. "The body bears all the usual hallmarks. Strangled, tortured, left breast hacked off, posed like a silly shampoo advert, but no calling card that I could see. Might be beneath her, though. He always leaves a calling card. Unless we've got ourselves a copycat, though I suspect it's too early for that. We've managed to keep most of the sordid details from the press so far."

The pathologist nodded. Jessica was known to run a tight ship. If any of her team was so foolish as to blab to the papers, they'd be out on their ear so fast they'd feel the g-force turning their brains inside out. She snapped on some latex gloves, the smallest size, which still flapped like empty balloons at the end of her fingers. Hennessy and the rest of the team fell back, as she began her tour of inspection, walking round the body in a circle, then squatting down for closer examination. She spoke into a digital voice recorder.

"Body is that of a young female, aged between fifteen and eighteen. Relatively fresh still. Time of death estimated to be not much more than four, five hours tops. Little in the way of lividity. Rigor mortis unapparent. Ligature marks around the neck indicative of strangulation. Obvious signs of torture. Left breast has been inexpertly removed." She indicated the ragged flesh to the onlookers. "At a guess, I'd say a switchback blade or some such." She picked up one of the dead girl's hands, examined it both sides. "Restraint marks round both wrists and ankles. Evidence of bruising to thighs; further examination required to determine if sexual interference took place. Little blood, even allowing for rainfall. Suspect victim killed elsewhere and the body dumped on site." She clicked off the recorder and jumped nimbly to her feet. "Okay, let's get her bagged, tagged and back to the morgue. I'll start work right away." She grinned impishly, turning a plainish face almost pretty. "George Clooney'll just have to take a rain check tonight. That's what happens when you date a career woman."

Jessica grinned back, but only in a half-hearted fashion. There was little chance of her seeing her own bed any time soon. First step would be to try and identify the dead girl, trawl through the misspers database, see if anyone fitting the victim's description had been reported missing. Assuming they got a match, her next job would be to land up on some unsuspecting parents' door, bearing the kind of news no one should ever have to hear. Aside from seeing murdered youngsters, informing the relatives was the one part of her job she truly loathed. As a DI, she could have outsourced it, fobbed it off on someone of lesser rank. But no rookie deserved to have such a weight thrust upon their shoulders, and the bereaved deserved handling with the sort of care gleaned only from bitter experience.

Jessica took out her mobile phone and called her home number. "David," she said, when her husband picked up. "Look, I know this is a real pain, but I'm going to have to cancel our date-night." She angled the phone away as her husband erupted in an angry tirade. She didn't need to look at the team to know that to a man they were all earwigging. "Yes," she said, when she could finally get a word in edgewise. "I do know you've gone to a lot of trouble, but it's really not my fault. David?" Silence. He'd hung up on her. Stone-faced, Jessica stowed the phone in her pocket. Inside, though, she was raging, but it was a guilt-ridden rage and she wasn't quite sure where exactly to direct it. At herself for letting him down again? At her husband for laying the guilt trip on her, when there was genuinely nothing she could do? It wasn't like she could wave ta-ta to the team. *Bye all. I'm off to wine and dine with my husband and, afterwards, bonk like a couple of sex-starved bunnies.* Disconsolate, her gaze went to where the young girl's body, now encased in an ugly grey body bag, was being loaded into the back of a private ambulance. Her real anger, of course, was reserved for The Director. Not only was the bastard hell-bent on murdering random girls, he was hell-bent on murdering her marriage too.

CHAPTER TWO

"There's nothing random about these victims."

Jessica suppressed a yawn as Robert Edwards, the forensic profiler, went into his spiel. His voice was dry as warped timbre. He had a real knack for turning what could have been a fascinating topic into something akin to the shipping forecast. "The killer has a definite type. The girls are all of an age, young adolescents, blonde, skinny and, most importantly, available." In case they were too obtuse to figure it out for themselves, he went over to the whiteboard, where pictures of the victims were pinned up in the order in which they were found, and tapped each one. "Melanie Potts, sixteen, a runaway from a care home. Jordan Flynn, another runaway, this time from home. Allegations of abuse by her stepfather." Edwards had a wide mouth. He stretched it into a kind of grimace. "Poor kid. Out of the frying pan …" He moved on to the next picture. Tap went his map-pointer finger. "Tara James. Barely sixteen and already on the game. Track marks on her arms. Started out by smoking weed with her mother when she was only nine, if you can believe it."

Jessica could well believe it. Some people weren't fit to have kids. It wasn't PC to admit it, but sometimes in the dark place of her soul, rarely visited even by herself, she thought there might be a real case for eugenics.

Edwards moved on to the most recent victim. He tapped twice beneath her photograph, as if for emphasis. "Kerrie Gray. A different scenario, in as much as Kerrie came from a well-to-do, non-dysfunctional family. Nice house in the Surrey commuter belt. Father a well respected GP. One sibling, a brother studying law at Cambridge. They worshipped the ground she walked on."

"Didn't they but!" Jessica thought, flinching as she recalled the screams of Kerrie's mother when she broke the news that their pretty little daughter had the dubious distinction of becoming The Director's fourth victim. Her father had simply stood there, staring in disbelief, before remembering his manners and inviting Jessica to sit down. "There's chocolate digestives," he'd said, clearly in shock, his mind quite unable to process the devastating news. "Coffee, or would you prefer Earl Grey?"

"They didn't like her boyfriend," Jessica filled in the team. "Young lad, black, lives in south London. Fill in the gaps."

"Not good enough for my daughter," Hennessy huffed.

"Something like that," Jessica agreed. "They had a massive row. Kerrie emptied her savings account, packed a small bag and took the train from Dorking to London. Who knows what happened then? The five days between her leaving home and her body turning up remain a mystery."

"Anyone interview the boyfriend?" That was Connors. DS Sarah Connors, so eager for her boss's job, Jessica swore she could feel the woman's breath scorching her heels.

"Only a quick prelim," DC Liversedge, the youngest member of the team volunteered. Mixed race, tall and bendy as a rubber band, he had one of those affable apple-cheeked faces that made him look ten years younger than his actual age of twenty-eight. "He's just got back from a short trip to Majorca with his girlfriend. His real girlfriend! He claims to know nothing about Kerrie's death. Claims she was just an easy source of money. They met at a concert in the O2, some rapper, Pee Jay. Jay Tee?"

"Jay-Z," Connors corrected smartly. "Where have you been living, under a rock?

Jessica refrained, but only just, from rolling her eyes. At thirty-four, Sarah was a mere two years younger than herself, but tried to kid herself she was down with the kids – cool, hip, or even hip hop.

DC Liversedge kissed his teeth in an exaggerated fashion. "Listen up, Connors. Just cos me Daddy Jamaican, don't mean manz all reggae, rap 'n' rice and peas."

Hennessy, the oldest member of the team and self-appointed patriarch, fried them both with a glare. "So it was the age-old cliché, bad boy from the wrong side of the tracks attraction," he remarked, when order had been restored. He licked his lips across a Rizla paper, tapped the ends of a rollie and added it to the line of small white sausages accumulating on his desk. Every first of January Hennessy gave up smoking. The following day, he took it up again.

"Clichés are called clichés for a reason," Jessica said. "Still, I've got a feeling Nimrod ...", she paused, while everybody snorted out a laugh. "Nimrod Peters may not be telling us everything. So, I'm popping out shortly for a word in his shell-like. She nodded to Liversedge. "Sedgie, you come with me."

The profiler cleared his throat. "The Peters boy is not your killer."

Jessica's lips narrowed. He was trying her patience. She lined him up in her cross hairs, took aim and fired off a verbal volley. "So, who the hell is, then? Name? Number? Rank?"

Edwards grated out a laugh. "If I knew the answer to that, I'd be sunning myself now on a Mediterranean island on the proceeds of my winning Lotto ticket." He bent her the kind of condescending look that made her want to pulp his face. "Profiling, DI Wideacre, is not an exercise in clairvoyance. I can't give you any of the aforementioned details. All that I can tell you, based on the information amassed from similar cases is that, most likely, he's aged somewhere between twenty-five and forty-five. He's educated, well-spoken, white-collar job, probably in the media or the arts. He feels under-appreciated, both at work and in life in general. He's a narcissist with grandiose ideas; hence his calling card, The Director. He wants to believe he's the one calling the shots, and the ultimate power trip is the power to mete out death. Sexually, he's dysfunctional. As I understand it, no semen was found either inside or anywhere on the victims?"

"Nothing we could find," Jessica confirmed. "Although, there was evidence of both internal and external bruising to the genitals in every case."

"Penetration by object or objects of some kind. Further evidence, I would suggest, that our man is unable to perform sexually. He may well be impotent." The profiler took out a handkerchief and dabbed at his large nose. "Perhaps, somewhere in his past, a young lady spurned his advances or laughed at him for his sexual inadequacy, thereby laying down the blueprint for his future killing spree."

"And the cutting off of the left breast," Connors asked. "Sadism, or symbolic?"

Edwards bent an approving eye in her direction. "A bit of both, probably. It may be significant that it is the left breast, i.e. over the heart. Throughout the ages, women's breasts have been lauded for their beauty, eroticism and, of course, nurturing abilities. Our chap might even have had a difficult relationship with his mother."

Fucking Oedipus again! Jessica suppressed a yawn. She'd had a maximum of three hours' sleep the night before, plus a massive dose of cold shoulder from David. Her engine was running on empty, and her patience, always in short supply, was fast disappearing. She cut to the chase.

"So, because he didn't get the titty as a baby," she said, "and some girl laughed at his dodgy todger, he's out for revenge?"

Edwards folded his handkerchief neatly and returned it to his pocket. "A somewhat vulgar over simplification but, in essence, yes."

"And he's aged somewhere between twenty-five and forty-five, works either in the media or the arts and is a narcissist with grandiose ideas." Hennessy enumerated the traits by picking up a rollie for each and separating it from the bunch on his table.

Connors raised a tweezed eyebrow. "A narcissist with grandiose ideas?" Sounds like every man I've ever known."

Jessica jerked her head at Hennessy. "Pop out, Sergeant, would you, and pick him up. You can take my car." Everybody laughed, except Edwards. She didn't care. Her faith in the breed was, at best, lukewarm. They were just another American import, to be taken with a grain of salt. Lolling back in her chair, she stretched her arms high above her head, then snapped forward again, all business.

"Sedgie. Go get the motor. Hennessy. Connors. Whip out your fine-tooth combs and go back over the case notes on all the victims. See if anything jumps out that we might have missed. Check again for a common denominator. Tinker. Tailor. Soldier. Spy. Someone with whom all the victims have had contact. She dismissed the profiler with a nod. "Mr Edwards, thank you for your time. You've given us a lot of food for thought." My Aunt Fanny! she thought, as he packed his notes away and headed stiff-backed for the door. He'd given them nothing, really, just wild conjecture and generalities. Still, it would keep Inspector Beckwith happy. Detective Chief Inspector Mark Beckwith. Beck-twit! Him and his full-of-herself actress girlfriend, whose first cousin, coincidentally, happened to be none other than Robert Edwards.

She was about to shrug on her jacket when, speak of the devil, Beckwith appeared at the office door. Jessica was dimly aware of Connors flicking her blonde mane and throwing back her shoulders so that her double D breasts strained against her shirt. The DCI had that effect on women – some anyway. Jessica had once heard him described as the love child of George Clooney and Brad Pitt. True enough, his looks were a cut above the ordinary, but his personality was somewhere down the U-bend. He was bumptious, arrogant and a misogynist, and those were his good qualities. He'd tried to shaft her once, scotch her recent promotion to DI. He didn't know she knew and, when the time was right, she had every intention of making him pay for chucking that particular wrinkle her way. Connors was welcome to him! As it happened, Beckwith didn't even glance her colleague's way. He bounded over to Jessica and loomed over her. His glance went to the jacket in her hands.

"I thought Robert Edwards was to address the team this morning."

"He just did," Jessica said coolly. "Although, if you want my opinion, the man is about as much use as a cat flap on a submarine."

"But I specifically told you that I wanted to be in attendance." A pulse, the barometer of the chief's moods, zigzagged in his temple. The more it pulsed, the greater the chance of stormy weather.

"I sent you a memo." The lie tripped easily off Jessica's lips. "Still, like I said, you didn't miss much, just a shitload of generalisations a nursery kid could have come up with." She feigned embarrassment. "Sorry, I forgot. Robert Edwards is Venise's cousin, isn't he?"

The pulse in his temple registered hurricane. Beckwith raised himself slightly on tiptoes – up, down, up, down – reminding her of the old *Dixon of Dock Green* stereotype copper. 'Ello! 'Ello! 'Ello!

"If you're implying, DI Wideacre, that my decision to canvass Mr Edward's expertise was in any way influenced by my personal relationship, I hugely resent the implication."

Not altogether successfully, Jessica suppressed a smirk. "Never even crossed my mind." And nobody else mentioned it either, or not in my hearing." The hostility between herself and the chief was palpable.

"Robert Edwards," he said, almost shouting, "is one of the foremost professionals in his field. *Decoding a Killer*, his last book, went to number one in the *Sunday Times* bestseller list. Added to that, he was senior profiler on several big-league murders, including the infamous Ben Bailey case."

Considering the wrong man had been jailed for that particular murder and the Met had almost gone bankrupt paying out a shedload of compo, it wasn't the best example to use. The thought seemed to strike the DCI at the same time, for he suddenly looked confused. And angry. Most definitely angry.

Luckily, perhaps for them both, Connors chose exactly that

moment to contribute her own pearls of wisdom.

"For what it's worth, sir, I thought Mr Edwards to be quite remarkable." She pushed herself slightly back from her desk, crossed one long leg over the other and laser-beamed equal parts sincerity and lust Beckwith's way. "He flagged up a number of interesting pointers." Her hand slid rhythmically up and down her smooth, tanned leg. Jessica cringed for her for being so shamelessly obvious. Connors would stop at nothing in her bid for promotion. Not even the fact that Beckwith had the beautiful, much younger, Venise Love-Davies as his squeeze, was enough to put her off. What price equality! Jessica threw her a look of disgust. She could have kissed Sedgie, when, with perfect timing, he leaned on the car horn outside, providing her with a legitimate excuse to leave the pair of them to it.

"That's Liversedge with the car," she said, trying not to look too exultant as she headed for the door. "We're off to grill Nimrod Peters. I'll leave you with DS Connors, sir, to fill you in on all the pointers she found so interesting." She tossed the last remark over her shoulder. Knowing her colleague's track record with the opposite sex, she almost felt sorry for Beckwith. "NMBP," she told herself, making a "cut" motion at Sedgie, as he rapped out a tune on the horn. "Not my bloody problem!"

CHAPTER THREE

As Shania Lewis struggled back to consciousness, the first thing she noticed was the dust motes whirling in the light filtered through the sacking covering the windows. Confused, she thought she must be dreaming. The curtains on her bedroom window were lipstick pink, her favourite colour. She'd picked them out of the Argos catalogue and customised them with little diamante gemstones from the 99p shop. Her mum said it was a waste of time, the stones would all come off in the wash, but Shania had gone ahead regardless. She'd made a flower design, a wonky daisy. When she put herself into voluntary care, she'd taken them with her, though the cunts wouldn't let her hang them up. The second thing she noticed was that she couldn't move. Something was holding her wrists and ankles; something strong that wouldn't let go; something that bit into her skin and hurt. She noticed the third thing when she tried to open her mouth to scream and found she couldn't. Someone had taped it shut.

···

"Stick on the blues and twos," Jessica instructed when they hit heavy traffic at Clapham North. Like much of south London, the area had gentrified over the last decade or so. Pricey cafés had sprung up, along with wine bars and designer boutiques that were solely the preserve of the City high-fliers who had flocked to the area because of its proximity to the Square Mile. Only fifteen minutes to Bank. Travel in London didn't get much better than that. The indigenous population of scroungers and smackheads had long been exiled to the country's rundown seaside resorts where housing was a fraction of the cost and where, ultimately, they'd be somebody else's problem. Dole-on-Sea, the papers dubbed it. A jogger bounded past on the pavement, a tall, tanned woman, blonde ponytail swinging jauntily from side to side, impossibly pert arse.

The DC's lips pursed to a whistle. "Nice," he said, then lights flashing, siren blaring, began to bully his way through the traffic.

As always in this neck of the woods, Jessica found herself looking out for the turn-off to Tremadoc Road, where she and David had had their first love nest. It hadn't been up to much, just one bedroom on the third floor of a bog-standard Victorian terraced house. Peeling walls, a windowless galley kitchen and a tiny living room with a 1960s tiled fireplace that belched out smoke on the one occasion they'd tried to use it. The furnishings were eclectic, i.e. the product of skips, charity shops and cast-offs from friends and family. Since they'd spent most of their time in bed, none of that had mattered one jot. Students, poor as the proverbial church mice, it was only with hindsight that she realised that what they'd had back then was far more valuable than money or status. They'd had paradise! Paradise, she had a sneaky suspicion they were on their way to losing. How long, given the pressures both were under, before one of them buckled and walked out.

Following the route of the Northern Line, the car screeched past Clapham Common, Balham and Tooting Bec Tube stations. At Tooting Broadway, Liversedge swung a right down Garratt Lane, narrowly avoiding an oncoming ambulance on its way to nearby St George's Hospital. A little further along, the traffic thinned and he killed the siren. As they shot past the four concrete tower blocks of the infamous Thatcher's estate, Jessica clucked in disgust. "Dante's seventh circle," she said, eyeing the concrete monstrosities with distaste as they receded in the rear-view mirror. The architects of those places should all have been taken out and shot."

"Weren't they seen as the Seventies solution to low-cost housing?" Liversedge asked, pulling into a tree-lined road on the borders of Earlsfield and Southfield.

"That was the idea," Jessica said drily. "Only it didn't quite work out that way." She looked around in surprise at the well-kept Edwardian houses surrounding them on either side. Each had a pretty pocket-handkerchief sized garden in front, and several had their own driveway, a definite bonus in traffic-clogged London. "Nimrod lives here?" Such genteel surroundings were not what she had expected.

Liversedge grinned. "Just opposite. No. 35." He led the way and, despite the presence of a doorbell, pounded imperiously on the door. Back at the station they called it the fear-of-God knock – FOG for short. As they waited for a response, Jessica took in the rest of the house: sparkling clean windows, a hanging basket trailing dark blue and pink lobelia, two small ornamental bay trees flanking the door. It certainly didn't look like skanksville.

As the DC raised his hand to knock again, the front door opened on a gangly young black man, clad unimaginatively in hoodie, baseball cap, low-slung jeans and Nike 110s. Jessica flashed her ID card.

"Fuckin' 'ell, ain't I the popular one." Peters stepped back to allow them entry. Under the glower, Jessica could see he was a good-looking lad, though the wispy goatee adorning his chin was something of a lost cause. He turned immediately left into a small living room and threw himself across a chintz-covered settee. He looked Jessica up and down, lingered deliberately on her chest. "So, what the fuck'm I supposed to have done now?"

Jessica kept him waiting as she took in her surroundings. The room was old-lady immaculate, a haven of potpourri and lavender furniture polish. Crochet antimacassars covered the arms of the settee and matching armchairs. A display cabinet showcasing Lladró and Royal Doulton figurines was set against one wall. Above it hung a selection of tasteful botanical prints. Below the period mantelpiece, the brass firedogs were polished to an eye-watering shine. The only jarring notes in the room were the open can of Foster's on the coffee table and the rollie burning in a plastic pub ashtray. Peters picked up the cigarette and took a long deliberate puff, before exhaling slowly. His eyes challenged them over the thin ribbon of smoke. "Fuck's sake, it's just a bleedin' fag. Can't arrest me for that."

"Kerrie Gray," Jessica snapped. "Tell me about your relationship with her and, just so you're clear about it, I don't do bullshit."

Peters rolled his eyes. He pointed the rollie at Liversedge. "I already told fuckin' string bean here everything I know." He glared at Jessica . "And there was no relationship, geddit? I didn't hardly know the stupid bitch."

"You knew her well enough to take money from her," Jessica said, itching to knock the smart-ass look off his face. "You a pimp, Peters? That what you do, take money from little girls?"

Peters took one last toke, ground the cigarette butt out in the ashtray. "You don't get it, do you, bitch? Girls like her, spoilt little white princesses, sometimes they wanna change." He grabbed his crotch "Know what I mean?" His eyes locked with Jessica's. "You wanna try it yourself, Miss Up-your-own-hole. No way you'll ever go back. Just sayin'."

Jessica stuck her arm out, automatically blocking Liversedge as he took a threatening step forward.

"Oh, I get it all right. Kerrie Gray was easy meat."

Peters shrugged. "*She* came on to *me*." He made a mouth with his hand. "Flappin' her beak. Rat-tat-tat-tat! How she could help me make it big as a rapper. How Daddy had contacts in the music industry." He gave a derisory snort. "Blagged on about how she'd actually met Puff Daddy and P. Diddy. Stupid cow didn't even realise they was the same person." He picked up the can of lager, held it a moment without putting it to his mouth. His eyes gleamed. "She'd dosh, though. More'n I've ever seen, 'cept maybe in the movies." He upended the Foster's, drained the can of every last drop, his prominent Adam's apple working hard as he swallowed. "And me, I ain't got shit." He crunched the tin with one hand, tossed it into a waste-paper basket on the floor beside him. He jerked his head round the room. "This yard belong my aunty. Manz only here on sufferance, so's she can look good in the eyes of the Lord 'n' cry 'bout me on Sundays."

"Did you bring Kerrie here?" Stony-faced, Jessica ignored his descent into self-pity. "Is this where you lured her?"

Peters looked shifty, less sure of himself. His hand rose seemingly of its own volition and latched on to a medallion around his neck, an oversized dollar sign on a golden chain. Gangsta bling.

Jessica honed in on the movement. "Gave you that, did she?" At his almost imperceptible nod, she pressed on. "What else,

Peters? What else did Kerrie give you?"

He rubbed his fingers and thumb together, nodded towards Liversedge. "I already told him. Squiller."

Jessica squinted her eyes. "How much *squiller?*" She used the slang word for money with contempt. "How much exactly did she give you?" Heavy emphasis on "give".

"Enough." Peters' body language had changed during her questioning, segued from cocky to defensive. He crossed his arms over his chest.

"Enough to take your girlfriend to Majorca?"

"Yeah. Like, so what? Wasn't like she couldn't afford it."

Jessica's lip curled. "That's hardly the point. Who gives money to a bloke she fancies so that he can take his other bird away on holiday? Doesn't make sense, Nimrod. And, as Judge Judy says, if it doesn't make sense, it's a lie." She leaned across the coffee table, getting up close and personal with his goatee. She had the satisfaction of seeing him flinch. "Which leads both me, and DC Liversedge here, to conclude that you're nothing but a nasty tea-leaf. She rocked back on her heels. "Which is why her handbag was missing when we found her. No purse, no phone, nothing."

Liversedge upped the ante. His affable face grew ugly with contempt. "Did you steal that poor little girl's handbag, Nimmers? Is that how you funded your holiday to Majorca, on the ill-gotten gains from a murdered girl?" He shook his head from side to side. "Man, that is some serious bullshit."

"She was so pretty, wasn't she?" Jessica said, taking up the reins again. She began to paint a picture of the innocent Kerrie, a deliberate ploy to stir his conscience. She was banking on at least a small part of his religious aunt's influence rubbing off on him.

"The apple of her parents' eye, hot-housed all her life. Poor kid, it did her no favours in the end." Her lip curled. "Then again, no one expects their naive, trusting kid to fall prey to scum like you. What a heaven-sent opportunity, eh, when this babe-in-arms rolls up looking to you for her first romance." Her hands fisted in rage. "She still had her My Little Pony and Bratz doll collections. There was a picture of pretty-boy Harry Styles on her bedroom wall. Her favourite TV programme was *Glee*. That's how much of a kid she still was. She'd believe anything anyone told her, especially a good-looking boy who knew all the right words."

Bullseye! She hit the target. Peters began to squirm. His eyes darted tellingly to the door. He was wishing he was anywhere else. Setting out to widen the chink in his armour, Jessica began to paint a different picture. "Poor little Kerrie. She wasn't so pretty when we found her, Nimrod. Not pretty at all. She'd been beaten, hacked about, her left breast cut off." She began to pace around the room. "She'd been tortured for hours. Days, maybe." She paused before the window, lifted the lace curtain to one side a little. Outside a kid was attempting to do tricks on a skateboard. He caught her looking, stuck out his tongue. Brat! Jessica let the curtain drop back into place and returned to stand over Peters, where she continued to pile on the agony. "That little girl. That naive little girl who fancied you so much she ran away from the safety of her own home, died an agonising death." She shuddered visibly at the memory, no need to act.

Peters cracked then. He held up his hand. "Okay! Okay! Enough! Fuckin' shut up and I'll tell you everything."

CHAPTER FOUR

For a change Jessica managed to get home before David. In an effort to score brownie points, she made up a pot of his favourite chilli con carne, threw together a mixed green salad and ran a clove of garlic over some buttered ciabatta, ready for popping in the oven. She uncorked a bottle of Shiraz-Viognier, middle of the road, but quite drinkable, and went upstairs to run a bath. While the tub was filling, she laid a sea-green wraparound dress on the bed, peeled off her standard working uniform of shirt, slacks and utilitarian underwear, and kicked her flat shoes under the bed. It amused her no end how on TV crime shows, especially the American ones, the female detectives were invariably tarted up in tight skirts and sky-high stilettos. Two and a half inches was as high as Jessica was prepared to go, and then only on special occasions like tonight, when she wanted to dress to impress. She rummaged around for her one pair of high heels and found them stuffed at the back of the wardrobe. Finally, she took a strand of jade and silver beads from her impoverished jewellery box and laid them on the bed too.

On her way back to the bathroom, she paused in front of the mirrored door and gave her naked body the once over. Her innate lack of vanity drove both her mother and her younger sister wild. The phrase, "you never make the most of yourself", uttered in varying degrees of frustration, had been a ringing refrain throughout her life. At five-foot eight, her body was athletic rather than curvy. Her breasts were on the small side, but high still with no sign of sagging. Her hips were slim and boyish, her stomach flat, though marred by an ugly appendectomy scar. Her legs were long and slender, the knees slightly on the knobbly side. She disliked her feet; they were too bony and too big, another good reason not to draw attention to them with fancy footwear. Jessica leaned closer to the glass and examined her face. She had the milky, non-tanning, easily freckling skin of her Scottish forebears, though, thankfully, the freckles on her face were confined to just a smattering around her nose. She also had the dubious distinction of being the only one in the family to inherit the red hair of the Celts, though again, thankfully, a tamer version – three parts copper to one part demon red. Left to its own devices, it fell in bed-spring spirals to her shoulders. Most days, she simply stuffed it all up in an untidy pile. David loved her hair loose. He loved her freckles. He loved every part of her, or so he said. Only she couldn't quite remember when he'd last said it. She turned away from the mirror, determined to put that right. Starting that very night.

...

Jessica's mobile went off at eight o'clock, fifteen minutes after they'd sat down to eat. David stopped chewing as she picked it up. His jaw clenched. His eyes asked a question over a forkful of chilli con carne. Three little words later – "On my way" – Jessica clicked off again, her own eyes guiltily meeting his. David threw his fork back on the plate and reached for his wine glass.

"I – I'm sorry," Jessica said, grating her chair back from the table and rising to her feet. David said nothing, but his face spoke volumes. She paused with her hand on the door knob, turned back. "Oh God, don't do this to me, David, I was really looking forward to us spending the night together too." She gestured towards the table, laid with unusual care. Proper linen serviettes. Crystal glasses. Flowers, which as a rule she didn't do, making a colourful centrepiece. "Would I have gone to all this trouble otherwise?" As David maintained his silence, resentment at being put on the back foot catapulted her into defence mode. Her eyes flashed. "For Christ's sake, this isn't a clock-on, clock-off job. You knew that when you married me. If you can't hack it, then -" She stopped abruptly. The last thing she wanted was to do was to plant ideas in his head.

David plonked his glass down so hard the delicate stem broke. So much for the crystal glasses. Waterford crystal too, a wedding present from her parents, who'd made sure she knew exactly how much they'd cost.

"I married you, Jessica, because I love you." His frustration rolled over her in waves. "I'm not asking for a nine-to-five wife, but you can't blame me for wanting us to spend the occasional evening together without your damn phone going off."

"It will get better," Jessica promised, frozen midway between fight and flight. "Once we catch the son of a bitch who's murdering all those young girls. They've just found another body. I need to be there."

David's shoulders slumped. "I'd look bad for arguing with that, wouldn't I? Cruel. Cold-hearted." He waved a hand. "Oh, look – go Jess! Do whatever you have to."

Jessica threw him a glance of despair, before hurrying upstairs to change. To be continued, she thought, assuming there was the chance to do so. She had a horrible feeling that there had been a subtext to his final words. "Do what you have to do *and so will I*." *Dear God*, she bargained, diving under the bed to retrieve her sensible brogues, *I'm trying to do the right thing here. Please, don't make me suffer for it.*

Considering most of May had been colder and wetter than average, the night was surprisingly balmy. Torrential rain, day after day, had conspired to wash away whatever evidence there might have been left at the crime scenes, making her job almost impossible. An ivory moon played peek-a-boo from behind a thin veiling of cloud, before shaking it off like a stripper and shimmying across the sky in all its voluptuous glory. Jessica climbed into her car and with a heavy heart set off for Wimbledon. As usual on Friday nights, the streets were thronged with young people determined to cut loose after the hard graft of the week. Girls in low-cut tops, miniskirts and skyscraper shoes wobbled past, some clutching bottles of blinged-up alcohol like they were Top Shop accessories. A clever marketing ploy, that, Jessica thought, manufacturing them in girl-friendly colours and sweet flavours like blackcurrant, orange and cola. Like lemonade, they slipped down easily. Too easily. Later the streets would be awash with pools of vomit and already hard-pressed A & E departments would be packed to the rafters with the detritus of another weekend's partying. If she had her way she'd ban all such drinks, or tax them to the extent where they were well beyond the scope of most kids' pockets. Like champagne.

Leaving the high street behind, Jessica began the climb upwards through the postcard-pretty village, making for Wimbledon Common where a courting couple had literally stumbled over the latest body. What were the parents of those girls thinking, she wondered, letting them out on the streets like twenty-pound toms? Didn't they read the newspapers, watch the news? Didn't they know there was a vicious killer on the loose? If ever she had a daughter, she'd make damn sure she knew enough not to put herself at risk. She shifted into second gear as the incline steepened. Kids! Another bone of contention between herself and David. He wanted them. She didn't. She doubted she ever would.

Pole lights were already in position when she arrived at the scene, and a tent had been set up both to preserve evidence and to protect the body from the rubberneckers that invariably appeared, no matter how remote the location.

Hennessy, puffing on a roll-up, trundled over to meet her. "We think we've already got an ID on this one. Fits the description of a Shania Lewis, fifteen, missing from Totterdown Children's Home in Stockwell. She took off a week ago, though no one thought to alert the police till yesterday."

"Care homes!" Jessica spat. "My mother's cat gets more care than the kids in most of those places."

The flap on the tent whisked back and Laura Shackleton emerged. Pulling off a pair of purple latex gloves, she greeted Jessica with a nod. "Before you ask, it wasn't Orinoco wot done it." Seeing Jessica look blank, she attempted to jog her memory. "The Wombles of Wimbledon Common? Hairy little bastards that went round cleaning up litter. They had a catchphrase. Make good use of bad rubbish? No?"

"Uncle Bulgaria. Tobermory," Hennessy contributed, showing his own knowledge of the popular children's show that aired way back in the Seventies and was repeated almost constantly on Freeview." He jigged about a bit, sang in a croaky voice. "Remember you're a Womble."

Jessica raised her hands in a gesture of surrender. "Sorry, no," she said. "I must have been doing something else at the time. Like having a life." The glare of the lights lent a greenish cast to her face. In no mood for levity, she jerked her head towards the tent. "How bad?"

"Steel yourself. This is the worst one yet." The pathologist headed for her ginormous vehicle. She turned back for a moment, all traces of her earlier humour vanished. "What the hell happens to someone to cause that much rage?"

Jessica shrugged. "Ours is not to reason why. Ours is simply to nail the bastards." Explanations and motivations she left to the bleeding hearts of the world. She took a deep breath and entered the tent.

...

It took several days to track down Shania's mother, Amber Lights-Lewis, an emaciated thirty-six-year old, whose face bore witness to a lifetime of heavy drinking. In the event the post-mortem had gone ahead without notifying her. It had been particularly gruelling and Laura's team had done their best to conceal the worst of the wounds. Shania's blonde hair had been brushed clear of leaves and dirt and a dusting of powder applied in an attempt to disguise the real extent of the bruising to her face. A cotton sheet pulled well up under her chin concealed both the damage done by her killer and the further hacking about incurred during the post-mortem. Shania's mother emerged from the viewing room and staggered blindly to a nearby seat.

Jessica's eyebrows lifted.

Amber Lights Lewis blinked tearfully. "Yeah, that's my gel, all right. That's my Shania." She dabbed at her eyes with a tissue that had turned soggy and black from runny mascara. Jessica passed her another from a box of Kleenex kept specifically for the purpose. "Silly mare. We fell out over of a pair of curtains, you know. Cheap, tacky curtains from fuckin' Argos." She sniffed loudly. "Pink, they was. On sale. She bought some of those little gemstone things and made a flower. She was artistic like that, Shania. Loved *Blue Peter* when she was kid. Went through bog rolls and sticky-back plastic like there was no tomorrow." She shredded the tissue. Bits fell like confetti to the floor. "I warned her, I did. Told her they'd come off in the wash, and when I washed 'em, some of 'em did." Her voice hardened. "Got a monk on then, didn't she; spun social services some yarn 'bout me being an unfit mum. Next thing the nosey gits are all over me business like flies on a dog shit. Last I seen of Shania, she was sticking her tongue out at me as they drove her off into care." A humourless chuckle escaped. "Her *and* her bleedin' curtains."

Jessica let the woman ramble on, understanding her need to talk, to get her head round the terrible thing that had happened. It was normal under the circumstances to run the full gamut of emotions, swinging wildly from one to the other and back again. Sorrow. Blame. Anger. Guilt. Remorse. Shania's mother, she knew, would be torturing herself with the "what ifs" and "if onlys" that might have changed everything. She would spend the rest of her life regretting that stupid, petty argument, wishing in vain she could turn the clock back.

"They'll have to pay, won't they, the bastards?"

Jessica was completely disarmed by the sudden change of tack. Gone with breathtaking swiftness was the grief-stricken mother, her place taken by a hard-faced, grasping creature with pound signs in her eyes.

"Compo." She wore an expression of almost feral cunning. "Social shit-faces! They had … what's that thing called – a duty of care, didn't they? That'll bleedin' cost 'em!" She nodded, and there was satisfaction in the gesture. Entitlement. "I deserve a big payout, me, losing me daughter like that. They should've taken better care of her."

...

"With a mother like Amber Lights Lewis," Jessica told the team in the incident room later, "it's no surprise Shania put herself into care. After only half an hour of listening to her bang on, I almost admitted myself into care."

"Amber Lights Lewis," DS Connors frowned. "Now why does that name ring a bell?" She sat on the edge of her desk, long legs swinging, feet encased, Jessica noted, in three-inch heels with red soles. She began snapping her fingers, presumably as some sort of aide-memoire. "Got it!" The clicking came to an abrupt end. "Amber Lights Lewis, real name the much less poetic Sandra Smith. Sandra was a well-known tom, back when I worked on Vice. Had a pimp, a Rasta, a real vicious bastard. He got his when he crossed swords with a Romanian drug baron, an even more vicious bastard than himself." She grinned. "Legend has it that, like others before him, he's currently doing time as part of one of the uprights on a motorway flyover bridge."

"No loss, then," Liversedge said. "Probably the only bit of honest work he ever did in his life." He grinned. "Death, I mean."

As jokes went, it was pretty lame, but it was enough to lighten an atmosphere that had grown thick with rage, disgust and the very real frustration that they were no nearer catching The Director than when his first young victim had turned up dead on

Streatham Common six weeks earlier.

Jessica excused herself and went to the Ladies, more for a chance to think than to relieve herself. She sat on the toilet and thought about Nimrod Peters, how he had gone into meltdown, spilling his guts after she and Sedgie leaned on him earlier. In Jessica's eyes, he was almost as responsible for Kerrie's death as her killer. She flushed the toilet, washed her hands and, without even so much as glancing in the mirror, went into the custody room where Peters had been taken for further questioning. All signs of attitude had completely vanished. Hunched inside his hoodie, he appeared to be making himself as small as possible, trying to disappear. No chance! Jessica took a chair opposite and leaned across the desk. A brief had been appointed at Peters' request, a bored-looking Asian woman who, judging from the amount of times she glanced at her watch, was longing to be elsewhere. Jessica knew the type – a box-ticker, going through the motions, no more, no less. If Nimrod Peters thought he had bagged himself a shit-hot lawyer, he was sadly mistaken.

The door opened. Hennessy, stinking of cigarette smoke, lumbered in and sat next to her. He switched on the tape recorder and ran through the prescribed script: time, date, those present at the interview. Formalities complete, cassette wheels rolling, Jessica began her interrogation.

An hour later, Peters walked. The cockiness back, he grabbed his crotch on the way out of the incident room and leered at Jessica. "Like I said, you ever fancy a change, you come get me." He struck a gay pose, hand on hip, and blew a kiss at Hennessy. "You too, sarge."

"Stay!" Jessica commanded, as Hennessy, his face brick red,

jumped to his feet and made a dive for Peters. "He'll get his comeuppance one of these days. His type always comes unstuck. Eventually."

"And when he does," Hennessy said, slamming his fist into the palm of his hand. "I'll be fucking waiting."

...

"I'm as mad as you lot," Jessica told the team later. "But, apart from banging him up on the grounds of being an immoral bastard, we've nothing concrete to charge him with."

"Not even theft?" Connors asked. "We know he skipped off abroad on the proceeds of Kerrie's bank account. Then there was her handbag and phone."

"According to him, Kerrie gave him the money. His word against that of a dead girl. No contest. And, since her handbag and phone are still missing, there's no proof he took those either. We'd need a lot more to go on before the CPS would even begin to entertain a case against him."

The door opened and DCI Beckwith came in on a waft of lemony aftershave. He folded his arms and leaned his behind against Connors' desk.

He nodded to Jessica. "You've released Nimrod Peters, I hear. Want to tell me why?"

News travels fast, Jessica thought, guessing Connors was the mole.

"Because, apart from being a useless twat and an insult to humanity, everything we've got is circumstantial." Her eyes met his; steady, but with the hint of a challenge. "Kerrie Gray emptied her bank account and ran away of her own free will. No doubt, Peters encouraged her to do both, but there's no evidence to suggest undue pressure was brought to bear. The kid was infatuated. She'd have jumped through fire for him." She raised an eyebrow, glanced quickly at Connors and away again. "Some women are daft like that. They let the great god One Dick Two Balls walk all over them." She paused both to let the barb sink in and the knowing sniggers die down. "Since Peters' God bothering aunty was unlikely to be receptive to the idea of him bringing Kerrie home, he took her to a mate's flat on the Thatcher estate." She paused to take a sip from the mug of coffee cooling on the desk beside her. It was a novelty mug bearing her favourite mantra: "Just so you know, I don't do bullshit!"

Hennessy took over. "Seems Peters' *boys* were all there too." He stressed the word to leave them in no doubt he wasn't talking boy scouts in shorts and woggles. "Kerrie, understandably, was shit-scared. But Nimmers, playing host with the most, soon put her at her ease."

Jessica put down her coffee. "By plying her with copious amounts of alcohol," she said drily. "Drugs too, most likely, though he only coughs to a little weed. Then, his mate's girlfriend came home and threw a strop when she saw Kerrie. Seems she's bessie mates with Charmaine Simpson, Peters' actual girlfriend. She threatened to spill the beans if he didn't lose the 'honky bitch' sharpish." Jessica encapsulated the racist term between her bent fingers. She shook her head in disgust. "So, they bundled poor little Kerrie into a van and chucked her out somewhere near Victoria train station. Still pissed and stoned out of her head, most likely."

"Peters swore she had her handbag and phone with her and enough money to get back home when the trains started running,"

Hennessy added. "Says they left her at around 3 a.m. Alive! His toerag mates confirm his story, as does his girlfriend, who hot-footed it over to the Thatcher estate to give him earache about Kerrie. I bet he wished he'd gone straight back to his aunty's in Earlsfield."

"What time was that?" DCI Beckwith asked.

Jessica consulted her notes. "Three twenty, which sounds about right. It doesn't take long to get from Victoria to Tooting at that hour of the morning. There's CCTV evidence to back him up, as well as a grainy capture of Kerrie sat on a bench outside the station, too grainy to make out whether she has her handbag with her. That was at 3.45 a.m., by which time Peters was already mid-bollocking."

"No sighting of Kerrie after that?" Beckwith asked.

Jessica shook her head. "She got up and walked out of sight of the camera a minute or two later. And that was the last anyone saw of her."

"Jesus!" Connors groaned in frustration. "It doesn't seem right that Peters should get off scot-free. Isn't there anything we can nail him on?" She addressed the question directly to Beckwith.

He eyed Jessica coldly. "Apparently not."

Jessica returned the look with interest. "Yes, it's frustrating. Peters is scum. But he's not the killer. Although we can link him to Kerrie, there is nothing at all to link him to any of the other victims. Let's keep our eye on the bigger picture here. The bodies are piling up and, so far, we've got naff all to go on."

"Well find something, DI Wideacre," Beckwith said. Then, after a pregnant pause. "And make it quick, or I may have to think about replacing you with somebody else. Somebody more experienced. Somebody … competent."

Liversedge grinned round at his fellow officers as, hot on Beckwith's heels, the door slammed shut behind Jessica. "I guess the boss needs to learn what the rest of us already know. DI Jessica Wideacre doesn't do bullshit!"

CHAPTER FIVE

Jessica was in bed when David came home. He hadn't phoned to say he'd be late. No text. Nothing! Twice she'd tried phoning him, but each time his voicemail had clicked on. By midnight she'd had enough. Concern changed first to anger and then to resentment. Presumably, this was his way of punishing her for the demands of her job. She dumped the remains of her microwave spaghetti meal in the bin, polished off half a bottle of Shiraz and, having left the washing-up for the morning, stomped upstairs to bed. Unable to sleep, she picked up a James Patterson thriller. Twenty minutes later, having absorbed not one word, she chucked it to the floor.

"David. David. David," she moaned, eyes roaming restlessly around the room. "Where the hell are you?" She toyed with the idea of phoning him again, dismissed it, hating the idea of herself as weak and needy. Fatigued to death, she eventually dozed. Shortly after 2 a.m. she was jolted awake by the sound of his key turning in the lock. She heard the door open, then click gently closed behind him. He wasn't drunk. She knew that immediately. His movements were too quiet, too controlled. There was a moment of complete silence. She pictured him standing at the bottom of the stairs, indecisive – should I go or should I stay – upstairs to her, or … ? He went into the kitchen. Ears cocked, she heard the tap running, the soft splosh of water in the kettle, the pop of the switch as he turned it on. She heard the scrape of a mug as he set it down on the granite worktop, the chink of a spoon as he measured out coffee and sugar. Her senses honed, each noise cut through her, sharp as a knife. The fridge door opening, closing again. His footsteps pacing back and forth on the quarry-tiled floors. He took his drink into the living room, making sure to close the door firmly behind him. Ears straining now, Jessica sat up in bed. She just about managed to make out the faint strains of Beethoven's "Moonlight" Sonata. She panicked then. That was David's go-to piece, his place of escape whenever the world got too much and he needed to shut it out. Was he shutting her out too? More than anything, she wanted run downstairs, reach out for him and feel him reach out for her. Once she would have, unhesitatingly. Now, it was as if an unbridgeable gulf had opened suddenly between them, each of them marooned on opposite sides. Stressed, tearful, oozing resentment, Jessica suddenly felt overwhelmingly lonely; lonely, empty and, she had to admit, scared too. Her world was imploding and she didn't quite know what to do about it.

Chilled to the bone in a way that had nothing to do with cold, she lay back down and tugged the duvet right up to her chin. Outside, a car drove past, its headlights throwing a misshapen square of light onto the ceiling. Jessica closed her eyes, squeezing them tightly shut. No way was she going to cry. But, she did.

...

DCI Mark Beckwith took off his black tie and laid it on top of the dinner jacket draped neatly over the back of a chair. He undid the stiff buttons of his dress shirt and pulled it free of the waistband of his trousers. Relieved to be home, he made himself a cup of camomile tea and bore it off into the conservatory to reflect on the events of the evening. It was shortly after 3.30 a.m. and pitch dark outside. The moon, enveloped in a vast blanket of dark cloud, gave not one chink of light. Steam from the tea, a pleasant aroma, both floral and fruity, spiralled upwards.

He switched on the radio, more for background noise than any real desire to listen. The news. A body had been found. He stiffened. A male. He relaxed again. Not The Director, then. His target was young women. The youth, the newscaster continued, was believed to have died from stab wounds. Mark immediately felt bad again. A killing was a killing, and somewhere some unfortunate family would be mourning the loss of their son. A robbery gone wrong, it emerged. Defending himself, the householder had turned the robber's own knife on him. Mark didn't feel quite so bad after that. It was the law of the streets that if you brought a knife to the party, you'd better be prepared to use it. If it ended up being used against you, tough shit! The news ended, segued into a piece of orchestral music – Bach, or maybe Beethoven. He wasn't big on classical, found it depressing. He twiddled the dial, found Gordon Lightfoot singing "Sundown". Much better. He settled into his seat, took a sip of the tea, thought about Venise, how she'd looked that evening. Beautiful. Serene. Like a younger Cate Blanchett, with a bohemian twist. Despite being up against some tough competition, actresses of far greater standing than herself, Venise had walked away with the most coveted title of all, that of Best Actress. Watching her graciously accept her award and deliver her thank-you speeches without any of the drama and over-emoting so in vogue amongst her peers, he'd felt a curious mix of emotions. Pride, of course – who wouldn't be proud to be the consort of Venise Love-Davies? Even her name had star quality. He felt guilt too. Despite her assertions that age was just a number, he sometimes felt he was little better than a dirty old man taking advantage of her innocence and youth. Others, especially DI Wideacre, did nothing to reassure him on that score. She made no secret of her scorn for 'sugar-daddies', managing with surprising frequency to drop the phrase into the most innocuous of conversations.

He was also uncertain as to what exactly he could bring to Venise's table. She was undoubtedly destined for great things, a place in movie star history. As Jack Kingsman, the director of *Raining in My Heart* said, she was a star in the ascendant. Her interpretation of DCI Merry Moore must surely rank as one of the greatest pieces of acting ever. Mark took his word for it. What he knew about acting and films could fit on the back of a postage stamp.

He laid aside his cup of tea and picked up an e-cigarette from the coffee table. Like Sergeant Hennessy, he too had been trying to wean himself off smoking for years, and this time it appeared to be working. He hadn't had a real cigarette in five weeks, two and a half days, fifteen minutes and three seconds. He pressed the button and a blue light came on, indicating it was fully charged. He inhaled deeply and it bubbled like a mini hubba bubba pipe. A moment later he exhaled a scentless cloud of vapour.

In the normal course of events it was unlikely that he and Venise would ever have met; they moved in two very different worlds. The actress and the cop, every bit as odd a pairing as the actress and the bishop, the subject of so many ribald jokes. In truth, he'd felt like a bit of a joke that evening, certainly an oddity. Even more so when Venise had thanked him from the stage for being her mentor and "the man to whom I owe so much". Never one to seek the limelight, he'd felt himself grow hot first, then cold. He'd started to sweat. His hands grew clammy. He felt a complete idiot, a fish out of water. Worst of all, he had a suspicion that the luvvie crowd knew it too and were collectively revelling in his discomfort. When Venise, gazing at him like – what was that expression Wideacre had used? – the great god, One Dick Two Balls – had beckoned him up on stage, it took every ounce of courage he possessed not to turn tail and flee. Thankfully, he'd managed to pull it together, but only just.

"I did very little," he assured the audience, as she linked her arm through his. "When Venise got in touch enquiring if she could shadow me in preparation for her role as DCI Merry Moore, what could I say? Well, what would you say if Venise Love-Davies asked to shadow you?" The last delivered wryly, earning a laugh and a smattering of applause from the audience.

The truth was it had taken a great deal of persuasion before he'd agreed to have anything to do with Venise, or any actor, come to that. Only when leaned on by those on high, and persuaded that it would be good PR for the force to be seen to cooperate in such a venture, had he capitulated. With very bad grace. It said a lot for Venise's charm that he'd seen it through to the end, particularly given the slings and arrows he'd suffered at the hands of the rest of his colleagues. For the most part, he'd put his big boy pants on, grinned and bore it. Not so when it came to DI Wideacre. That woman had a way of needling him like no one else could. Personality clash wasn't big enough to cover it. They were polar opposites; fire and ice, sunshine and shadow. He took a sip from his tea, thinking about it. No, scrap the last thought. Neither one could claim a sunny outlook. They were both dark, both strange in their own way. Jessica was more than that, though. She was a loose cannon. A maverick without a clue, which made her reckless. Strange how she seemed to inspire so much devotion in her team, any one of whom would, in a trice, take up the cudgels on her behalf. With the possible exception of DS Sarah Connors.

He put down the cup, stood up and stretched. Outside, the sky had changed into the grey-pink of half-mourning. A bird with a faulty alarm had already clocked on and was revving up for the dawn chorus. Determined to grab some shut-eye for the few hours of the night that remained, he switched off the lights and went to bed. Annoyingly, the last face he saw before he drifted off was not that of Venise, but Jessica Wideacre. Scowling. No change there.

...

David came to bed just as dawn was breaking. Jessica hadn't slept a wink all night. Instead, she'd spent it with a devil on one shoulder, an angel on the other. "Go down and kick his ass, have it out with him once and for all." That was the devil. Straight and to the point. Jessica was tempted. The devil spoke her language. The angel – cool, calm and collected – counselled caution on the grounds of making a bad situation worse. She took the angel's advice, and was glad she had when David finally slid into bed, curled into the warm curve of her body and dropped a kiss on her naked shoulder.

"I love you, Jess." A whisper, a mere breath, but enough to make Jessica's heart sing. His draped his arm around her waist and, within moments, his breathing had slowed to the even rhythm of sleep.

Jessica smiled and closed her eyes, grateful that the storm, for now anyway, had passed over.

CHAPTER SIX

"Saw you on TV last night, guv." That was DC Liversedge, first off the blocks when DCI Beckwith arrived at the incident room the following morning.

"It's all right for some, schmoozing with the stars." The lugubrious Sergeant Hennessy this time, getting in his own dig. "The tux your own, sir, or did you hire it specially for the occasion?"

A snort, quickly muffled. No surprise where that came from. Beckwith's eyes narrowed. He glared at Jessica, if-looks-could-kill. Serene, she gazed back, innocent as the day is long, except for the derisory glint in her cat-green eyes. No hiding that.

Not even two minutes had elapsed and she had already contrived to piss him off. Two could play at that game.

"Wideacre, see me immediately after you've briefed the team." It was a verbal snap of the fingers. A master/slave, jump-to-it command. "I want a full update on The Director murders."

"Yes, sir," Jessica said, just about managing to refrain from clicking her heels and saluting. Problem was, she had nothing of any value to add to what he already knew. No more bodies had turned up since Shania Lewis ten days earlier, but they were still no nearer to catching the killer. The press, moderately well behaved until now, had begun upping the ante big time. Since first light the phones had been ringing off the hook. Amber Lights Lewis, starring in full make-up and low-cut blouse on the front page of that morning's edition of the *Daily Mail*, was responsible

for lighting that particular fuse. Jessica glanced in disgust at the
lurid, designed to shock headline on the tabloid lying on her desk.

DIRECTOR OF DEATH
In an exclusive for the Daily Mail, Amber Lights Lewis (36) revealed
the details of the murder of her sixteen-year-old daughter, Shania,
latest victim of the killer who dubs himself, The Director.

"My Shania was a good girl," Ms Lights Lewis told our reporter,
wiping away tears. "Little did I know that our last row over a pair of
cheap pink curtains would lead to her death."

Ms Lights Lewis said that she felt Social Services had failed in
their duty of care towards Shania, and indicated that she would be
taking legal advice on the matter.

The grieving mother went on to describe in graphic detail how the
killer had sadistically tortured her young daughter prior to her heinous
murder.

"Jesus!" Jessica said, tossing the newspaper into the waste-paper
bin, without bothering to read the article in full. "The depths
some people will sink to, and all for fifteen minutes of fame and a
couple of bob."

"She's a nasty piece of work, all right," Connors said, fishing the
paper back out and running her eye over the column. She snorted
out a laugh. "Thirty-six! If she's thirty-six, I'm still swimming
up the birth canal." She checked her watch. "Five minutes DCI
Beckwith said. Isn't it time you faced the firing squad, guv?"

She didn't have to sound so bloody smug about it, Jessica
thought, gathering up her notes and heading into the lion's den.
Another thing, she wished Connors would lay off the Eau So

Expensive. It smelt like she bathed in the damn stuff.

As it happened, Jessica escaped from Beckwith's lair after a relatively minor mauling. Clearly, something had happened in the short interval between his summons and her arrival to deflect his attention elsewhere. Whatever it was, she hoped it was a royal pain in the arse. Judging from the way he dismissed her with a distracted "get on top of things, Wideacre" – no threat about replacing her, no snide comments as to her competence – she guessed it was something pretty major. She would have been very surprised to know that the problem exercising Beckwith's brain was nothing more than a dinner invite.

After his DI's departure, he sat glaring at the telephone as if it, and not Venise, was personally responsible for the dilemma in which he found himself.

"But darling," Venise had wheedled when he'd pronounced himself less than charmed by the idea of joining Jack Kingsman for dinner, "Jack is a wonderful director and I owe him so much. Do it for me, Marky, please."

Marky! It made him sound like a prat. "In the end he'd given in, of course, and she'd rung off, billing and cooing and burbling on about what an amazing *duck* he was. He shook his head, once more questioning the wisdom of their relationship. Thank Christ Wideacre hadn't been privy to the conversation, particularly the duck remark. Not, he told himself, as he pulled a bundle of paperwork towards him, that he gave a rat's arse what the red-headed tyrant thought.

...

Jessica, Liversedge and Connors attended the funeral of Shania Lewis, as they had the funerals of all the young victims. They were there not only to show respect, but to observe. Since killers didn't go about advertising their presence on sandwich boards, their eyes were peeled for anyone who might pique their interest. Their training had equipped them to look for possible giveaways: a face, not connected with the family, seen at two or more of the funerals, preferably all five in this case. That, of course, would be the most simplistic and unlikely scenario, since any idiot would know to don disguise and, whatever he was, this killer was no fool. So far, he'd left them nothing, not a single clue as to his identity. However, it was the little things that could prove to be a game changer. To the expert eye, an individual's gait and posture could prove almost as useful in ID-ing them as a fingerprint. Those who did opt for disguise rarely thought about this aspect and, if they did, generally elected for an unoriginal shuffle, limp or hunch, thereby immediately earmarking themselves as potential persons of interest. In exactly such circumstances as these, Jessica had once collared a murderer disguised as an old lady, complete with Zimmer frame.

The mourners at Shania's funeral were disappointingly stable on their feet, their postures finishing-school erect, not a hunchback among them. Nowhere did Jessica and her team spy so much as the hint of a villainous moustache, nylon wig or latex face mask. The only person to generate any real interest, for all the wrong reasons, was Amber Lights Lewis, whose OTT displays of grief threatened to upstage her daughter at her own funeral.

"God in heaven," Jessica snarled in an aside to her colleagues, as the woman's wails threatened to drown out the sound of the vicar, "can't somebody please get her a muzzle." It was a crass remark, immediately regretted. Regardless of the fact that the

Lewis woman had her eye firmly fixed on the compo pot, she was still a bereaved mother and had lost her daughter in appalling circumstances. Liversedge and Connors shot Jessica a disapproving look. It was merited and she owned it. "Sorry," she whispered. A gleam in Connors' eye told her she had just provided the woman with another bullet for Beckwith's armoury. "Bad call, Jessica," she reproved herself mentally. Add mouth almighty to the list of inheritances from her Scottish forebears.

The church service was brief, the requiem at the graveside similarly short, no longer than fifteen minutes start to finish. For reasons best known to itself, the insensitive sun had chosen that day to put on its hat and come out to play. As the coffin, its brass plaque glinting in the sunlight, was lowered into the contrasting gloom of the earth, Jessica vowed justice for Shania – and for Melanie, Jordan, Tara and Kerrie. No matter what it took. No matter what the price. Neither they, nor she, could rest so long as The Director, the murdering son of a bitch, was still large.

"I'll get him," she whispered, turning away from the grave. It was both prayer and promise. One thing about Jessica Wideacre – she always kept her promises.

CHAPTER SEVEN

Jack Kingsman's residence was palatial; a three-storey mansion house just off Berkeley Square. A former embassy, it was the kind of house DCI Beckwith, on his police salary, could never in a million years hope to own. His own house being more than adequate for his needs – two of the three bedrooms were empty – he wasn't remotely envious. Venise, though, was awestruck.

"Wow!" she said, gazing up at the Queen Anne facade, her expansive thespian's repertoire briefly deserting her. "Awesome! I expected it to be nice, but this is, like, really amazing."

Beckwith felt a jolt go through him. Venise's youthful expressions served only to underline the age gap between them. She relished it, insisting it didn't matter one bit. He was less convinced. Lady Gaga was as much foreign territory to him as the Rolling Stones were to her. And music was the very least of it.

She flew up the flight of marble steps leading to the door. "I bet there'll be champagne and caviar and lobster and everything."

Mark felt his stomach turn. He was an honest-to-God beer or whisky drinker, with an intense hatred of anything fishy, both the literal and the metaphorical. Feeling like he was about to enter the portals of Newgate Prison, albeit a stunningly posh version, he glanced in despair at the building towering above him. Rows of crystalline windows gazed blankly back, except for one at the very top where a white face materialised for a split second before melding back into the glossy facade. How many minions, he wondered, did it take to run a place of this magnitude?

"Marky!" Venise urged, a note almost of panic in her voice. "Hurry up. Mr Kingsman doesn't like to be kept waiting."

His inner curmudgeon coming to the fore, Beckwith deliberately slowed his step.

...

At the same time her boss was dallying on Jack Kingsman's doorstep, Jessica was psyching herself up to enter her parents' house. When she emerged again, she knew it would be with the demeanour of one for whom the gallows would seem a happy release. Larkin, she sometimes thought, had her in mind when he wrote the immortal words, "they fuck you up, your mum and dad". Guilt! That was Jessica's overriding emotion whenever she thought about her parents. Guilt that she didn't measure up to their expectations. Guilt that she never could measure up to their expectations. Guilt that if each and every one were suddenly to disappear, she probably wouldn't miss them. The door opened suddenly. Her mother's hand shot out like a music hall crook and pulled her into the hallway. As always, whenever Kathleen Reid spoke to her eldest daughter, the dominant note in her voice was one of irritation.

"Jessica, come inside! We've been waiting ages for you." Denim-blue, slightly faded eyes squinted over Jessica's shoulder. "Where's that husband of yours?"

"Finance convention," Jessica muttered. "He sent his love. He'll pop round later if he can get away." Hell would freeze over first. Reserved, occasionally puritanical, David found Jessica's family a trial. She used to joke it was a good thing she'd hooked him before introducing him to her very own version of the Addams family.

Her mother sniffed. "Thinks he's too good for us, I suppose." It was a tune so familiar, Jessica could whistle it out her nostrils. "I don't know what you ever saw in him. Or him in you, for that matter."

"Nice!" Jessica murmured beneath her breath, trailing after her into the dining room, where her father, sister and brother-in-law were already ensconced at the table. A small pile of gaudily wrapped gifts were stockpiled by her father's elbow. Jessica, irreverently noting that he grew more and more like Toad of Toad Hall every day, handed over a crumpled W.H. Smith paper bag.

Happy birthday, Dad," she said. "I couldn't think what to get you, so I got you that book by Ali Dizaei."

"The bent copper?" Her father peered briefly into the bag, shoved it unenthusiastically to one side, huffed, "I hope you kept the receipt. In my day, the likes of him would never have been allowed in the force."

Jessica took a chair. "Yeah, yeah, and women would never have had the vote, and slavery would be alive and well and living in East Acton. Oh, sorry it is. I was forgetting about you, Mum." She waved an airy hand round the table. "Hi, all. Sorry I'm late."

Her brother-in-law smiled, picked up the wine bottle and poured her a glass. "Get that down your neck. Jessica," he said. "You look like you could use it."

Jessica returned the smile. "Thanks, Ted. Only the one, though. I'm driving." She looked at her sister, whose pregnancy was so far advanced her stomach looked as though it might be about to stage a bid for world domination. "Hi, Carol. How's junior coming along?"

Carol looked sulky. Carol always looked sulky. "Slowly. David not here?"

"He's busy," Jessica explained for the second time. "Finance convention." She reached for a bread roll to go with her soup – thick green algae, masquerading as pea and ham. It tasted foul, but a refusal to partake would have resulted in the outbreak of World War III.

"Ted's busy too," Carol snapped. "Funny how he always manages to make time." She wasted no time lunging for her sister's jugular. "David's not very supportive of you, is he? Or the family." She made it sound like they were the Corleones, only the mob was way nicer.

Jessica chewed on a pink piece of rubbery ham. "Like I said, he's busy. So am I, so I won't be staying long." Not if she could help it.

"Oh yes, busy *not* catching, what's that creep called, The Director?" Carol unleashed a little trill of laughter. "It's so gratifying to know we can all sleep easy in our beds knowing DI Jessica Wideacre is on the case." For someone who was doll pretty, she couldn't half look ugly. Her rosebud mouth flat-lined to spiteful. "Not!"

"Fuck off and die, bitch," Jessica said, but only in her head. Aloud she said, "You're welcome to come along and give us the benefit of your wisdom, Carol. I'm sure we'd all be very grateful for the insights of an ex trolley dolly."

Her mother, whose Scottish temper was legendary, slammed her hand down on the table. "Don't start, the pair of you," she warned. "Let's, just for once, have a nice, civilised dinner."

"Sorry, Mum," Jessica said. Calmly, she spooned some more

of the green goo into her mouth. Inside though, she was raging for allowing herself to be sucked into the usual family bullshit.

Carol glared across the table. "Never mind 'Sorry, Mum', it's me you should be apologising to."

"For what?" Jessica snapped. "Living?" And with that remark, the gloves were off. Carol banged her spoon on the table and screamed the old refrain Jessica had heard since forever.

"Oh, shut up, you! You're just jealous... . *just because I've got blue eyes... . just because I've got blonde hair... . just because I'm prettier ... more popular ... everybody loves me ...*"

Wishing she'd had the sense to bail on the stupid dinner, Jessica pushed her barely-touched soup bowl away. Her eyes sought the heavens. "Oh, for fuck's sake, Carol," she said wearily, "grow up would you, instead of just out!"

Swearing - the signal for her mother's hand to go into overdrive, slicing through the air like a deranged windmill.

"Jessica Wideacre! That is enough of that language, thank you. You're not down the station now."

Carol stirred the pot. "Huh! Now that she's made DI, she's worse than ever. Funny how all that swearing never sounds right coming from a woman. Makes them sound as if they're trying too hard. Trying to be one of the lads."

Women in the force – her father's favourite subject! Bang on cue, he came wading in with his flat-footed size 12s. "I must say I don't hold with this ladette business, myself," he said. "There's nothing more guaranteed to turn me off my dinner than a foul-mouthed woman."

Jessica eyed his empty bowl. "Looks that way, all right," she said. "Look, can we not get started with all this women-don't-belong-in-the-force garbage. Things have moved on a lot since ye olde days."

"Not for the better. All this equality of the sexes and PC bollocks!"

Jessica smirked. "I don't think I've met him."

The witticism passing right over him, her father pressed on. "The world's gone mad. In my day, men were men and women were women and never the twain met, except in the kitchen or the bedroom. Proper order, if you ask me. Am I right, Ted?"

Typical, Jessica thought, as he called on her brother-in-law for back-up. All boys together. To give Ted his due, he looked uncomfortable, reluctant to declare his hand one way or the other.

Carol did it for him. "Oh, come on, Ted," she shrieked. "You know you agree with Dad. You're always complaining about the women at work. You're just trying to spare Jessica's feelings." Disproportionately angry all of a sudden, she pushed her own bowl away, sending a wave of green slop over the edge. "Well, I bloody won't. That promotion you got should have been Ted's. The force is his career. It's only a stopgap for you till you have children. If you thought anything of this family, you'd never have put yourself forward for it in the first place."

Jessica lost it then. "Oh, get over yourself, you silly cow," she yelled. "Just because you want to stay home playing wifey doesn't mean we all do." She turned her attention to her brother-in-law. "I'm sorry you're disappointed, Ted, but we both know me turning the position down wouldn't have meant you were an automatic shoo-in." She glared at her father. "And you can shut up and all, Dad. Just because I don't have a prick doesn't mean I'm no good at my job. I put in a lot of hard graft for this. It wasn't just handed to me on a plate."

Jessica's mother threw in the towel. Stiff-backed with indignation she rose to her feet and began collecting up the dishes.

"Trust Jessica to cause anarchy and chaos wherever she's goes," she said, speaking about her in the third person. "It's her m.o. Her modus operandi." A cop's wife for more than forty years, she'd picked up some of the lingo herself. "But then, you only have to look at the state of her to see the way her mind works." She rounded on Jessica. "Tell me, did you even brush your hair today? Those jeans, were you painting in them, or what? Why don't you just become one of those lesbian creatures, and be done with it."

Jessica grated her chair back from the table. No way was she going to stay and listen to the well-worn litany of failings coming her way. Not, when she could already recite them by heart. Secretly, she was delighted to have been given the excuse to leave. On her way out, she swiped the book back from her father and stuffed it in her oversized satchel. "I'll take this back for you, shall I, Dad? Replace it with that other one you're always banging on about, *In My Day*.

As she slammed the front door behind her, she could hear her mother protesting, Carol whining and her father blustering.

She was about to pull away from the kerb when Ted emerged from the house. He hurried over and tapped on the car window. Reluctantly, Jessica lowered it.

He leaned in. "Listen, Jess," he said. "I'm happy you got the promotion, really I am. Carol's hormones are all over the place right now. She doesn't really know what she's saying."

Jessica raised an eyebrow. "Do me a favour, Ted. We both know the real reason Carol has her knife in me, and promotion has very little to do with it."

Ted dropped his gaze. "I know. And I also know I shouldn't say this, but do you ever wonder what would have happened if we … if we hadn't split up?"

"No!" Jessica made her voice brusque. "That's ancient history, not that Carol believes it. She'll never forgive me for dating you first."

"We were good together, though," Ted insisted. "Weren't we? Remember that time –"

Jessica cut him off abruptly and sighed at the inappropriateness of the question. They were both married now, and Carol, by the look of it, was about to give birth to a hippopotamus any day. The past, as the old adage went, was a different country. "Look, I don't mean to be hurtful," she said, "but you were just a rebound for me when David and I were on a bit of a break. I was never serious and I don't believe for one moment that you were either." She pressed the button and the window began to rise. "Go, Ted," she told him through the rapidly shrinking aperture. "Go back inside to Carol, before she comes out and knifes us both."

She sat for a moment as he returned to the house. Turning briefly, he gave her a little wave. She twiddled her fingers in return, switched on the ignition and, feeling as drained as if she'd been the main course at a vampire's dinner party, shot off down the street. The further away from that house she got, the better.

Lowering, unseasonable rain clouds darkened the sky on what should have been a pleasant evening in early June. A persistent drizzle peppering the windscreen added to the air of despond. Jessica turned on both wipers and headlights, glad to be heading back to her own home south of the river. The roads were pretty clear, light traffic only as far as Wandsworth Bridge, where a set of temporary traffic lights was causing chaos. Fingers drumming on the steering wheel, ironically to the beat of "Mr Blue Sky", Jessica glanced idly out the window, her gaze skipping over, then back, to where a young girl sat huddled in a bus shelter. Strands of lank blonde hair poked from beneath the hood of a tatty green parka. As Jessica watched, she pushed them impatiently out of sight, her nails a striking fluorescent pink against an otherwise darkly monochromatic backdrop. She looked to be around fifteen, sixteen at most, exactly the type to fit The Director's warped criteria. Worried suddenly, she wondered if she should get out of her car, offer the girl a lift home. Ahead, the traffic lights changed to green and the moment was lost in the impatient blare of the horn of the motorist behind. Jessica glanced in her rear-view mirror, relieved to see the girl on her feet as a bus approached. On the radio "Mr Blue Sky" faded into a commercial for Mr Muscle, in which the presenter bellowed about the wonders of its limescale-removing properties. She switched off the radio, and with only the swish of the windscreen wipers for company crossed slowly over the murky Thames.

As Jessica's car was rolling off the bridge, a white Transit van was just beginning to make its way across. Like Jessica, the driver had seen the young girl waiting at the bus stop. He'd seen the bus arrive and depart, without taking her on board. He'd watched her slouch back to her seat, shoulders slumped, disconsolate. Today, did the little cow but know it, was her lucky day. He turned the volume on his stereo up full blast.

"Make all the damn noise you want, darlin'," he taunted the girl trussed up in the back. "No one can hear you."

CHAPTER EIGHT

DCI Beckwith had met Jack Kingsman only briefly on the night of the awards ceremony when everyone was wearing black tie, so wasn't quite sure what to expect from the famous director. In his mind he had a vague idea of someone arty-farty in velvet smoking jacket and cravat, lots of air-kissing and "dahlings". He was pleasantly surprised to find he was none of those things. Somewhere in his fifties, he was casually dressed in jumper and chinos, his grey hair well overdue for a trim. Wire-framed glasses gave him a slightly nerdy look.

He greeted them in person at the front door, his handshake firm and welcoming, and led the way into a comfortable sitting room cum office.

"I hope you don't mind," he said. "The rest of this place is a bit of a mausoleum, acres of rococo plasterwork and marble, more to my interior designer's taste than my own. He smiled conspiratorially. "As an East End lad from a two-up, two-down, I sometimes feel like a bit of an imposter." He gestured round. "This is where I like to relax with friends." It was a charming remark which, had it not been uttered with absolute sincerity, might have come across as contrived.

The lack of pretension put Beckwith at ease, and he relaxed further when Kingsman waved him into a leather chesterfield sofa.

"You look like a whisky man," he said, producing a bottle of Glenfiddich. "Or, there's beer, if you prefer. I tend to leave champagne and all that poncey stuff to the ladies." He threw a smile at Venise, whose attention was already caught by a wall covered in black and white photographs of various actresses. "You're there too," he said. "Third row from the top, two from the end." Eschewing false modesty, Venise hurried over for a closer look and Kingsman turned his attention back to Beckwith. He held the bottle. "So, DCI Beckwith. What's it to be?"

"Scotch, please. And it's Mark."

Kingsman smiled. "And I'm Jack." He was generous with his measures and, because he liked to keep a clear head, Beckwith added water to his drink from a jug left for the purpose. Kingsman took his straight. "I'd like to personally thank you," he said, "for mentoring Venise. Her utterly convincing performance as DCI Merry Moore was, in no small part, down to you."

Beckwith smiled modestly, said what was expected of him. "It was a pleasure. Venise isn't exactly hard on the eye."

"No, indeed," Kingsman said.

Sensing their gaze on her, Venise spun round. "Oh, Jack, these pictures are wonderful. Especially the one of—" Hesitant suddenly, she broke off.

"Of Marissa? It's okay, you can say her name. It was all such a long time ago. My late wife, Marissa Bloom," Kingsman explained to Beckwith, who was looking blank." There was an accident on set. She died of her injuries. But, like I said, it was all a long time ago. Twenty-five years, to be exact. One mustn't wallow for ever." He poured a glass of champagne for Venise, who left the pictures and came to sit on the sofa. "Actually, Venise, that's the main reason I asked you here tonight." He paused as she looked expectant, broke into a smile. "I'm going to remake *Killer Queen*, and I want you to play the part of Lorelei Turner."

...

Venise could not stop talking on the cab ride back to her apartment. "This is big," she assured Beckwith. "Like, really, really big. *Killer Queen* was the movie that shot Marissa Bloom to stardom. It was one of the biggest grossing movies of all time. Her name was everywhere." She paused, glanced at him sorrowfully. "You must be the only one on the planet who hasn't heard of her."

He shrugged. "Sorry, that's never been my area of expertise. Anyway, you must only have been a baby at the time."

Venise nodded. "True, but my mother was her number one fan. She queued for six hours once in blizzard conditions outside the Empire Cinema in Leicester Square, just to catch a glimpse of her."

"And did she?" Beckwith asked, not because he was remotely interested, more because he felt he had to.

Venise beamed. "Better. She got a signed photograph. It takes pride of place in my bedroom. Right over my bed, in fact." She grinned at him. "You know, Marky, for a policeman, you can be remarkably unobservant."

When it came to charm, DCI Beckwith was more Gordon Brown than Tony Blair. The opportunity to slip her a "I only have eyes for you" compliment went entirely over his head.

"What happened to Marissa?" he asked.

"Her veil caught on fire from a candle sconce on the set of *Mistress Boleyn*. The gauze went up in a blaze, spread to the rest of her costume, and, in seconds, she'd turned into a fireball. She died of her injuries a week or so later. Probably just as well. "She was so beautiful ..." Venise's voice trailed off.

Beckwith suppressed a smile. Clearly, Venise thought death preferable to losing one's looks. He dreaded to think what DI

Jessica Wideacre would have made of that philosophy, considering how she, herself, seemed to have been born with not one whit of vanity. Her mop of untamed hair, dowdy clothes and make-up free face were testament to that. What Wideacre lacked in grooming, though, she more than made up for in pig-headedness. She made no secret of her contempt for Venise. Not that she came right out and said it. The odd low snort in his hearing, curl of the lip, or disdainful flash of her green eyes put it better than words ever could.

Venise's mood of introspection lasted no longer than the beat of a butterfly's wings.

"I can't believe Jack chose me to play the part of Lorelei," she said for the umpteenth time, a huge smile splitting her face. "That's, like, Marissa's part. The starring role."

"You're not worried about the pressure?" Beckwith asked. "It sounds like you'll have a lot to live up to."

Venise pooh-poohed his concerns. "Not in the least. If Jack Kingsman thinks I can do it, then I can." She gave a little whoop, said again, "I can't believe it. It's like a dream come true." The cab pulled up in front of Du Cane Court, an art deco apartment block in trendy Balham. "Coming up?" Venise asked.

Beckwith shook his head. "Much as I'd like to, I've got an early start." He'd also drank way too much scotch and wasn't quite sure he could rise to Venise's – rather high – expectations. Wasn't sure he wanted to. Wasn't sure why that should be.

"Your loss," she grinned, far too happy to give him a hard time.

He dismissed the cab and saw her safely to the front door of the building, waiting till she'd disappeared inside the lift. His house, in Nightingale Lane, was less than a fifteen-minute walk. The night air felt good on his face, cool after a recent shower of rain, but not cold. He used the time to think about the evening, pleasantly surprised to find that he'd actually enjoyed himself. Kingsman was good company. He had a dry wit, was mildly self-deprecating and full of humorous anecdotes about the film industry. The more he heard about it, though, the more Beckwith was convinced that it was a world of round holes, in which he, the square peg, would always be an outsider. A loner by nature, that aspect didn't worry him, but Venise did. There was no role for him in her future. Stardom. It was time to end things. The actress and the cop was a saga that should never have got past the pilot episode. She was a bird of paradise; he was a dull old crow, happy with his lot. If, on the very slim off-chance, she was actually hurt by the break-up, there would be any amount of far more suitable admirers only too willing to glue back the pieces of her broken heart. Decision made, a weight lifted off his shoulders. By the time he arrived at his house, he was whistling.

As Beckwith closed the front door behind him, a white van was prowling up the street in the opposite direction. The driver was singing along to Tammy Wynette on the radio. "Stand by your man," he bellowed, "give him two arms to cling to."

In the back of the van, the young woman lying on the floor would never cling to anyone again. He and the boss had made damn sure of that. He braked sharply as a fox dashed across the street in front of him. The sudden motion sent the girl's body thumping hard against something. The fox skittered off into the night, eyes backlit to amber by the glare of his headlights. He was glad he hadn't hit it. He liked foxes. They were vermin, like him.

CHAPTER NINE

A new face had joined the five young victims on the whiteboard. She was Monika Jakubowska, and she had just turned seventeen. In the photograph, she was smiling, all glammed up for a night on the town with her mates. Her parents were Poles. Ten years earlier, they'd come to Britain to make a better life for themselves and their only child. They'd worked all the hours God sent, picking cabbages and living ten to a room on a farm in rural Kent. Eventually, they'd scraped enough together to move to London, where Josef got a job driving minicabs and Grabda found work as a hospital cleaner. They paid their taxes and made it a point of pride never to take a penny they didn't earn. Monika was intelligent and beautiful. Never gave a moment's trouble. And now she was dead, number six on the killer's ever-growing toll of murders. He'd left her on Mitcham Common and this time he'd stapled his card to her right breast.

Jessica, hair sticking up at all angles, stalked up and down in front of the pictures. She rubbed at her temples, forcing her brain up a gear.

"This Director bastard is not superhuman," she told her equally frustrated team. He doesn't operate in a vacuum. This is London, for God's sake. No matter what hour of the night, there's always someone around: cabbies, overnight couriers, drunks staggering home, tea leaves out on the rob. Someone must have seen something."

"He'll slip up," Connors said, looking a whole lot less perfect than her usual self. Bags which Jessica had never noticed before were prominent beneath her eyes, the fine lines around them cruelly exposed by the sunlight shining through the dusty window. The case was getting to them all, giving them sleepless nights. "They all do, eventually."

"But, in the meantime, the bodies are stacking up." Jessica shook her head. "No, eventually just doesn't cut it. We need to nail him and we need to nail him now."

A sudden barrage of shouting from outside focused their attention on the window. Following this latest murder, the press had descended upon them in force. Jessica was glad it was Beckwith who was scheduled to be thrown to the lions later on and not herself.

"I want all hands on deck today," she told the team. "Hennessy, see if you can't draft in more help from the other departments. This case must take priority over everything else. Knock on every door of every house, flat and dog kennel within a mile radius of Mitcham Common. If the occupants aren't at home, make a note and come back until such time as you find them in. I want everyone questioned – plant, animal and mineral. If they don't speak English, get an interpreter and fuck the expense. Someone somewhere has seen something and I want to know what it is." She turned back to the whiteboard, signalling that the briefing had come to an end. "Oh, and one more thing." She turned swiftly back. "All leave is cancelled until further notice. But, on the plus side, there'll be no quibble about overtime."

Hennessy punched the air. "Thank fuck for that," he said, beaming round as if he'd just scooped the Lotto. "We were due to spend a week with the wife's sister next week. Blackpool," he added, nose wrinkling as if from a bad smell. "Now, there's sweet FA she can say to me."

"What's wrong with her sister?" Liversedge asked.

"Nothing. It's that fucking Tower Ballroom I hate. Wife tries to drag me round it like I'm bleedin' Fred Astaire. And I fucking-well am not. Look at me," Hennessy implored, pointing to his corpulent stomach. "Is this the svelte physique of a poxy dancer?"

Everyone laughed, and that's the picture DCI Mark Beckwith carried with him on his way past to confront the press. Jessica Wideacre and her team laughing their arses off, while his was about to receive a very public mauling.

...

"How do you do it, Laura?" Jessica asked, as the pathologist pulled off her latex gloves and ran her hands under the tap. "All that blood and gore, doesn't it get to you?" Behind them, on a stainless-steel mortuary table, lay the lifeless body of Monika Jakubowska. Autopsy finished, Laura's assistant was doing the final tidy up, prior to releasing the body for burial.

Laura grinned. "Hey, it's a dirty job, but—"

"Right," Jessica said. "Seriously, though, how do you get into something like this anyway? It wasn't one of the career choices presented to me when I was at school."

"Coffee?" Laura jerked her head towards her office at the back of the mortuary, where a percolator was kept permanently on the go. Jessica nodded and followed her past a family of four sheet-covered corpses killed in a road accident the night before. "It all started," Laura said, "when my father bought me a pet rabbit for my birthday. Thumper." She grinned. "Originality wasn't my strongest point. Neither was pet care. The next day, I gave him back, all nicely jointed, his tiny heart, lungs and liver removed, weighed and written up in my diary."

"Jesus!" Jessica looked at her, horrified. "What did your father say?"

"Thank you very much, that'll do nicely for a rabbit stew."

Jessica's face relaxed, as the other woman burst out laughing. "You had me going just then," she admitted. "Rabbit stew, my eye!" Laura handed her a mug of coffee and she helped herself to the sugar bowl, adding two large spoonfuls. No milk.

She cradled her own mug, her dainty hands putting Jessica in mind of a squirrel cradling a nut. "I don't know how I got into it, really. I started out as a surgeon. The problem is live people tend not to like pain and sue you when things go wrong."

Jessica grinned. "You're impossible, you know that." She liked this woman, she realised, not entirely sure when the change from simply tolerating her had occurred. She could imagine them kicking back together and having a good laugh, which was strange, since Jessica wasn't a circle-of-friends type woman. Never had been, really. Never did the nightclub thing, the hen-do thing, the male-stripper thing. She'd had one or two best friends growing up, wasn't in touch with anyone anymore. David and her career were her whole life.

Laura went over to a small TV in the corner of the room and switched it on. It was a few seconds short of twelve o'clock and the music for the BBC news bulletin was on the countdown.

"Your man Beckwith was on this morning, wasn't he?"

Jessica grinned. "Yes, for his sins. I hope they didn't pulverise him too much." It was clear from her tone that she wished exactly the opposite.

"Beckwith's all right." Laura came back and leaned her bottom against the counter next to Jessica. "Better than some of the types I've gone out with. At least he's got this own teeth – I think."

Jessica laughed, and made a mental note to ask her out for a drink some time. The thought warmed her; then, because it was such an alien idea, also made her slightly nervous.

"Here he comes now," Laura said, as the cameras panned in on the front of Rosewood nick, where Beckwith was standing at the top of the steps, reporters surging below him like piranhas at feeding time. Both women listened intently as, no sign of nerves evident, the DCI gave his statement. Yes, the body of another young female had been found and, yes, he believed her to be the sixth victim of the man calling himself The Director. They'd know more when the pathology report was to hand. In the meantime, the police were doing everything possible to catch the perpetrator and were following a number of lines of enquiry. Blah! Blah! Blah! All the stops were being pulled out, more officers drafted in, no expense being spared. Having trotted out the same tired old tune countless policemen had sung since time immemorial, he paused for questions and found himself in the sights of a notorious hack from one of the gutter tabloids. Unsurprisingly, the hack's angle was salacious.

"DCI Beckwith, how do you justify schmoozing with film stars and attending movie premieres when you should be entirely focused on catching this killer? Last night, you dined with Venise Love-Davies and Jack Kingsman at his mansion in Mayfair. How can the public have faith in a chief inspector who puts his private life ahead of his duty to the public?" Encouraged by his fellow reporters and members of the public baying their approval at the question, he added what was supposed to be an aside, but which came out loud and clear over the microphones. "Bet she's bloody good in the sack. I wouldn't throw her out of bed for eating biscuits."

Jessica chuckled as Beckwith blanched visibly. "Dear, oh dear, he should have seen that one coming."

"You really don't like him, do you?" Laura looked at her curiously.

"Hate him," Jessica said. "Loathe him. Detest him."

Laura put down her mug. "And yet, love and hate are two sides of the same coin."

"No! No! No! No!" Jessica laughed. "Don't try that psychobabble on me. I do not, never have and never will fancy him. That man is his own fan club."

Laura said no more, but there was a smugness radiating from her that made Jessica rapidly rethink their developing friendship. No way would she ask the poisoned fucking dwarf for a drink now!

On screen, DCI Beckwith neatly side-stepped the question and brought the press conference to a close. "I have nothing more to add," he said. "I can only reiterate that we are doing all in our power to apprehend this killer."

"And getting absolutely nowhere," Jessica said, as the news switched to the troubles in Syria. "Wasn't there anything at all on Monika's body?" she asked now. "A hair? A fibre? Maybe you missed something."

Her professionalism called into question, her companion's lips thinned with annoyance. "DI Wideacre, you'll have my report tomorrow morning in full, all relevant boxes neatly ticked, all relevant sections filled in, t's crossed and i's dotted. As per usual."

"I … I didn't mean …" Jessica began, then tailed off. What was the use, the woman was ice from the forehead down. Any sign of thawing had been purely imaginary. "Thanks for the coffee," she said, hurriedly rinsing her mug under the tap. "I'd better get back to the nick."

As she walked away, she was uncomfortably aware of Laura Shackleton's eyes boring into the back of her head. Oh well, back to tolerating each other again.

...

Beckwith was royally pissed off. First he'd been bollocked by the press, then called in by his commanding officer, Superintendent Green, and subjected to a further bollocking for his "colourful" love life. A bit rich this, considering how, when he had voiced his objections to mentoring Venise, Green had been one of the most vociferous in persuading him of the value of it in terms of PR. Oh, he'd loved the publicity then – PC Plod being seen in a romantic light, reflecting glory on his fellow plods – but now that the fair wind had turned foul, Beckwith was the one getting it in the neck. His instinct was to go shit on someone else – Wideacre, maybe – but his innate sense of fairness held him back. The lack of progress in The Director murders was no more Wideacre's fault than it was his own. The woman was clocking up more hours than anyone else, losing weight off her already skinny frame and looking haggard beyond her years. Rumour had it her marriage was under strain.

His stomach rumbled, reminding him he'd had nothing to eat since breakfast, and it was already gone three o'clock. He headed over to a Subway across the road, still pondering his colleague's marriage. In some ways, it was as odd a pairing as him and Venise.

He'd met David Wideacre at a couple of police socials and thought him standoffish and humourless. He'd held himself apart, nursed the same drink all evening and responded to friendly overtures with a curtness that sent most people scuttling off in search of more convivial company. Jessica invariably looked uncomfortable, faintly embarrassed and usually, before too long, the pair made their excuses and left. It was rare these days that she even showed up to an event.

The shop assistant finished serving the customer in front. Beckwith gave his usual order for a large chicken and bacon melt, stuffed with salad and sauces. David Wideacre was some sort of hot-shot financier. His suits were bespoke, his shoes handmade. He drove a Jag, top of the range. Never in a million years would he have put him together with a woman like Jessica. He felt a brief pang of sympathy, suspecting she was every bit as out of her depth in the company of her husband's peers as he was in Venise's world of luvvies. His stomach rumbled again.

"I'll have a chocolate chip cookie, too," he told the shop assistant, willing him to hurry the hell up. "And a large coffee." As he fell upon his sandwich, all thoughts of Jessica Wideacre vanished, as though they had never been.

CHAPTER TEN

When her phone rang at 2.30 a.m., Jessica's first thought was that there had been another murder. She was almost relieved to hear that her father had had a stroke and had been rushed into hospital.

"It's Carol," she mouthed, as David struggled up beside her. "Dad's had a stroke."

"Is he okay?" David asked, when Jessica put the phone down.

"He's in Hammersmith Hospital," Jessica said, climbing out of bed. "I'd better get over there."

"Want me to come?"

Easier if he didn't. The truth was her family never really got David. They, like many others, made the classic error of misreading his reserve as arrogance. Carol summed it up pithily. "David Wideacre thinks his poo doesn't pong!" They were so wrong. Behind her husband's sophisticated exterior, he was warm, loving and gentle. His background was one of culture, privilege and stiff upper lips that made it hard for him to open up, especially to people like Jessica's family, who made a virtue out of inverted snobbery.

"There's no point in both of us losing our beauty sleep," Jessica told him, picking out jeans and a top from the wardrobe. "I'll call you if – if anything else happens."

David's relief was palpable. He wished her luck, blew her a kiss and snuggled back beneath the bedclothes. Envious, Jessica headed for the bathroom.

...

The temporary traffic lights on Wandsworth Bridge were stuck on red, apparently. Jessica seethed as she waited for them to change. Ridiculous how they didn't reset the timings for when the traffic was light, like now, when there was a mere handful of cars on the road and most God-fearing people were at home tucked up in their beds. A van approached on the opposite site of the road. Jessica took a keen interest in the driver, a young man in his twenties. A courier service. He noticed her looking, picked his nose in an exaggerated fashion and flicked it her way. Nice! No manners, but that didn't make him a murderer. Hot on his wheels was a black cab, the interior in darkness, probably reeking of vomit from the drunks it had ferried about all evening. Last up, before the lights changed, was a small hatchback. A young couple in that, heads nodding to the beat of something on the radio. Jessica switched on her own radio. Snow Patrol, "Chasing Cars". She loved that song. Ten minutes later, she pulled into a parking bay in front of Hammersmith Hospital.

Ted was outside, having a cigarette. He jerked his head at the no smoking sticker on the window behind him. "I know I shouldn't, but fuck it!"

"How's Dad?" Jessica asked.

He took one last pull, chucked the dog end into the night. It glowed fire-fly bright, then died. "Conscious. Grumbling. It was a TIA. In layman's terms, a mini-stroke. Carol's hysterical, of course."

She would be, Jessica thought. Everything was always about Carol. When she reached her father's room, her sister was already baring her fangs and poised to strike.

"Well, you didn't break your neck coming, did you? Dad could have been dead and buried in the time it took you to get here."

"Hardly," Jessica returned mildly. It was late. She was tired, and the last thing she needed was to get into it with Carol. She leaned over the bed. "Hi, Dad," she said. In the harsh light from a neon strip overhead, he looked sickly. His skin had a yellowish cast and bagged loosely over his cheekbones as if the skull inside had somehow shrunk. His eyes were dark-rimmed, sunk back in his head. For the first time in her life, Jessica pitied him. He muttered something unintelligible, and her mother, sitting on the opposite site of the bed, shushed him gently. Jessica noticed she was cradling his hand in both of hers. Her heart clenched a little. Her parents were in the puritanical camp when it came to public displays of affection. Even as a child, Jessica could never recall seeing them cuddle, let alone kiss. And yet, she was in no doubt that they loved each other. "All right, Mum?" she asked gently.

In times of stress her mother's accent changed to broad Glaswegian.

"Och, dinnae worry aboot me." She gazed over Jessica's shoulder. "Where's your man? He didnae come, then?"

"David's away on business." It was easier to lie. Behind her, Carol snorted, not buying the story. Jessica gritted her teeth. "Shall I get you a cup of tea?"

"Aye," her mother nodded. "A cup of tea would be grand." She turned her attention back to her husband, looking fragile, old beyond her sixty-six years.

...

The cafeteria was closed, but Jessica found two vending machines, one dispensing drinks, the other confectionery and packets of crisps. She dug in her purse for change, tensing as Carol materialised beside her.

"I'd give the coffee a miss," she said. "It's vile. The tea's fine, though, and the hot chocolate's okay, a bit watery but drinkable."

Jessica made a non-committal noise, suspecting that the point of the exercise was to labour the fact that Carol had been hanging round long enough to sample them all. She was proved right when her sister added, "Of course, you'd know that if you'd got here sooner."

"I got here as soon as I could." Damn it! Jessica cursed herself for taking the bait. "I do live in south London, you know, and I don't have a helicopter."

"Yes, well you're here now, anyway," Carol said, moving swiftly on to her real agenda, Jessica's husband. "So, David's away on business, you said."

"I did, didn't I?" Jessica inserted some coins in the drinks machine, shoved a cup beneath the spigot and pressed tea/white/sugar. She swore as the scalding liquid spurted out splashing her.

"But he's not, though, is he?" Carol pressed. She narrowed her eyes. "Are you even together anymore, the pair of you?"

Jessica took her time answering. She put a plastic lid on the cup of tea and put it to one side. She selected hot chocolate for herself. "And what exactly is that supposed to mean?"

"Well, we never see him these days. He's always working or *away* on business." She did that inverted comma thing with her fingers. Jessica guessed they were now coming to the real meat of the conversation. "Or … so you say."

A cup in either hand, Jessica turned to face her. "Spit it out, Carol," she said. "I know you're just itching to tell me something."

"He's having an affair, isn't he?" She could see the "gotcha" in her sister's eyes.

"You tell me," Jessica said, stone-faced.

The words spilled out of Carol then. "Ted saw him in a restaurant in Piccadilly last week. He was with some blonde woman, much younger than him. Ted said they looked very … cosy."

Jessica laughed gaily. "Oh, Emily, you mean. His *niece*, Emily – he took her to lunch to celebrate her twenty-first birthday."

The wind went right out of Carol's sails. "Oh," she said, her face falling. "I didn't know he had a niece."

"Clearly, you don't know everything." Jessica said. She began to walk away, turned on her heel. "What, for instance, was Ted doing in Piccadilly at the time?"

Carol bristled. "He was working under cover."

Jessica winked. "Ah yes, but under *whose* covers?" Smirking, she left her sister standing in the corridor, her mouth opening and closing like a goldfish.

…

"Are you having an affair?" Jessica demanded the following morning, when she returned from the hospital to find David sitting at the breakfast table, *The Times* propped up on the teapot in front of him. He paused, a slice of toast halfway to his mouth.

"Of course. I'm almost forty. It was either that or a Porsche."

"If you were wise, you'd have chosen the Porsche," Jessica said. "Seriously, though, my spies reported you wining and dining a mystery blonde in Piccadilly last week."

"Saskia. And it was actually a sandwich and a cup of coffee in Pret. We were going over some notes for a meeting that afternoon. Sorry to disappoint."

Jessica relaxed. She should have known better than to let Carol rile her. Saskia was David's happily married assistant. They had attended her wedding not six months before. Her lesbian wedding.

"Jess." David regarded her steadily over his toast. "Do you seriously imagine I'd cheat on you?"

"'Course not, but it's been difficult lately for both of us. All work, no play. I couldn't blame you if you were tempted."

"I'm not," David said. "Besides, these things too shall pass. The Director will get caught and the markets will recover. We've just got to hang on in there." He made a silly face. "In the meantime …"

Smiling, Jessica completed their silly catchphrase. "We've got each other."

Later she thought about that, wondering if it was still true. Her family were right about one thing. David and she were in many ways worlds apart, the proverbial tomayto/tomato couple. He liked sushi. She liked fish 'n chips. He liked Beethoven. She liked Steppenwolf. He liked Sudoku. She liked Scrabble. He read military history and maths books for entertainment. She read, James Patterson and Stephen King. On paper, the relationship should never have got off the starting blocks. It had, though, and they were genuinely happy. Lately, however, each had come under increasing pressure. David, as a result of the downturn in the financial markets. Her, as a result of The Director murders. Jessica was neither scientist nor mathematician, but even she could figure out that something or somebody subjected to sustained pressure will eventually crack.

•••

"Can't you stay a bit longer?" Venise ran a long-nailed finger down

Beckwith's back as he sat up in bed.

"'Fraid not," he said. "I'm running late as it is." He smiled down at her, feeling like a real shit. In truth, he'd intended to break things off the night before, but he'd been tired and depressed and she'd been so warm and appealing, balm to his sore ego. Almost before he knew it, they'd ended up in bed. Fuck! Fuck! Fuck! He'd have to hang in there for a bit now.

Venise mock-pouted. "Well, I'm sorry if I've kept you late, Marky." She giggled. "Maybe you should get out the handcuffs."

Beckwith forced himself to smile. Christ! He didn't have time for games. "Well worth it," he said gallantly, hating himself for his duplicity.

"Will I see you later?" Venise sat up in bed, totally naked, her skin gleaming like Golden Syrup, no attempt whatsoever to cover that amazing body of hers. He liked that about her, her honesty. She was gorgeous. She knew it. He knew it and the world knew it. No need for false displays of modesty.

"I don't know," he said. "Maybe. I'll call you."

She settled down again as he headed to the bathroom. By the time he emerged, she had drifted back to sleep. Thankful, and guilty for feeling that way, he let himself out.

...

Jack Kingsman had been up drinking all night. An empty bottle of scotch lay tipped on its side on the floor. Another, one quarter empty, stood on the table before him. Fuzzily, he examined the wall opposite where only two pictures of his leading ladies remained. The rest of the gallery was reduced to little more than confetti: lips, eyes and sultry expressions strewn about in a grotesque Picasso-esque jigsaw. His psycho period!

He rose unsteadily to his feet and lumbered across the room, whisky bottle in hand. Mad! He must have been mad to have embarked on the remaking of *Killer Queen* when the definitive version of the film had already been made. Venise Love-Davis was a great little actress, with a wonderful career ahead of her, but she would never be Lorelei Turner. That was Marissa's role, the one that had catapulted her into the stratosphere of acting royalty. There could never be another Lorelei Tuner. Just as there could never be another Marissa Bloom.

Sweat that had nothing to do with the temperature of the room beaded his forehead and upper lip. He upended the bottle of scotch and gulped at the contents, realising he was up to his neck in shit with no way of digging himself out. The investors had already come on board. The cast, including some of the best-known faces in the industry, was already assembled, as was the production crew. The hype machine was having a field day, spewing out the usual movie guff. All the elements that went into making a blockbuster were moving inexorably into place. To pull the plug at this stage was to commit career suicide. Jack Kingsman, award-winning film-maker, would be lucky if he ended up making skin flicks in a filthy garage in deepest, darkest Leytonstone.

"Fuck! Fuck! Fuck!" He dashed the bottle to the ground. Unmoved, Marissa smiled sweetly down from the wall. Beside her, Venise Love-Davies mirrored the smile, only in her case the effect was somewhat marred by the shattered glass of the picture frame and the dagger piercing her right eye.

Jack sank to his knees, unaware he was being observed through a gap in the door.

CHAPTER ELEVEN

Ed loved his job. Fucking loved it! When the boss was finished setting up the shot, it was his turn to move in. Then it was lights, camera, action. He grinned. And cut! With a sharp blade!

"Won't be long now, luv," he told the terrified girl, who was tied to the bed. "All be over soon."

He watched the boss arrange the girl's hair, clipping in extensions to make it longer and thicker, spreading it out like a bleedin' fan around her head. He'd no idea what the fuck that was all about, didn't give a flying one neither. Ordinarily, these girls were way out of his league. He'd be nothing more than shit on their shoe. A figure of fun. Guess who was laughing now.

The boss removed the girl's gag, moved away behind the camera. Ed cracked his knuckles and waited for the signal. The red light came on. The camera was rolling. Take one! Action!

"Please," the girl screamed, as Ed loomed over her. "What did I do? What did I do wrong?"

He thought about it a moment. "Nothing," he told her, grinning. "Nothing at all." Twenty long minutes later when the girl's screams had died to a final groan. Ed moved away. The camera panned in on her bloodied face.

"Fade to dead," the boss called. "It's a wrap."

•••

Jessica Wideacre looked like shit. Her eyes were slitty from lack of sleep. Her hair was a bird's nest, chucked up any old way. Her clothes looked like she might have slept in them – for a week. Frustrated to the point of madness, she leaned across DCI Beckwith's desk, hands clutching the edges for support.

"Short of putting teams of coppers on every common in south London twenty-four hours a day, I don't know how else we're going to catch this guy."

Beckwith recoiled slightly, both from the light of battle in her eye and her breath, pungent from her last meal – garlic prawns, at a guess.

"Not possible," he said. "We've not got the resources."

"Of course not," Jessica snapped. "Funny how there's always enough bodies to escort minor royals, toerag politicians and Z-list celebs about the place, though. In the meantime, those of us who are actually invested in these murders are going around like zombies through lack of sleep."

He wasn't going to argue with that. 'Twas ever thus! With successive governments cutting back on the police force and a recruiting embargo currently in place, it stood to reason there was nowhere near enough manpower.

"Tell me about the latest victim," he said. He waved his hand. "And you can sit, if you like."

"What? Oh!" Jessica backed off a bit, lowered herself into the chair facing him. "Same as the others. Young, blonde, pretty. Susan Kelly, eighteen years old. Called herself Shoshana. Dreamt of being an actress, hence the pretentious name. Ran away from Leeds to London. Got a job waiting tables. When the manager got frisky she chucked a cup of hot coffee over him and took off again. Her money ran out before she could get another job. Fell into arrears on the pig-sty bedsit she rented in the arsehole of Colliers Wood." Jessica paused for a breath. "Suddenly, she's out on her ear and living rough. No permanent address, so she can't get benefits. Nowhere to go but the gutter." She put her head in her hands. "Jesus, it's all so fucking predictable." When she looked up again, there were tears in her eyes.

Beckwith cleared his throat. "Go home, DI Wideacre," he instructed. "Go home and get some kip."

Jessica kicked herself for her weakness. She shook her head. "I can't. There's far too much to do."

"It's an order." Beckwith was firm. "You're running on empty, which makes you a liability and bugger all good to anyone." He checked his watch. "I'll see you back here tomorrow, 0800 hours."

Jessica gave up. She *was* all burnt out and, though she didn't appreciate him pointing it out to her, it did make her a liability. Her head was spinning. Her limbs felt like lead and her brain was so tangled there wasn't a coherent thought to be found there. She felt guilty leaving the building, felt as though she was slinking out and leaving her team to cope with all the flak. They were just as wasted. Connors had fallen asleep at her desk earlier, giving everyone a good view of the half-inch growth of black roots in her normally immaculately coiffed blonde hair. Curiously, this chink in her glamorous colleague's armour served to soften Jessica's attitude towards her slightly. When push came to shove, Connors was every bit as willing as the rest of them to get her manicured fingernails dirty. That went a long way in Jessica's book.

...

At home, she kicked off her shoes, slid into bed fully clothed and closed her eyes. Despite her exhaustion she was still wide awake an hour later. Her mind was amped to fever pitch. Images of the seven young victims segued with pictures of her father as she'd last seen him in hospital, his habitual bluffness subsumed by age and infirmity. In turn the carousel shifted to David looking at her, puzzled, as if he didn't quite know who she was any more or what to make of her. Infuriatingly, he morphed into Beckwith gazing at her ... how? As if ... as if he actually gave a shit. As if he cared that she was tired and stressed. She rocketed up in bed and sloughed off the thought like a dirty shirt. No! Beckwith didn't do caring. His agenda, his only agenda, was that she was fit for purpose. Even he recognised that occasionally people need to rest and recharge their batteries. It was naive to attribute any finer human feelings to the man. As an aide-memoire, she leaned over and pulled a dog-eared piece of paper from the top drawer of her bedside table. It was the memo she'd found stuffed down the back of her predecessor's desk, the one in which Beckwith tried to trash her chances of promotion. She didn't need to read it, not really. Every word was indelibly burned into her brain, especially the last two sentences, which made her sound like some sort of hysterical maiden aunt and not the competent, conscientious, hardworking copper she knew herself to be.

It is my considered opinion that DS Jessica Wideacre is volatile, hasty in her actions and prone to the kind of excesses of emotion that lead to poor judgement and rash decision-making. I recommend that promotion be withheld pending further assessment.

Her immediate instinct had been to beard him in his den, kick his head in, but sensible, rational, David had persuaded her otherwise. It would serve only to prove Beckwith correct in his reading of her character. His advice was to play the long game, give one hundred per cent and make the bastard eat his words. Jessica really didn't think she could work harder than she already did, considering how she routinely sweated blood and tears for the job, putting her health, sanity and marriage at risk. When eventually she cooled down, she realised her husband was right. The memo had never been meant for her eyes and there was no point in adding fuel to Beckwith's fire. The urge to kick his fat head in, however, went straight to number one on her bucket list. Where it remained.

Giving up on the idea of sleep, Jessica climbed out of bed and stomped down to the kitchen for a cup of tea. She grabbed a biro and pad and, while the kettle came to the boil, began to jot down the details of the seven murders, searching for that elusive clue they might have missed, the all-important lead that would help them nab their man. Ten minutes later she threw the biro down in disgust and got up to make the tea. Same old same old. The victims were all female, young women on the cusp of adulthood, all of a type: blonde, attractive and accessible. Each had been dumped on common land in south London, suggesting the perp was a local man with local knowledge.

She added milk and sugar to her tea and sat down again. A plain white business card bearing the words "The Director" had been left at each scene. The cards were generic, printed on a home computer, so no chance of tying them to a particular manufacturer. Sedgie, who knew about such things, reckoned they'd been done on a bog-standard inkjet printer, the type that was being offloaded in charity shops and car boot sales on a daily basis. It was the price of the ink, he said. People were literally giving them away. So, there was no chance of obtaining a name and address and just nipping round and picking the scumbag up. That would have been way too easy. Jessica massaged her temples with the tips of her fingers.

A headache was brewing. Rigid with tension, her shoulders were up around her ears. It felt as though she was balancing an anvil on each. Idly, she drew a heart, zigzagged a line through it, all without noticing. If the killer was local, it followed that the actual kill site was also relatively near, south of the river anyway, since only a nutjob would risk driving round for hours with a dead body in his vehicle, especially in the dead of night. Too many variables, getting pulled up by the cops for one reason or another not the least of them. *You don't mind if I breathalyse you, sir? Oh, and perhaps you could explain why there's a dead girl rolling about in the boot of your car.* The Director was indeed a nutjob, but he was no fool. He'd got his routine down pat. The quicker he could get rid, the less chance of being caught. The bastard had thought of everything. Until he cocked up and left a major clue or someone happened upon him disposing of one of the bodies – and what were the chances of that? – his killing spree could continue ad infinitum. Unless he grew a conscience and found God. Flying pig time!

Jessica picked up her cup of now lukewarm tea and glared at her notes, willing the paper to magically transform itself into a map with a helpful arrow: "your murdering git is here". It didn't, so she scrunched it up, chucked it away and started from scratch. When David arrived home several hours later, he found her sound asleep at the table surrounded by a mountain of crumpled paper balls, the biro still tightly clutched between her fingers.

CHAPTER TWELVE

Ed Hatcher was used to being low man on the totem pole. A person of no account, he glided through life – anonymous, unmemorable, never disturbing the air, leaving not a ripple. People looked through him like he was a ghost, as if he didn't exist, too unimportant, too insubstantial to cross their radar. Which was just how he liked it. Now! It hadn't always been like that. It used to piss him off royally. A Johnny No-Mates all his life, things really went down the crapper when puberty came calling. Girls, even the really butters ones – the cripples, the ones you wouldn't touch with someone else's prick – refused to give him the time of day. Once, out of sheer desperation, he'd sunk so low as to put the moves on a blind woman he knew and – Christ on a bike! – got knocked back. Like the dozy cow had 'em queuing round the block. He'd taken her white stick and chucked it in the nearest dustbin. The memory gave him a chuckle still, looking back seeing her head spinning like that bird in *The Exorcist*, not a clue which way to go. She'd got a dog after that, one of them Golden Labradors. He went round and poisoned it. Nice bit of rare steak with a jus d'arsenic. He'd hung around till she came out in the garden calling it – "Honey, Honey" – and pissed himself laughing when she fell over the fucking thing. Splat! Flat on her face.

Then he got the mumps, because his slut of a mother had been too lazy to have him inoculated as a kid. After that, he couldn't have got it up even with the help of a crane, all the king's poxy horses and all the king's men. Now, thanks to his boss, he was getting his own back. Someday all the bitches who had knocked him back would know his name. Someday all the fuckers who had ignored him would see him peering out of their newspapers and monopolising their TV screens. Someday every cunting one of them would realise that he too was *somebody*. For now, though, he was just a ghost, a person of no account. Happy days.

...

DCI Mark Beckwith was in hell; his girlfriend, in heaven. The reason for both extremes of emotion was *Killer Queen*, the DVD playing on Venise's 50-inch flat-screen television. "Wasn't she wonderful?" Venise sighed, as the late, great Marissa Bloom strutted her stuff on screen. "So beautiful and talented. Do I look like her?" She knew she did. Jack Kingsman had told her as much. Beckwith suppressed a sigh of his own. Venise's constant need for reassurance was playing on his nerves. "And her voice," she continued, "it's so distinctive. Sexy, low, with a little throaty purr." She batted her eyelashes in an exaggerated fashion. "Have *I* got a distinctive voice, Marky? If you closed your eyes, would you know it was me speaking?"

If he closed his eyes. God, if only he could! The long hours he was putting in down the nick were beginning to take their toll, and still they were no nearer to catching their man. Not only was he dog-tired, but Wideacre and her team were fraying round the edges too, snapping and snarling at each other like rabid dogs. Even the normally unflappable Hennessy had been surly of late, his twenty-a-day fag habit inching closer to forty. Venise hit him with one of the many ornamental scatter cushions on her bed, prompting him to a response.

"Of course, I'd know it was you," he said. "You only have to say 'hello' on the phone and I know it's you."

"You've got caller ID," she remarked acidly. Accusation in her beautiful blue eyes, she froze the action on screen. "Marky, you're not taking me seriously. I know I'm just an actress and my job's not as important as yours, but it's important to me." She paused. "And if you love me, *really* love me, it should be important to you too."

Jesus H. Christ! Mark swallowed rapidly. For ages he'd been working up the courage to break things off with her, (yeah, right, how's that going, he asks himself, lying beside her, stark bollock naked). Love! That shot things into a different dimension. He wasn't sure he even knew the meaning of the word. According to his ex-wife – the marriage had been mercifully brief – he was an emotional cripple and "withholder". Despite a lack of medical training, she'd diagnosed him as suffering from full-blown Asperger's and prescribed having his fucking head examined, pronto – either that, or shoving it up his arse. Now she was happily married to someone else and popping out kids like they were Smarties.

His mouth opened as he fished around for something gallant, but not misleading, to say. His eyes ping-ponged around the room. Venise hit him with the cushion again and unleashed a trill of laughter.

"Aw, relax, Marky," she said. "It was only a wind-up." She picked up the remote control and took the DVD off pause. She settled back then, her head resting on Beckwith's chest. "I really want to do her justice," she said, as Marissa Bloom came to life once more on screen, wicked, seductive. "See," she said in perfect synchronicity with the voice of the character, "I told you I'd steal your heart." The camera pulled back to reveal Lorelei Turner, the killer queen holding up a still beating, bloody heart. Venise clapped her hands. "Did I do it right?" she asked. "Did I catch her intonation?"

...

Jessica dabbed some Blistex on the cold sore at the corner of her mouth. It did nothing to improve her looks. She grinned sourly at her reflection in the mirror. Her eyes were red-rimmed, smudged beneath with dark shadows. Her face was gaunt, the skin stretched drum-tight across her cheekbones. On her skinny frame, her clothes hung shapelessly loose. She'd pinned her trousers at the waist to prevent them from mounting a spontaneous descent around her ankles. Just as well she wasn't the vain type, she thought, grabbing a hank of hair at the back of her head and spiralling it into a scrunchy. She picked up her watch and, still buckling it on her wrist, ran down to the kitchen. It was 6 a.m., high time she left for the hospital. Since evenings off were becoming as rare as hen's teeth, she'd taken to visiting her father before going on duty. She knocked back half a cup of super-strong coffee, reflecting that it was an arrangement that worked on several levels, not least because it meant that she avoided Carol and her endless sniping. Also, and she felt a bit guilty about this, it meant that she wasn't round to witness the daily disintegration of her tough old Glaswegian mam into a pale, wizened creature with big frightened eyes. While in hospital, Jessica's father had suffered a second stroke, this one serious enough to put him in mortal danger. If he did survive, there was more than an outside chance that he would be left permanently disabled.

Jessica wasn't selfish, she told herself, as she went outside to her car. She just didn't have the reserves of strength needed to take on anyone else's emotional bullshit, not when she had more than enough of her own to be going on with. Not that it stopped her sister from dumping on her with endless voicemails and texts. *How come she and Ted were doing the lion's share … acting as unpaid taxi drivers … ages since they had a night out together… and –* this always delivered in an outraged squeak – *didn't Jessica realise she was pregnant!* Since there hadn't been such fanfare since the birth of the Messiah, it was unlikely that Jessica, together with the whole wide world, could have escaped such earth-shattering news. Especially when it was being drummed into her at every opportunity.

She paused a second on the driveway and looked up at the window of the guest room, where her husband was sleeping. The separate bedrooms had been a recent innovation, made at her own suggestion. She'd been so restless lately, tossing and turning, disturbing David and robbing him of his much-needed sleep. She kind of wished he'd put up more of a fight, though, instead of acquiescing with nary a punch pulled. Disappointing, but she didn't blame him, not really. All work and damn all play had turned her into the very definition of a miserable, angst-ridden bitch. Hell, she'd avoid her own company if she could. Piss off into a different room. Take a holiday from herself.

As she climbed into the car and jammed the key in the ignition, she caught sight of the recycling bin, the lid propped part-open by the mountain of newspapers and cartons inside. Also, known only to her, and cunningly hidden at the bottom, a large pile of empty wine bottles. Jessica jerked her gaze away. One thing at a time. She'd tackle her growing alcohol addiction when The Director had been caught and everything had settled down. Right now, though, she needed all the help she could get, and red wine helped a lot. As she drove away, she was aware of the curtains twitching at Mr Singh's, her neighbour. The poor old sod lived in fear that she would have his elderly mother deported for overstaying her visa. Having a cop living directly opposite must have seemed like his worst nightmare.

...

Arriving at Rosewood later, her mood, already verging on bad, was in no way improved by the sight of DCI Beckwith and Laura Shackleton playing bessie mates in the corridor. The pathologist had her head thrown back, laughing uproariously at something Beckwith had said. She started slightly as she caught sight of Jessica, leading her to suspect that she was somehow the butt of their joke. Beckwith saw her too and nodded a grudging acknowledgement.

Jessica nodded coolly back, damned if she was going to give either one of them the satisfaction of seeing her rattled. After a final word, Beckwith disappeared into his office and Jessica swung a left up the corridor, making for the incident room and the morning briefing. A moment later, her shoes echoing dully on the linoleum-covered floor, Laura Shackleton caught her up.

"Jessica. Wait!" she said. "It was actually you I came to see. Here!" She thrust a buff-coloured folder into Jessica's hands. "The Monika Jakubowska report, not that you'll find it of any great interest. In short, the poor kid met the same fate as all the rest. No hairs, fibres, semen, bodily fluids or the slightest clue as to the identity of the killer." She grinned. "And, just so you know, I did look again. Hence, the slight delay in getting it to you."

Jessica made a mental note to work on her paranoia. So Beckwith and Shackleton had had themselves a little joke, so what! Personally, she found Beckwith as funny as a slap round the chops with a wet kipper. To each their own. "Cheers;" she said. "I look forward to reading it."

"As one does," her companion said wryly. "Perhaps I should think about entering one of my reports for the Booker Prize. I'm sure the judges would find it riveting."

Jessica laughed then, the last of her prickly reserve melting away. There was something appealing about Laura Shackleton's dry sense of humour and self-deprecation. She was professional to her fingertips, yet didn't take herself too seriously. "I heard about your father," she said. "I am sorry, Jessica. What's the prognosis?"

Jessica thought about how he had looked that morning, the yellowness of his skin, the pronounced beakiness of his nose as the flesh slid off the supporting structure of the skull beneath. He'd looked smaller too, as if his body was being absorbed bit by bit into the mattress as a prelude to disappearing altogether. She'd sat quietly, watching his eyes flicker under eyelids thin as rice paper while, around them, the busy hospital sprang to life. She hoped his dreams were happy ones. When she left, it had been with a deep sense of sadness – for him, for her, for not being the son he had wanted to carry on his name.

She put her head on one side and answered the question. "Technically speaking, he's fucked." She patted the file. "Well, work to do ..."

The other woman put her hand out to detain her, withdrew before making contact, no more the touchy-feely type than Jessica herself. "Listen, I'm here for a few hours," she said, seeming faintly embarrassed. "You don't fancy grabbing a bit of lunch later, do you? My treat."

Jessica looked equally uneasy. Such overtures rarely came her way. "Yeah, why not," she said, after an awkward pause. "But only if we go Dutch."

...

The incident room was a hub of idleness. Hennessy, lolling back, feet up on his desk, was taking forty winks. Connors was mooning over some God-awful women's magazine that looked suspiciously like *Hello!* Liversedge was texting on his iPhone, checking in with one of his admirers, no doubt, of whom there were more than just a few.

"Fuck's sake!" Jessica yelled, slamming down the forensic report on Hennessy's desk with a bang. Where do you think you all are? Fucking Center Parcs? "Get to work, the lot of you, before I kick your arses out on street patrol." The threat acted like a gun. Before you could say "back in uniform", Hennessy had ratcheted up ramrod straight, Connors' mag was filed in the bin, and Liversedge's phone was tucked safely out of sight. Jessica retrieved the report and stalked to the top of the room. "Monika Jakubowska," she said, indicating it with disgust. "Sweet FA in there, so I hope you lot have some good news for me. What happened with the house-to-house? Anybody see anything? Any nosey bastard spying on their next-door neighbour?"

"Plenty of those, guv," Connors said. "One old dear wanted us to go round and arrest her neighbour; said his ears were too low. Sign of a bad character, apparently."

Jessica grunted out a laugh. "Jesus, in that case we'd better go round and nick everybody on the Thatcher estate." Her eyes scanned the room. "Surely we've got more than that? Anyone coming and going at dodgy hours, dragging a blood-soaked body behind them? Sound of a spade digging in the night? No? Disobliging bastards!"

"A few were away," Hennessy offered, heavy-eyed from his catnap. "I've made a note to go back."

"As many times as it takes," Jessica ordered. "I don't want anyone slipping through the net." At the far end of the room, the telephone shrilled. Liversedge picked it up, spoke quietly into the receiver. Jessica continued, "I can't stress enough how vital it is that we leave no stone unturned. Right now it seems that we and not The Director are Public Enemy No. 1. And the politicians, fucking vultures, are taking every opportunity to do a bit of political grandstanding, making us out to be the Keystone Cops, while crippling us with cuts." Jessica slapped the report savagely down on the desk. "Perhaps if they got their snouts out of the trough long enough to look around they'd make the connection between the lack of bobbies on the beat and the rise in crime."

The clatter of Liversedge replacing the telephone diverted Jessica's attention from what was a favourite topic, the failure of successive governments to provide adequately for the police force.

"What?" she asked, as, exultant, he punched the air.

"I think we've got something, guv. A possible witness. He's coming in now to make a statement."

"Not a headcase looking for a spot in the limelight?" Jessica asked, scarcely daring to hope they'd finally caught a break.

"He didn't sound like a nut," Liversedge said.

"Bastards never do," said Jessica, thinking of the one who had turned up the week before demanding his mother-in-law be arrested for practicing black magic. Hennessy had made short work of him.

"All mothers-in-law are fucking witches, mate," he'd said, marching him out by his collar. "Deal with it. The rest of us fucking have to."

"Right," Jessica said with relish, "you and I will see him together, Sedgie. Let me know when he arrives. In the meantime I'll be in my office reading the Jakubowska report. The rest of you, do something productive." She wagged her finger at Hennessy. "And if you want to sleep, do it at home. Tell Mary to give you a sodding break, you're not as young as you used to be."

Hennessy looked sheepish, muttered, "Chance would be a fine thing."

...

Their potential witness was not a nutter, but a smartly dressed, articulate man. That in itself was no guarantee of sanity, David Icke being a case in point. However, Alex Watchester advanced no lizard theories; neither did he claim his mother-in-law was a practising witch and, on those two grounds alone, Jessica was disposed to give him a fair hearing. Disappointingly, it was also a short hearing, since he didn't really have that much to tell them, and seeing it written up in her report for Beckwith later made it look even more scant.

At 2.30 a.m. on June 23rd 2014, Mr Alexander Watchester, of 22B Underwood Street, Mitcham, was driving to Heathrow Airport to catch a flight to Miami. As he proceeded down Croydon Road, past Mitcham Common, a light-coloured van, possibly white, possibly a Ford Transit, emerged at high speed from Cedars Avenue, cutting him up on the roundabout and causing him to brake sharply. Mr Watchester was unable to provide a good description of the driver, other than to say he was a white male, wearing a baseball cap. There was a logo on the side of the van he described as a "clown face" or "funny face". It was not until he returned home several days later and learned that

Monika Jakubowska's body had been found on Mitcham Common that he wondered if the incident might be connected in some way.

Beckwith tapped on the report with his biro, disgust writ large on his face. "And he didn't think to report the driver for dangerous driving?"

"The man would have missed his flight," Jessica said. "You know what Traffic are like. Takes them ages to write down a sentence, then they have to rub it out and start all over again."

Beckwith said nothing to that. He knew she was right. "A clown face," he mused, then with an unusual flash of humour that lit up his dark brown eyes, "Not Ronald McDonald, I don't suppose?" His humour died as swiftly as it had been born. "There's not a lot to go on here, really, is there? This might have no bearing on the Monika Jakubowska killing whatsoever. Ubiquitous driver in baseball cap. Ubiquitous white/light-coloured Ford Transit van. Ubiquitous white van dangerous driving. We've all been cut up by one of those at some point or another."

Ubiquitous fucking moaning Minnie! Jessica gritted her teeth. "It's *something*, sir," she said. "Got to be worth investigating, anyway. I don't suppose there are all that many vans around with funny-face logos on the side, so it shouldn't take up too many man hours to track it down. Besides, it would be negligent not to." There, she'd let slip the "n" word, the one that struck fear in the hearts of all those in charge. Beckwith reacted as if she'd farted in his face. "Just saying," Jessica said, as the vein in his temple accelerated from twitch to vigorous drum solo.

"I don't believe I ever suggested otherwise." He glared at her across the desk. "*Tempus fugit*, Wideacre. Chop-chop!"

CHAPTER THIRTEEN

It was 14 July, a baking hot day, the temperature somewhere up in the late 30s, threatening to climb all the way to 40 by midday. At home, Jack Kingsman dabbed beads of sweat from his brow, only for a fresh batch to pop up straight away. His discomfort had nothing to do with the oppressive heat – he had state-of-the-art air conditioning – and everything to do with the anonymous note he had received that morning. Two words only, capital letters, sketched out in thick black marker on a torn sheet of spiral-edged notepaper.

I KNOW!

He examined the envelope in which it had arrived; plain white, bog-standard, no stamp, suggesting it had been hand-delivered. Shakily, he went into his office to examine the CCTV footage from the camera monitoring the entrance to his house. He scrolled back all the way to the previous midnight, when he had come home from an evening out. 12.05. There he was entering the house, a little the worse for wear, but definitely not drunk. He zoomed in on the floor by the door. No sign of an envelope. He moved the footage forward, scanning it intently. 3.45. A neighbour's cat, filthy moggy, stopping to use his flowerbed as a toilet, eyes luminous green in the night-vision camera lens. Nothing after that till 7 a.m. when the staff started arriving for work: cook, housekeeper, two young Turkish domestics – twin sisters, Melis and Mahlika – arriving together arm-in-arm. Next up at 8.30 a.m., the gardener, who didn't even come in, just disappeared round the side of the house and cracked on with mowing the lawn. Finally, at 9.30 a.m., the shorts-clad postie cycling up on his Royal Mail bicycle. Jack watched him dismount, lean it carelessly against the gate post and scrabble inside his satchel for the legitimate post: bills, junk mail, a couple of invitations to various industry events. He exchanged a few pleasantries with the gardener, who had come out with a bag of garden waste, and went on his way. In any case, Jack had already received the letter by then.

He wiped the sweat from his brow again. *"I KNOW!"* The words circled round and round in his brain, magnifying, pulsating, bullets of fear striking at his very heart. "Who knew? Exactly how much did they know? And just what did they propose to do about it?"

...

Jessica and Laura bypassed the nick's greasy spoon canteen in favour of O Sole Mio, a small Italian restaurant reputed to make the best seafood risotto anywhere outside of Italy. It felt oddly decadent to be dining out in the daytime, Jessica thought, giving her order for the famous dish. Not that she dined out much. Last time had been 14 February, St Valentine's Day, when David had taken her for a romantic meal in the West End. That had gone tits-up when a call came from Beckwith, abruptly ordering her back on duty. A body had been found. Melanie Potts, The Director's first known victim. Little had she known the chain of events that murder would set in motion.

"Wine?" Laura asked, when she had placed her own order for lobster salad. "I won't tell if you don't."

Jessica shook her head. "Water for me." If she started on the wine, she wasn't entirely sure she could stop. The press was full of it these days, articles on professional women like her, dubbed the nation's new binge drinkers. At first, she'd pooh-poohed the idea. Fucking scaremongering! There was nothing wrong with a relaxing glass of wine in the evening. It was the demarcation line between work and winding down. Except, in her case, one glass soon morphed into two, then half a bottle, and now she could quite easily dispatch an entire bottle a night without any help from David. Somewhere, at some point – damned if she knew when – Jessica's brake line had been cut. She was intelligent enough to know she was veering dangerously out of control.

When the waiter, a good-looking young stud in crisp white shirt and too-tight black trousers had bustled off with their order, they sat for a moment, unsure of exactly what to do or say next.

Laura grinned suddenly. "Sorry, I missed the class on small talk. Looks like, maybe, you were truanting too."

Jessica started to relax. "I think we're supposed to start with the weather and move on to shades of lipstick." She smiled absently as the waiter returned with a basket of focaccia and a small bowl of olive oil and balsamic vinegar for dipping.

Laura helped herself to a slice of the still-warm bread. "Really? Well, thank God I missed it, that's all I can say. I must have been doing something more interesting, like squeezing a blackhead."

"I had a large collection of those," Jessica offered. "And acne. Everybody avoided me like the plague."

"You cleaned up nice," Laura said. She dipped the bread in the oil and vinegar, bit into it and rolled her eyes ecstatically. "I'd kill to have hair like yours."

Jessica shook her head. "Believe me, it's a nightmare. The

slightest bit of damp in the air and I end up sporting an afro."
They froze as the same thought struck them both. Jessica brought
her hands together in a loud clap, startling the other diners. "And
that, I believe, is small talk!"

When she returned to Rosewood an hour later, her spirits were
considerably revived. For someone who cut up dead bodies for
a living, Shackleton was surprisingly good company. Despite her
reputation as a ball-breaker, she had a far more active love life
than Jessica, and wasn't at all shy about sharing the details. More
than once, Jessica had found herself spluttering into her sparkling
water. When they got up to leave, the pathologist had slipped her
card to the sexy young waiter.

"Know the sexiest thing about him?" she'd asked, leaving a not
insubstantial tip behind. "A pulse!"

They split up, promising to meet again soon. Therefore, when
Laura's number flashed up on her mobile within minutes of
getting back to the nick, she was slightly taken aback.

It was uncanny how the other woman read her mind. "Don't
worry," she said. "I'm not stalking you. This is about your brother-
in-law. Ted, isn't it?"

"Yes," Jessica said. "Ted Carling. Christ, he's not on your slab
is he?"

Laughter on the other end of the phone. "Not yet. I just forgot
to mention that last night's lover boy, who's based at the same
nick, mentioned he's been suspended. Some allegation about
drugs going missing after a bust or some such, usual pillow talk
stuff. Anyway, just thought you might want to know. It's all a bit
hush-hush, so the news might not yet have filtered through."

She rang off and Jessica accessed the latest accusatory voicemail from Carol. "You're a selfish bitch, Jessica. How come Ted can take time off from work and you bloody can't? Just because you think you're indispensable. Well, you fucking-well are not. You're—" She pressed delete . Seemed like her bro-in-law was telling porkies. She didn't blame him one bit.

...

Ed sat in the cab of his van watching a bunch of schoolgirls cross the road in front of him. Most were nothing to write home about, too dumpy or too skinny, fat ankles or flat chests like ironing boards. One, though – a flaxen blonde, fifteen-years-old or so – caught his eye. She was taller than the others, graceful, her body language showing she was already aware of her womanly wiles. She was animatedly tossing her hair, laughing at something her uber-plain mate said, flashing her perfect Scarlett Johansson smile. Her skirt was hitched up several inches to reveal long, tanned legs, her school shirt open to the middle button, revealing a swell of bosom. Ed had no doubt that every man watching her wanted to do her, though, of course, they wouldn't admit it. Underage schoolgirl? Hands thrown in the air, shrieks of horror. What is the world coming to! Hypocritical bastards! Give 'em the chance and they'd rip her knickers off in a heartbeat – and her heart out in another. If no one was watching and there was no chance ever of being caught, they'd be in like fucking Flynn. They did it in war situations, didn't they, raping and pillaging, unleashing their darkest fantasies under the guise of doing right by their country. Each giving the other license. When could it ever be right to rape a ten-year-old? Wasn't like some little girl or boy was a threat. But they did it, anyway. Why? Not for freedom, but because beneath that paper-thin veiling of civility they showed to the world, they were all just like him, fucking animals. Difference was, he was honest. Ed was no kiddie-fiddler, neither. That was a point of pride. None of his "girls" was under the age of fifteen – that was a woman, that was.

"Scarlett" saw him watching. He waggled his tongue at her, amused when her veneer of sophistication fell abruptly away, giving a glimpse of the childish vulnerability beneath. Confused, shocked, a little bit frightened, she almost ran the rest of the way across the road. Ed chuckled. Maybe he'd seek her out again, when the boss sent him out on a fresh mission. For now, though, Missy Long-Legs was safe. The lights flashed amber, then green. Ed drove slowly away, conscious of the delicate load in the back of his van. Wouldn't do to fuck that up. Five minutes later he turned down a side road, pulled up outside a number of warehouse-type buildings. A sign attached to the gates read "Kingsman Film Productions".

CHAPTER FOURTEEN

Demi Carter was running late, thanks to the bleedin' Tube train grinding to a premature halt. She wasn't quite sure what the problem was this time; probably some sad bastard who'd decided to end it all at salubrious Stockwell. Selfish prick! Turned out, it was actually a fire and, given what happened at King's Cross back in 1987, way before she was born, the staff weren't taking any chances.

"Everybody out," came the shouted instruction and, almost before she knew it, Demi found herself propelled out onto the pavement, alongside the other stragglers from the late-night train.

"When can we go back in?" she asked, commandeering a bored-looking guard. He shrugged, already starting to walk away.

"No more trains tonight."

"Well, how am I supposed to get home?" Demi demanded, trying not to sound scared. Inside, though, she was freaking out.

A sigh. A roll of the eyes. "Where you going?"

"Far side of Streatham Common."

"Night bus." The guard pointed across the road. "That'll take you as far as Streatham Hill; your ticket's valid for the bus."

Demi's heart sank. Streatham Hill. That was, like, miles away from where she needed to get to. What could she do, though? The guard was already walking back into the station. Moments later he and his colleagues had barricaded themselves behind the heavy iron gate concertinaed across the station entrance. Clearly, no one gave a fiddler's fart that a fourteen-year-old was stranded miles from home, in the middle of the night, in a shithole area of south London.

Of course, Demi knew she looked far older than fourteen with all the slap she was wearing, the stripper heels and tarty bodycon mini dress. How else would she and Stacey have got past the bouncers at Starz, where there was a strictly enforced over-18s admission policy? As it happened, they'd breezed through, and it had been one sick night right up until Stace had got a monk on and buggered off. Like it was Demi's fault the Justin Bieber lookalike fancied her and not her mate. She hobbled over to the bus stop. The shoes that had made her feel so fabulous and grown-up earlier in the evening had rubbed her heels raw to the point where she could feel blood trickling down the backs of them.

Stacey was a fat cow, she thought. She was also her BFF, and she was supposed to be on a sleepover at Stacey's house, following a fun-filled evening of popcorn and Hannah Montana. Like they were fucking twelve years old! Demi quailed at the prospect of her parents finding out what they'd really been up to. She'd be grounded for life.

The bus, already full to bursting, rolled up and Demi battled her way on. The inside stank of piss, vomit and weed. She didn't dare go upstairs, usually a hot spot for trouble. Instead, she stood next to the driver's compartment, where she felt safer. She was uncomfortably aware of being the focus of several pairs of eyes, in particular a group of wannabe gangsters in ridiculous oversized hoodies and jeans with the crotch bagging down round their knees. She tugged the hem of her dress lower and wrapped her arms tightly about herself, achingly conscious of her youth and vulnerability. Thankfully, the gang left her alone, except for a few kissy-kissy noises and smart-arse remarks as they exited the bus at Brixton. By the time the bus reached Streatham Hill, there were only two passengers left, her and an office type, who bounded off clutching his briefcase like it was the receptacle for the Holy Grail.

"Got far to go, luv?" the driver asked, switching off the lights and plunging the bus into darkness. "Only, it's not a good idea you walking around on your own this time of night." His eyes ran over her, appraisingly. "Tell you what. I'm clocking off now. Gimme a minute and I'll run you home in my car."

Demi wasn't completely stupid. She knew enough not to get into cars with strange men. "You're all right," she said. "My da's picking me up just round the corner." She wished he was. She had a helluva long walk ahead of her. Briefly she considered phoning home and risking her parents' wrath, but she had no poxy credit on her mobile, and the chance of finding a working public telephone was somewhere between zero and it'll never happen. Tired, dispirited, in agony from the sodding shoes and more than a little nervous, she started the long walk up Streatham High Road, keeping close to the shadows. By the time she reached Streatham Common, she was near to tears. She hesitated at the entrance. If she cut across, she could shave at least fifteen minutes off her journey. Going the long way round would take closer to half an hour, especially in her stupid heels. It was risky, though. Everyone had heard about that bloke, The Director, who was going around dumping girls' bodies on commons all over south London. Still … She glanced quickly round. A white van had passed her a while back. Since that, nothing. Nobody. A painful throbbing in her right heel decided her. If she lost the heels she could run all the way, be home in the blink of an eye. She was a good runner, even won a medal once. She kicked them off, sighing in blissful relief as the velvety dewiness of the grass caressed her feet. She left the shoes where they lay – she didn't plan on wearing those bastards again - and started to run. She was halfway across the common when she thought she heard a noise behind her. Panicked, she sped up, desperate to get home now, not caring if her parents grounded her for the next hundred years. Another noise, louder this time; real or imagined, Demi wasn't sticking round to find out. Her heart began to pound; she could feel it vibrating against the thin walls of her chest. Her head was reeling, the blood scooting round and round, making her dizzy. Her gorge rose, a mixture of greasy chips and the illicit booze she'd knocked back earlier in the evening. She began to sob, harsh, gut-wrenching sounds born of pure terror. Flecks of spittle flew from between her lips. She was tiring fast, her legs turning to rubber. Something sharp pierced the sole of her right foot, tipping her off balance. She managed to stay upright, but only just. Then she was stumbling forward again, her pace jerky and uneven, as though she had forgotten the mechanics of running. In the near distance she could see the line of trees marking the far side of the common, the street lights just beyond, beckoning her on towards safety. She gave one final push, tripped over something on the ground and crashed to her knees. Sobbing, terrified, she put out a hand to steady herself, touched something soft and yielding. Demi Carter started to scream like she'd never stop.

...

Jessica gave herself a quick blast of Gold Spot before exiting her car, hoping it might mask the giveaway smell of alcohol on her breath. Luckily, she'd only had one glass of wine when the call came in. Other nights, she might well have finished off the bottle.

Shackleton was there ahead of her and already peeling off her gloves. "Not the same," she said, gesturing to the small mound on the grass behind her. "Not The Director's m.o. Although this one's been strangled too, there's no obvious signs of torture or sexual assault. She's fully clothed, no stupid hair extensions. No business card." She tucked the gloves in the pocket of her overalls. "I can't rule him out, of course, till I've conducted a full PM back at the morgue. Weary, she rubbed her eyes. "Initial thoughts, though, it's a domestic. Sad, but as you know, it happens."

And all too frequently. If Jessica had a quid for every woman strangled to death each year by her boyfriend or husband, she'd be well on the way to setting up home somewhere in the Med. Despite what the public thought, attacks by strangers were in the minority. Most women who came to grief did so at the hands of someone they knew well, often the very person who had vowed to love and cherish them for the rest of their lives.

"Do we know who she is yet?" she asked as Connors approached, notebook in hand. "Married? Boyfriend?"

She's only fourteen, guv," Connors said. "*Was* only fourteen, I mean."

"Fourteen!" Jessica's mouth slackened with dismay. She gazed down at the young girl's body, the smeared make-up, clownish in the harsh glare of the arc lights, the cheap, inappropriately short dress. Primark, probably. "She looks older, at least eighteen."

"Friend says she's fourteen," Connors said, gesturing to where a young girl sat slumped against a tree stump, her head buried in her hands. Someone had draped a foil blanket around her shoulders. Even so, she was shaking like a leaf. "Seems they went to an over 18s club in town, hence the slap and bum-freezer dresses. A bit of argy-bargy ensued when one got off with a bloke the other one fancied. They split up, and sometime between then and now, this one met her Waterloo."

"She was killed here?" Jessica looked to Laura for confirmation.

She fanned her hand in front of her mouth, suppressing a yawn. In the distance the sky had just begun to lighten.

"If not, then extremely close by and not so long ago." The girl's core body temperature had fallen by no more than a couple of degrees, leading her to estimate time of death as little more than an hour, two at the very most. "I suspect her friend only just missed running into the killer. That makes her one lucky young lady, if you ask me."

"The friend couldn't have done it?" Jessica glanced over to where the other girl was now being fussed over by a man and a woman – her parents, presumably.

"Not a chance. Our victim is the bigger and heavier of the two, and manual strangulation takes a surprising amount of strength."

"Plus, the kid's in genuine shock, practically a basket case," Connors contributed. "We couldn't get a word of sense out of her for a full ten minutes. Mind you, it's not every day you stumble over your mate's dead body."

"Bit of a coincidence that," Jessica said. "What the hell was a fourteen-year-old doing on Streatham Common at that time of the night anyway?"

Connors relayed the rest of the story, extracted piecemeal from the hysterical girl. When she finished, Jessica shook her head. Which of them, as an underage kid, hadn't snuck into a nightclub?

Smoked weed? Got shit-faced. Got laid. Her heart went out to the young girl.

"Christ, poor kid," she said. She started across for a word with the victim's friend. "What's her name?"

Connors consulted her notebook. "Demi," she said. "Demi Carter."

...

Ed was livid. He'd well and truly ballsed up, but how was he to know the little slut was only fourteen? She'd looked way more, arse and tits hanging out, slap all over her face like a fucking Barbie doll. Brazen, too. It hadn't taken much to persuade her into his van. It was only when he was slapping her round a bit in the back of it and her school bus pass fell out of her purse that he discovered her true age. And nearly shat himself. Stacey Herbert – that was the kid's name – was only fourteen and way too young. Ed had standards, low as a limbo dancer's fanny, maybe, but standards nevertheless. Problem was, he couldn't let her live, not now that she could recognise him. He'd been merciful, though, put a swift end to her. She'd have blacked out pretty quickly, wouldn't have felt much. He was sorry to have to do it, but Ed couldn't afford no witnesses. It wasn't only *his* arse that was on the line.

He was on his way home, having dumped the body on Streatham Common, when he'd spotted another likely prospect, wobbling along the pavement on stilt-like heels. She'd fitted the criteria to a tee – young, but not too young, blonde, skinny, fit as a butcher's mutt. Ed considered grabbing her, but only briefly. Truth was, he was rattled by recent events. Experience had taught him that when one door closed, another slammed right in your fucking face. Better safe than sorry. He drove on.

CHAPTER FIFTEEN

Jessica conducted only the briefest of interviews with Demi Carter. As Connors had indicated, the girl was in a state of total shock and exhaustion. Tears had long since washed her make-up away, revealing the youthful features underneath. Her eyes, though, were old. They had witnessed the dark side of life. Any residual spark of childish innocence had fled, for ever. At fourteen years of age, poor little Demi Carter had learned one of life's most painful lessons – shit happens! And, quite often, to good people.

Jessica sent her home in the company of a family liaison officer and her distraught parents. She was glad she didn't have to deal with the dead girl's parents yet. They were away down the country somewhere, celebrating their sixteenth wedding anniversary. A romantic weekend. Champagne. Roses. It was an anniversary they would remember for all the wrong reasons.

Connors gestured to where the scene of crime officers were finishing up – bagging, tagging, searching the area for clues.

"First time the parents left her home alone, apparently. Thought they could trust her. Thought she was mature enough to cope for a couple of nights. An only child, too. Jesus! Life-long guilt trip coming their way."

"Could happen to anyone," Jessica said. "I was forever skiving off, and my parents didn't have a clue. By the time I was fifteen, I knew the first names of most of the bouncers in every pub and club in south London."

"I lost my virginity at thirteen," Connors admitted. "Alcohol-fuelled. Can't even remember the bloke's name. Just recall thinking, right that's that over with, like I was checking it off a to-do list."

The last of the night receded under a strawberry-tinged blanket of cloud. In the surrounding trees the birds revved up for lauds. A small breeze ruffled the yellow scene-of-crime ribbon cordoning off the area where the body had been found. Soon, the first, heartbreaking, floral tributes would start to arrive; some spelt out in text speak. "Miss u Stace, hon." "So soz, babe. Wit da angels, now, innit." "RIP mate, u woz da best." Along with the flowers, a small mountain of soft toys that Stacey would never get to cuddle. And, underlying the tears, Jessica knew from experience, would be a strange atmosphere, an almost tangible air of suppressed excitement. This murder would be the most newsworthy thing to happen to many of these people in their entire lives. Their association with the victim, no matter how tenuous, would somehow imbue them with a vague air of ghoulish glamour. It would become a story to tell, to mull over with friends, at work, or down the pub. Any real sensitivity would, eventually, be lost in the telling and retelling. A young girl's horrific death would cross genres from tragedy into the realms of entertainment.

Jessica's exhaustion knew no bounds. Weary and dispirited, she massaged the muscles knotted at the back of her neck. They ached so badly, it was difficult to keep her head erect.

"Go home," she said tiredly to Connors. "You look done in."

"You too," Connors said. She looked as though she wanted to say more, but Jessica was already walking away.

In the car, Jessica glanced at her watch, tempted to give her routine hospital visit a miss and go straight home to bed. It wasn't as if her father would notice; he hadn't been conscious for several days. She switched on the radio for a traffic report. Queues were already starting to build on Wandsworth Bridge. That decided her. She headed for home.

David was already up, suited and booted and smelling divinely of grapefruit and toothpaste. He'd had his hair cut, revealing a little more grey around the ears. Her husband was turning into a silver fox, an extraordinarily handsome silver fox, and somehow Jessica had managed to miss the transition. Now it struck her forcibly like a hammer blow in the guts. The contrast between them both couldn't have been more marked. David – suave, handsome, immaculately groomed, right down to his clipped and spotless fingernails. Her – an exhausted mess with a case of severe bed-head, even though she hadn't yet been to bed, her breath stale, her antiperspirant a distant memory. Christ! She could smell her own armpits.

Then she noticed the suitcase at his feet. It was open, filled with his neatly packed clothes. Packing – another thing she was useless at! Her eyes flew to his.

"Paris," he prompted, seeing her all too apparent confusion. He bent down to place a forgotten item inside the suitcase, then zipped it closed. He straightened up, a flash of impatience crossing his face.

"The merger I told you about, Jess. Hazeboittes and Delois. I'll be away for five days, remember?"

Jessica wracked her brains and vaguely recalled him telling her something of the sort all right. The problem was there was so much crap going on in her head that she was finding it difficult to keep everything straight.

"Now?" she asked, as outside a car horn blared. "You're going to Paris, now? Like, right this minute, now?"

"Yes," David confirmed. He picked up the suitcase. "And, as that's my taxi outside, I'd better get going." Hastily, he leant down and pecked her on the cheek. "Go to bed, Jess. You look done in." Then, he was gone.

Jessica stood a moment, assailed by a sense of unreality. Had David really left her with little more than a peck on the cheek? As if she was his mother or an older female relative, someone of whom he was fond. Fond of, but not in love with. She touched her cheek with her fingertips and, suddenly galvanised, sprinted for the door. No way could she leave things like that, so cool, so casual. Telling him that she loved him suddenly seemed like the most important thing in the world and having him repeat it back word for word. She needed his reassurance that they were all right. They really were. They were just fine.

There was someone else in the car besides the taxi driver. Female. Blonde. A cliché. Not Saskia, his lesbian assistant. Carol had been right, after all. David was cheating on her. Jessica waited just long enough to see the couple's heads turn towards each other and David lean intimately inward. Jessica didn't wait to see their lips connect. Instead, she spun on her heel, bolted for the loo and was violently sick.

...

DCI Beckwith slammed down the phone, keeping his hand tightly on the receiver, partially to act as a stress aid, partially to stop himself from picking it up and chucking the damn thing against the wall. He'd made that mistake before and been roasted by his commanding officer.

"What?" he snapped, as DC Liversedge appeared at the door.

"The … the parents are here," the constable replied, stammering slightly. Still young enough to be cowed in the presence of higher ranking officers, his eyes were wary, his pose one of flight, one foot in front of the other. Beckwith had a fleeting moment of amusement, thinking that if he were to stamp his foot, the young policeman would be gone like a shot.

"No sign of DI Wideacre, then?" he asked. It was a forlorn hope. The woman seemed to have vanished off the face of the earth. Though he'd wished for this on more than one occasion, now wasn't one of them. Not when he had a couple of grieving parents on his hands wondering why the hell their fourteen-year-old daughter's killer was still at large. He sighed and rose from his desk. Wideacre would rue the day. Beckwith had about as much bedside manner as Dr Crippen. He didn't *do* grieving parents. A marked man, he forced his expression into something vaguely approachable and set off to meet them.

…

Filming had started on the remake of *Killer Queen*. On set, it was nothing short of pure chaos as last-minute adjustments were made to the set, the lighting, the actors' make-up, the cameras, everything. The leading lady, Venise Love-Davies, had suffered a wardrobe malfunction – something to do with her veil.

"Oops," Jack Kingsman heard someone say. "Better get that sorted out, Venise, darling, unless you want to go up *phut* like your famous predecessor."

It was a crass thing to say, particularly in his hearing, but perhaps the speaker hadn't noticed he was there. Jack stepped outside and lit a cigarette. Over the course of the last few weeks he'd gone from twenty years' abstinence to a full-blown twenty-a-day habit. His fingers shook slightly as he lit up. There'd been no further correspondence since the first note, but he hadn't had a full night's sleep since. He simply couldn't get the words out of his head. *I KNOW!*

He sucked hard on the cigarette, his eyes roaming over the studio lot. Briefly, they locked with those of Ed Hatcher, who was unloading props from the back of one of the studio's vans. They went back a long way, him and Hatcher, all the way back to Marissa's glory days, when both men had been her willing slaves. She used to laugh about her burly admirer, the way he mooned over her. *He'd do anything for me*, she'd say. *Ask him to jump off a cliff and he'd do it with bells on.* Poor Ed. He'd been young back then, never a looker, never a threat to the handsome, sophisticated Jack. Neither acknowledged the other, and Jack swiftly shifted his gaze. To everyone else, Hatcher was just another worker and Jack was just the boss. They were far more than that, of course. They shared a secret, never to be told. Jack took a final pull on his cigarette and tossed it into a water-logged plant pot. He turned and went back inside.

Ed continued unloading the van, taking great care not to damage the delicate painted panels that were needed for one of the palace scenes later that week. There was also a consignment of Limoges china in one of the packing cases, and some valuable oil paintings on loan from a nearby stately home. When it came to things delicate and valuable, Ed was the only employee entrusted with their care. With good reason. He'd never fucked up an assignment yet. Hands like shovels, his supervisor laughed, but you could cradle a newborn in Ed's palms. Silly mare! She'd pass out if she knew exactly what his shovel hands were capable of.

He removed a painting of Elizabeth I and propped it against the side of the van. A fellow employee wandered over for a look.

"Christ, that's ugly," the man said. "Thing I could never understand is why those Tudors never had any eyelashes. Made them look like cancer victims." He bent forward for a closer look and pointed. "Got some hair or something there, mate, stuck to the frame."

Ed caught sight of it at almost exactly the same time – a couple of strands of long, blonde hair glinting in the sunshine. Quickly he reached across and pulled them free.

"Must have picked them up in the van," he said, his heart starting to pound immediately the words left his mouth. Fuck's sake! What had possessed him to say that? His colleague nudged him, slyly.

"Oy, aye. And just who exactly have you had in the back of your van, Eddie-boy? Vinyl Vicky? Rubber Rita? Plastic Pam?" Sniggering, he wandered off, anxious to share his little joke with the rest of the staff on the lot. For once, though, *Eddie-boy* had no problem with being a figure of fun. Hell, he'd cop to being bent as a nine bob note if it kept the nosey bastards from discovering the real truth about him. His wanker workmate had done him a favour, really. It was a wake-up call, a reminder not to get sloppy. The hair on the painting may or may not have belonged to one of his girls, but no way you could be too careful. As soon as he'd unloaded the rest of the props, Ed intended to give the van a proper valeting; inside, outside, full back and sides.

A shout of laughter told him the man was already bandying his wit about the place. Ed turned back to the van. Vinyl Vicky?

He grinned into the interior. Make that Melanie, Jordan, Tara, Kerrie, Shania, Monika and, he always had problems with this one, Susannah? Shoshana, that was it! A baker's half-dozen. He didn't count Stacey Herbert. She was just a blip. Collateral damage.

Ed removed the last item from the van and closed the doors. He stacked everything on a trolley and trundled over to the studio. The cast were taking a break between scenes, and some of them, including Venise Love-Davies, had left the stuffy studio and come out into the sunshine outside. For a moment their eyes met, and a small, polite smile trembled on her lips. Bitch! Probably thought he was after a poxy autograph. As if! Far as he was concerned, Venise Love-Davies was as much like Marissa Bloom as he was like George Clooney. An old phrase from the Sunday school he had rarely attended came back to him. *Not fit to kiss the hem.* His hands fisted round the trolley handle, the cords on the back of his hands visibly straining.

CHAPTER SIXTEEN

Jessica surfaced, bleary-eyed, to the sound of the telephone ringing off the hook. Her head was pounding. Her brain felt like it had been used for target practice by the Taliban. She picked up an empty wine bottle and chucked it in the general direction of the noise.

"Fuck's sake, shut up!" Miraculously, it stopped, only to start up again a moment later – shriller, louder, more persistent than ever. Whoever it was, wasn't taking no for an answer. Resigned, raging, Jessica levered herself out of her chair. Immediately the room started to pitch and spin. She fell back with a thump. A tsunami of nausea rolled across her. Bile forced its way up her throat. She could see at least two of everything, and everything seemed to be waving at her. Even the ceiling seemed to be moving, breathing in and out, in and out. And still the phone continued its relentless summons.

Jessica made another attempt to get to her feet. It wasn't happening. Gingerly, she got down on all fours and began to crawl across the kitchen floor. She was pouring with sweat when she reached the far side, only metres away. Hauling herself upright against the worktop, she snatched the receiver off its rest. "Whaaaat?" she screamed into it. "What the fuck do you want?"

On the other end, a cool, clear voice, "DI Wideacre, we need to talk."

...

DCI Beckwith banged the telephone back on its cradle. Wideacre was skating perilously close to the edge. His misgivings regarding her promotion were proving well founded. The pity was that no one had listened when he'd voiced those concerns. Too busy ticking all the right equality and diversity boxes to pay any heed as to whether the person being shoe-horned in was actually the right fit for the job. In his view, Wideacre was not. Off-hand, he could think of half a dozen men who had more than earned their stripes. Given the chance, he had no doubt any one of them would have made a better fist of leading the investigation. They'd probably have had a capture by now, instead of the big fat zero chalked up by Wideacre.

He picked up a biro and tapped it angrily against the edge of his desk. All that manpower on virtually unlimited overtime, squeezing an already cash-strapped police force and, so far, sweet FA to show for it. He tossed the biro away. It rolled off the desk and into the waste-paper bin. He left it. She'd better have a damn good explanation for her absence these past twenty-four hours or, by God, he'd stomp all over her like a turd on fire.

"Sir?" Sergeant Hennessy stuck his head round the door. "The team are waiting in the incident room. Are you? ... Is DI Wideacre? ... Who's taking the briefing this morning?"

"DI Wideacre." Mark kept his expression neutral. "She's on her way in. Until then, carry on as normal, Sergeant."

Hennessy retreated, returning a couple of minutes later with a mug of strong coffee. He placed it on Beckwith's desk. "If you don't mind me saying, sir, you look as though you could use this."

Could he ever! Beckwith nodded his thanks. Hennessy was a bit of an old curmudgeon, but his heart was in the right place. He took a sip of the treacly coffee that had obviously been stewing for hours. His stomach churned slightly. He was tempted to add a splash of the Glenlivet single malt he kept in the drawer for just such occasions. He didn't, solely because he wanted to be stone-cold sober when Wideacre showed up. All the better to bollock her, my dear!

...

Beckwith's phone call acted like an icy shower. If Jessica didn't quite snap back to sobriety, she met it more than halfway. With a clearer head came the memories from which she had sought alcoholic oblivion: Stacey Herbert, strangled on Streatham Common, David buggering off to Paris with a nubile blonde. The peck on the cheek for her. The kiss of death for their marriage?

The answerphone was flashing red with a wealth of new messages. Predictably, the majority were from her whiny bitch of a sister. Without listening, Jessica pressed delete. The rest were from work – enquiries as to her whereabouts, curious at first, a note of concern creeping in, followed eventually by sheer exasperation. The last work message had been from Beckwith, a weird note in his voice. If Jessica hadn't known better, she might have misconstrued it as panic. With great satisfaction, she pressed delete. The final call was from David. Her finger hovered over the delete button, came within a fraction of pressing it. She played it.

"Hi, darling, just to let you know I've arrived safely. Work is hectic, so I doubt I'll get to see much of gay Paree. I won't bother phoning again. You're probably busy anyway. See you in five days." Finished off with a big smacking kiss.

What the hell? Confused, Jessica played it again. *"Hi, darling?!"* Didn't he realise she'd seen him? Him and Blondie getting it on in the back of the taxi? It made her wonder if she'd imagined the whole thing. Could her exhausted mind have been playing tricks? Yes, she'd been, still *was* exhausted. But, delusional? No! What she couldn't figure out, though, was why David would risk the woman coming to their house, where she might easily bump into Jessica? The answer came to her in a flash. Because on other mornings, she had already left to visit her father. David must have nearly crapped himself when she'd arrived home unexpectedly. No wonder he'd beaten such a hasty retreat.

Bastard! Wait till he got home and then – and then, what? Stumbling a little, Jessica headed for the shower. No time to dwell on it now, not with the shit storm brewing at the nick. Beckwith first. Then David. Fun times!

...

Twenty minutes later, head still aching, but sober enough to drive, Jessica nosed her car into the rush-hour traffic that usually got her blood boiling. Today, she was grateful simply to inch along. It gave her time to plan an excuse for Beckwith. An unexpected death in the family? No, that was tempting fate, especially since her father was already booked on an imminent flight to the hereafter. Food poisoning? Dodgy prawns? Salmonella? Peanuts! Anaphylactic shock. Except he'd have been sure to have seen her cramming them down her throat in the staff canteen. She was a sucker for the dry-roasted ones. She gave up on the idea. She wasn't one of life's natural liars. Her mother had always known when she was fibbing, swore her left eye turned inward. A kind of ocular lie detector. Nonsense, but Jessica was taking no risks. Nothing for it but to face the music. Worst case scenario: she'd lose her job. The way things were going, that might be a blessing in disguise. She'd go out on a low, though, beaten by the bastard who called himself

The Director. So what? She wouldn't be the first to leave the force under a cloud.

She changed her mind as she passed the incident room and saw the pictures of his victims pinned to the whiteboard. A new one there too now, off a little to one side. Stacey Herbert. A large question mark over her death. All those young lives – so much promise, brutally cut short. Jessica steeled herself. Getting fired was not an option. She'd promised justice for those young women. She *would* deliver.

She told Beckwith the truth, whole and unvarnished, left nothing out. It was humiliating, especially the bit about the other woman. She'd seen something flash in his eyes at that point. *Schadenfreude?*

He did her the courtesy of waiting till she was all done, then leaned back in his chair, his gaze level. "So, what you're telling me, Wideacre, is that you let the complications of your private life take precedence over your professional duties."

"In a nutshell." Jessica met him eye-to-eye. "I got hammered. Rat-arsed. Drank the whole fucking vineyard." Another flash in his eyes. Contempt? Fuck him. She'd started, so she'd finish. "I screwed up," she said. "First and last time." That was his lot, nothing further to add. No way was she going to prostrate herself. Whatever the fallout, she had her big girl pants ready and waiting. She'd pull them all the way up to her neck, if necessary.

Beckwith said nothing, just leaned further back in his chair and laced his hands behind his head. His eyes lanced her. She had the feeling he was trying to access her brain, all areas. Then, he snapped forward and pointed to the door.

"Go!" he said. "You've kept the team waiting long enough."

Go! Jessica stared at him in shock. What? Was that all there was? Where was the bollocking? The recriminations? The "pull your socks up or you're out on your ear" speech he'd perfected to a fine art. Suspecting a catch, she remained in her chair. The seconds ticked slowly, almost audibly, by. She didn't move.

In the end, he gave her a searching look. "Was there something else?"

Suspicious still, she shook her head, rose cautiously to her feet. She'd got as far as the door when his voice lodged like an arrow between her shoulder-blades.

"Just a second, Wideacre."

Jessica froze. Fool! She'd walked straight into his trap. She tensed, waiting for the *coup de grâce*.

"Word of advice. Don't bare your soul to the team. Give them an excuse – dog ate your homework or some such. Food poisoning is always popular. Dodgy prawns, especially."

Jessica was actually smiling as she closed the door behind her. Who would have thought it?

...

DCI Beckwith was smiling too, and puzzled as to why that should be. He'd fully intended giving her both barrels, hanging her out to dry, doling out the bollocking to end all bollockings, attacking her with every hard-hitting cliché in the book, yet somehow she'd disarmed him. She'd looked so brave, so defiant, those big green eyes sparking at him like a naughty schoolgirl caught skiving. As it happened, she'd hung *herself* out to dry, made no attempt at white-washing. He admired that. Courage such as hers was rare. Jessica Wideacre, however frustrating, was an intriguing woman – and her husband was an absolute ass. How he could even look at another woman when—! Refusing to go there, Mark reversed his earlier decision and added a large splash of scotch to his, now tepid, coffee. He picked up the phone to dial Venise. As an antidote to Wideacre? He slammed down the receiver, found himself grinning again. There *was* no antidote to Wideacre. *Drank the whole fucking vineyard.* You had to laugh.

...

Soon everyone else will know!

Jack Kingsman turned the latest note over in his hands. As before, there was no clue as to its sender. Same spiral-edged notepaper. Same sinister scrawl. This one had been placed beneath one of the wipers on his car window. The car had been securely locked in the garage. Logically, all fingers pointed to an inside job. After the first note, Jack had interviewed each member of his staff. All denied knowing anything about it. He believed them too.

The chef, Mansour, was a Moroccan Jack had lured away from his favourite eatery in Chelsea. Though a whizz in the kitchen, the man's grasp of English was rudimentary at best. He was ill-equipped to embark on a campaign of harassment. Besides, he was extremely happy with his lot. His job was easy. Unless Jack was entertaining company, which wasn't often, there was only him to cater for, and Jack's tastes thanks to his modest East End roots were fairly simple. Mansour was paid well over the odds and got his accommodation thrown in for free. No way would he risk upsetting the apple cart.

The housekeeper went all the way back to Marissa. Sheila Walters was a distant relative of hers – second cousin, twice removed or some such. Jack wasn't big into genealogy. The plain, impoverished woman had been employed by Marissa as wish-fulfilment for her favourite role of Lady Bountiful. She'd got her money's worth too – thought nothing of calling on the poor woman's services regardless of the hour, and often on the most spurious of grounds.

"But she enjoys it, darling," Marissa would protest, wide-eyed, whenever Jack suggested she might actually try doing something for herself once in a while. "Don't you, Sheila?" The housekeeper had no choice but to agree, the hard glint in her cousin's eye leaving her in no doubt that it was either Marissa's way or the highway. After his wife's accident, she had carried on in the role, content with her lot, especially now that there was no diva to answer to. Jack knew she regarded him as something of a saviour and possibly even fancied him a little. She'd certainly never shown any signs of wanting a husband or children in her life. Selfishly, he was glad. He liked to maintain the status quo.

No suspects left other than the young domestics, Melis and Mahlika. They were employed for more than just their dusting skills, of course. While there had been no question of remarrying, Jack still had his needs, and the beautiful twin sisters were not averse to meeting them, sometimes singly, sometimes together. It was every red-blooded male's fantasy. Since they could barely speak English, let alone write it, he had never seriously suspected them. Besides, when it came to intimidation, he held the winning hand. A word to immigration and they'd be back in Istanbul before you could say shish kebab.

His mood improved slightly as he thought about the previous night, which had been particularly memorable. The girls, exhausted by their endeavours, were at that very moment curled up in his bed like a couple of dark-haired kittens. Sheila, on her way to do something or other, had caught a passing glimpse of them as he'd emerged from his room. She'd said nothing, of course, but her gimlet glare had said it all. Jack made no apologies. His money. His choice who he employed and for what purpose. He wasn't accountable to his housekeeper or to anyone else. Besides, the housekeeper was no fool. Sheila Walters knew which side her bread was buttered on. And Melis and Mahlika weren't the first. A succession of pretty young things had come and gone, while she remained a permanent fixture.

Jack's mood took a nosedive again as he stowed the note in his safe along with the first. Someone was out to get him, and if they knew what he thought they might, it was game over. Benjamin Franklin had once said, "Three may keep a secret, if two of them are dead." He went to fetch his car keys, already late for the start of that day's shoot. However, the three including himself who knew this secret were very much alive. He also knew for a fact that none of them had blabbed, which brought him full circle. Who the hell was behind the notes?

...

Jessica's team near as dammit laughed in her face. Food poisoning? Dodgy prawns? There wasn't a one of them that hadn't tried that one on at some time or another. Still, they could hardly call her a liar outright; being the boss had some advantages. When they'd finished exchanging knowing looks and, in Connors' case an audible snigger, Jessica walked to the top of the room and clapped her hands sharply together. Her head immediately kicked in with a dull thud and her stomach churned a little in sympathy. She forced the bile down. Enough! Time to get a grip.

Her glance swept around the room. "So, what have we got on Stacey Herbert? I take it one of you lazy bastards has already checked the records for known perps in that area? Anyone released recently?"

Hennessy adjusted the little pile of rollies on his desk. "I did, guv. No joy. The usual faces are all accounted for, some dead, some on tag, others reformed – those ones are few and far between – the remainder enjoying the hospitality of Her Maj's budget hotels."

"And the love angle," Jessica asked. "Rumours of a secret boyfriend? No? Facebook stalker, then? Troll? Bully? A fucking clue of some sort? Come on, folks, give me something. Anything!" She sighed at the row of blank faces. "Listen," she said, "girls of that age are teeming with secrets." She flung a dart in Connors' direction, who had somehow managed to squeeze in an appointment with her hairdresser and was back to her usual immaculate blonde self. "I'll bet Connors had a few in her day, didn't you Connors, eh?"

The DS came back, shooting from the hip. "No more than yourself, I'd guess, guv. And probably none so recent."

Jessica glowered. She'd pay for that. The next particularly vile autopsy was all Connors'. She was known to upchuck at the first cut of the scalpel.

"Barring her big night out, it looks like Stacey Herbert was a good kid." Liversedge put them back on track, palming the anger out of the atmosphere like a magician. "Did well at school, according to her teachers. Good attendance record. Popular with the others."

"What about her laptop? iPhone? Tablet thingy?" A self-confessed technophobe, Jessica contented herself with a ten-quid mobile phone from Tesco, so old the battery spent most of its time on life support.

"Nothing," Connors said, white-lipped with annoyance. "A couple of raunchy music videos – Miley, Rihanna et al. And a topless shot of Justin Bieber."

"Bet the techies are suffering PTSD after that one," Liversedge quipped.

Jessica could have hugged him, as the others grinned and the atmosphere lightened further. In truth, she was annoyed at herself for baiting Connors. No wonder men thought women were bitches. She and Connors were certainly fulfilling that stereotype, sharpening their claws on each other like a couple of mangy cats. Unfortunately, the DS reminded her of the girls in the charmed circles at school, the spoilt Queen Bees who had it all. It wasn't good enough, and she knew it. Point scoring had no place at work, not when there was a monster, possibly more than one, on the loose. She couldn't afford to lose focus, but there was something about Connors that irritated the hell out of her.

"Presumably that leaves us looking at murder by stranger," she said, when the jokes about Justin Bieber ran out of steam. That was a bugger, since stranger cases were by far the hardest to crack. Unless fate intervened in the shape of an eye witness or someone coming forward with a good lead – a name or some such – it was like looking for a Polar bear in a snow storm. At last count, the official population of London numbered nigh on eight and a half million. Add to that an unofficial population of Christ knew how many more and you got some idea of the scale of the difficulty. Media coverage was what was needed. Tons of it. "Any chance of a *Crimewatch* re-enactment?" she asked.

"I'm working on it," Hennessy said. "Trying for this week's edition. Takes a while, though, to get the shooting crew, actors and things in place."

"Wave a magic wand," Jessica said. "I don't care what else they're running, this needs to take priority." She smirked. "Perhaps DCI Beckwith can bring some influence to bear? All that hobnobbing with film stars and film directors has got to be good for something." There was a collective intake of breath. Unwittingly, Jessica had cast her bread on shark-infested waters and Jaws, in the guise of DCI Beckwith, had just swum in the door.

He threw an unamused glance her way. "I've called a press conference this afternoon, DI Wideacre," he said. "Tough questions will undoubtedly be asked about The Director murders, and whether there's a direct link to this case. See to it that you have the right answers."

Jessica nodded and compounded her previous transgression by writing furiously in her notebook. "Note to self," she read aloud. "Consult with Oz, the great and all-powerful wizard."

Beckwith's professionalism slipped slightly. She really did know what buttons to press. He threw out a question to the team, ignoring the half-suppressed titters. "Gut instinct, everyone – is there a connection, or not?"

The response was a round of blank expressions, leaving Jessica to dig deep.

"Copper's nose, yes it's him," she said, "though we haven't a shred of evidence to back it up. Stacey, unlike the other vics, was killed and disposed of in only a matter of hours. Demi Carter last saw her in Starz at around ten thirty. She turned up dead at twelve forty-five, a little over two hours later. We have no reason to believe it was a sexually motivated attack. The body was fully clothed – in other words half-naked, as is the fashion these days. Yes, she was strangled, but that's hardly an unusual method of murder. There is no other evidence to suggest it's him – no evidence of torture, no business card left, no weirdo hair extensions." She fanned the pages of her notebook, causing a mini draught to send a twist of loose hair spiralling about her face. "Still, gut instinct, it's our man all right. Proving it? That's a different matter." She flashed a grin "Anyone got Miss Marple on their Facebook friends list?"

"Could be he was disturbed before he could molest her further," Hennessy ventured. "Her mate arrived on the scene shortly after the murder took place, didn't she? For all we know, someone else might have stumbled upon him first."

"Still doesn't add up," Jessica mused. "Characteristically, the bastard holds his victims hostage for several days, so that he can do a real number on them. Only after he's had his fun does he dispose of them at the dump site." She sighed. "For the moment, I think we have no option but to treat this as a separate case. Keep an open mind, though. If anything occurs to you, no matter how small, I want to hear it. Okay?"

Beckwith nodded. "Right, keep me informed. We need to get a handle on this, before any more bodies turn up."

"Real statement of the obvious, that," Jessica muttered quietly, but not quietly enough.

Beckwith ramped up his earlier glance to glare status. "Seems that food poisoning really took its toll," he said. "It *was* food poisoning, wasn't it, DI Wideacre?"

"Salmonella," Jessica deadpanned, wondering if she was the only one to detect a glint in his eye. Somehow it made her want to laugh, and that simply couldn't be right. Laughing at Beckwith twice in one day, when in the normal course of events she dreamed of eviscerating him. She placed a palm against her forehead, checking for signs of a temperature, but found only the remains of her hangover, which thudded a painful reminder. It triggered a chain reaction in her queasy stomach; she only just managed to hold it together long enough to get to the loo. When she emerged, Connors was outside washing her hands. Rosewood was a no-frills, old-style nick, built in an era when men were the hunter-gatherers and women were chained to the sink. It made sod all allowance for the fact that sisters were now doing it for themselves. Formerly a small store room, the women's toilets were roughly partitioned into three small cubicles. There was one sink, a cracked mirror and a broken Tampax machine. The plumbing gargled for no reason, the toilets often backed up and, on a good day, it was stocked with toilet tissue. Most days were not good days; generally, if you forgot to bring your own personal supply of bog roll, you were stuffed.

Connors flicked the excess water from her hands and moved out of the way to make room for Jessica. She pulled out a tissue from a packet beside the sink and began to pat herself dry. She didn't speak, her huffy attitude making it clear she was still rankling from Jessica's earlier dig.

Jessica apologised, but only in her head. Somehow the words couldn't quite force themselves past her lips. Instead, she sneaked a look at the other woman, now busy renewing her lipstick. Red lipstick in the daytime. How very daring. And yet Connors could carry it off without it looking either harsh or slutty. On Jessica it would have looked like copious blood-letting in a slasher movie.

Next to her colleague's perfect reflection in the mirror, her own face looked like God's practice piece. Everything seemed slightly skew-whiff, as if it had been cobbled together out of a collection of spare parts. Her nose had a slight bump and the tip seemed hell-bent on following a route directly in line with her left ear lobe. A drunk had once described her eyes as opaline-green, but really they were a very ordinary green and nothing to get excited about.

She looked for the packet of tissues, only to realise they were Connors' own and that she had already secreted them in her expensive leather handbag. Her colleague gave no sign of noticing her dilemma. Instead, she gave a last perfunctory glance at her immaculate reflection, turned on her high heels and marched out. There was no toilet paper left. Jessica shrugged, and wiped her hands on her thighs.

By the time she got home that evening, she felt fit to collapse and ready to sleep for a fortnight. She could have cried when she saw her sister's car parked outside her house. Fisticuffs with Carol was the last thing she needed. Her agony was only slightly alleviated when it turned out to be her brother-in-law in the driver's seat.

"Shit! Shit! Shit!" she swore mentally, as she forced her face from murderous to neutral. A rogue thought made her briefly consider reversing back out of the drive and screeching off again. Too late. Ted was already out of the car and approaching fast. Jessica summoned her last reserves of strength and climbed out of her own vehicle. She dipped her head in greeting.

"Ted. What brings you to this neck of the woods? Everything all right with Carol? She hasn't popped yet, has she?"

Ted waved a distracted hand. "Carol's fine." There was a moment's silence while he examined her face. Disbelief crept over his own. "Oh, come on, Jess, you must know why I'm here. Even the fucking nuns up at St Jude's have heard about my suspension. I can't believe you haven't."

St Jude's was an enclosed order, with a strictly enforced vow of silence. For all anyone knew, the nuns might all have been dead for years.

Jessica stuck the key in her front door, stepped inside and quickly disabled the alarm system, amazed she'd actually remembered to set it that morning. "Oh, that," she said, leading the way into the kitchen and throwing her bag onto the table. "Yes, I did hear something, all right. But it was all very vague and, to be honest, a lot of shit's gone down in the last few days. It went completely out of my head." She fished a couple of dirty mugs out of the sink and gave them a perfunctory rinse beneath the tap.

"Bet my shit's worse than your shit," Ted joked feebly. "So you haven't heard any of the details?"

She tipped a teaspoon of coffee into each mug. "Something about drugs going missing, wasn't it? Milk? Sugar?"

Ted nodded yes to both. He scrutinised her as she made the coffee and passed him a mug. He sat at the kitchen table while she chose to remain standing, leaning back against the kitchen counter, her own steaming mug cuddled between her fingers. Her fingernails were bitten, he noticed, the tip of her nose red. She looked as though she'd been pulled backwards through a bush and yet, for reasons Ted Carling couldn't fathom, Jessica Wideacre was hot as all fuck. Given the chance he *would* go there, even at the risk of Carol finding out and turning his balls into earrings.

Jessica grew uncomfortable under the intensity of his gaze. "Ted!" she snapped. "You're not having one of those *petit mal* seizures or something, are you, only I really don't have the energy to deal with that right now."

"Sorry, no," he said. "It's just that you … you look …"

Jessica rolled her eyes. "I am *so* not in the humour, Ted. Just get to the point, and let me get myself off to my bed. *Alone!*" she added, wondering what trick of the brain had ever caused her to think him handsome once upon a time – worse still, to actually shag him. Today, he looked positively seedy; dough-faced, greasy-haired, his belly straining against his shirt. His eyes, a watery blue, were bloodshot. She tried to make allowances for the fact that he was under a lot of pressure, but for the first time in a very long while, her sympathy was all for Carol.

"They're fucking hanging me out to dry!" Ted burst out suddenly. He slapped his coffee mug down on the table, slopping coffee everywhere. "Some drugs have gone missing from a consignment captured in a recent bust and the finger is pointing squarely at me."

Jessica tasted her coffee, made a face, and added some more sugar. "Oh, someone's likely to have cocked up with the records." She pointed the teaspoon at him. "You know the default position is always to suspend pending full investigation. You'll be cleared in no time." In the meantime, she wished he'd clear right off.

Ted frowned. "What if I was to tell you the raid was on Nub Hollingbroke's place and that Nub and me go back a long way?" He looked sly. "Bessie mates at school and beyond."

Jessica's heart sank. "How much beyond? Are you still in touch?" She'd almost said "cahoots".

"Births, marriages, deaths." His lips twitched, the approximation of a smile. "The occasional phone call. Pint down the pub. Game of darts. It would be rude not to."

The coffee went sour in Jessica's mouth. "Christ, you can't be serious, Ted!" she said. A serving policeman consorting with a known villain. Correction. A notorious villain. One of the Met's most wanted. Are you completely stupid? Did you think it wouldn't get out? That's not the kind of association that goes unnoticed. Somebody, somewhere, is bound to have spotted you and spilt the beans." Her mental summing-up of the situation was that he was royally fucked.

"I'm bent over with my trousers down, aren't I?" he asked, reading her mind.

Jessica shrugged. "Unless there's some faint chance that your association hasn't actually been discovered and that it really is just an accounting error. In which case, once it's settled, I'd make sure you never set eyes on your scumbag mate ever again."

Ted's eyes fastened for a moment on a small stain in the corner of the ceiling before returning to her face. "I've been a twat," he conceded. "But Jess, I'm not a dirty cop. I've always been proud to serve." He licked his lips, a nervous gesture. "Any chance you could put in a good word for me with the powers that be?"

"Me?" Jessica gave a disbelieving chuckle. "Ted, I'm flattered you think my word would count for anything but, Christ on a bike, I've got no sway over this. Think logically. You're in a completely different division in a different nick, working under a different set of chiefs and Indians."

Like a sulky child, Ted pushed his coffee cup away. "So, you won't help me." His voice was measured, flat, toneless.

"*Can't* help you," Jessica sighed. "An important distinction."

"And yet, you do owe me. Kind of."

Jessica had the odd sensation of her skin creeping. She felt cold, hot and clammy all at the same time. "You what?" she asked, unable to believe her ears. "And how exactly do you make that out?"

Her brother-in-law's eyes narrowed to slits. All traces of reasonableness vanished into the ether. He looked thoroughly unpleasant. "The promotion," he said, his jaw tightening. "Carol was right. It should have been mine, *would* have been mine if the fuckers at the top hadn't been so intent on shunting in a token woman – that would be you, Jess, – even though nobody believes you're fit for the job." His voice rose. "Face it. You're a disaster. A joke! The only one who doesn't get it is you." Ted leapt to his feet. His hands clenched to fists, though he kept them by his sides. "Don't think people don't hold you personally responsible for the last few murders of those young girls, because they do. Just as if you tortured and killed them yourself. You're scum in the eyes of the world. A thick incompetent, whose only qualifications for the post are a pussy and a pair of tits." He sneered. "And they're nothing to write home about."

Jessica's bile rose. An icy hand squeezed her stomach, even as the rage inside her ignited into a blast of red-hot fury. She pointed to the door. "Get out!" she said, hating the fact that her hand trembled, even if only from the tail-end of her hangover. "Get out *now*!" When he made no move to go, just stood there staring at her in contempt, her voice rose to a shout. "I said, get the fuck out of my house, before I—" She raised her coffee cup to throw it, but Jeff closed the distance between them in two strides. He caught her roughly by the wrist, wrenched the mug out of her hand and dashed it into the sink smashing it to pieces. "You'll what? Read me my rights? Arrest me? Earn your stripes by shafting your family?" He let her go, raked her in disgust. "Don't worry, *DI* Wideacre. I've got the message, loud and clear. Just remember this, though – one day, you'll get yours. It won't be today, or even tomorrow, but somewhere out there, over the fucking rainbow and way up high, payback is on its way and my name is stamped all over it."

After he had left, slamming the door behind him so hard every pane of glass in the house rattled, Jessica sank wearily into a chair. She rolled her eyes heavenward. "Any more crap you'd like to throw my way?" she asked. "Or are you saving the rest for a rainy day?" She got the distinct feeling God was laughing at her.

...

Venise Love-Davies was not a happy bunny. More than once lately, it struck her that she might have exercised a bit more caution when putting her wishes out there to the universe. Following in the hallowed footsteps of Marissa Bloom was not easy. Everyone expected her to fail. *Killer Queen* was nowhere near in the can yet, but already the critics were queuing up to condemn it as a stinker. She got sick of hearing them ask the same question, "Why try to remake a classic? The definitive version has already been made. It will never be bettered." Then they'd invariably go on to list a number of remakes that had died a box-office death: *The Wicker Man*, *Psycho*, *Sabrina*. It really hacked her off. To add to her woes, Jack Kingsman seemed to have undergone a personality transplant. Gone was the easy-going, encouraging director she'd met on the set of *Raining in My Heart*, to be replaced by a sarcastic bully, determined to undermine her on every possible occasion. It was obvious that he considered her not a patch on his late wife, but, to be fair, no one could have measured up to those lofty standards. Consequently, Venise's strategy had been to try and bring something new and fresh to the part, imbue it with something of herself. Herself wasn't good enough. Desperate to fathom out the secret of her predecessor's appeal, she had become borderline obsessed with the movie icon, reading every book and article she could get her hands on, watching Marissa Bloom films over and over and often back to back. Mark was losing patience with her, though he claimed to understand. He didn't. He'd snapped the head off her when she'd recently suggested having plastic surgery to look more like her heroine. It was too late now, anyway. The time for surgery was *before* the film started shooting. She'd started experimenting more with her look, though, studying Marissa's make-up closely, practising over and over till she'd managed to perfect the little cat eye flick at the corners of her eyes that were the actress's trademark. She traded in her usual "natural" make-up for mauve eyeshadow and frosted, candy-pink lipstick. She'd taken a trip into a famous hair salon in Covent Garden and left with a set of thick, blonde, real hair extensions, having almost had to mortgage a lung in order to pay for them.

Mark had been genuinely perplexed. "You're already blonde. Your hair is already long. Seriously, I just don't get it."

Venise just shrugged. He'd never get it. How would he? He wasn't her. He didn't have to prove himself to anybody. DCI Mark Beckwith was already top monkey on his tree. She, on the other hand, had yet to make her mark. *Killer Queen* had given her a marvellous platform, but now she had to prove she was worthy of it. Many of the actresses who had been passed over for the role were all but praying for her to fall flat on her face. She wouldn't give them the satisfaction. Whatever Kingsman threw at her, she was in till the bitter end.

...

Beckwith, who had popped in to see Venise on his way home from work, spent a long time thinking about her on the drive home. Her growing obsession with Marissa Bloom was taking a turn for the creepy. He wondered briefly if he should have a word with Jack Kingsman, deciding on balance that the other man would be quite within his rights to tell him to take a hike. He didn't understand showbiz. He didn't understand showbiz types. He certainly didn't understand Venise, and he wanted out. Except, there was no out, not until she had conquered her demons on the set of *Killer Queen* and moved on to starry pastures new. He pushed the CD button on the console dash, relaxed as he heard the reassuring whirr of a Gordon Lightfoot CD slide into place. "Summertime Dream", the first song on the album. He relaxed into the melody, sloughing off his worries for three and a bit peaceful minutes.

...

Venise Love-Davies' attempts to emulate Marissa Bloom twenty-four hours a day were not lost on Ed Hatcher. He'd heard of getting in character, but the silly bitch was taking it to extremes. The hair extensions, the make-up, it was pathetic. She thought she was somebody, but really she was just a cheap slut. One day she'd get hers. When would people learn? – there could only ever be one original.

CHAPTER SEVENTEEN

Gaz Brown was out on the rob. Facebook and Google Street View had combined to make his chosen career something of a doddle. People were so thick. They had no idea who was reading their statuses. A simple boast that they were going out for the night or away on holiday paved the way for people like him to come in and rob them blind. Following the FB trail, any amateur sleuth could work out the number of occupants in a house and make their plans accordingly. Street View came into its own with a close-up on the property. Gone were the days of having to go out and physically case a joint. It was perfectly possible to zoom in on the windows and doors to check out any security issues. He had already determined that tonight's chosen property was a breeze. It was detached from its neighbours and surrounded by a high hedge, which would screen him perfectly from the road and the surrounding houses. There was no alarm system. The door was bog-standard uPVC and, sure as Tyson had bollocks, the lock would be a straightforward Euro cylinder. An expert lock-snapper, Gaz knew he could be in and out in a matter of minutes.

He whistled soundlessly as he parked his car a couple of streets away. It was late, around 3.10 in the small hours, and the streets were deserted. Still, you couldn't be too careful. He continued his soundless whistle and kept close to the shadows, glancing quickly to left and right, before shearing off down Burntwood Close. A wide, tree-lined road, bordered by a green on one side, it provided Gaz with all the cover he needed to break into the house. A cat shot suddenly across his path. He hissed at it and aimed a vicious kick. The cat disappeared unscathed over the garden wall. He stood a while letting his eyes roam over the 1930s facade of No. 13 – lucky for some, but not these particular house owners. The unlit windows gave nothing away. There was no garage and no car in the drive. The signs were good, but Gaz knew from bitter experience that he could still come unstuck. There was always the risk of the unexpected – a dog, say, not factored into the equation, a house-sitter or even cancelled plans. He'd already spent two stretches in Sheppey; Elmley Prison was no fucking joke. He didn't have the stomach for a third.

He approached the front door cautiously. A motion sensor light came on. He stepped quickly out of range, picked up a stone, and expertly took it out. The crack of breaking glass was louder than he would have liked. He froze where he stood, relaxed when nothing happened. He approached a second time, ears pricked for signs of life. He rattled the letterbox, gently at first, then slightly harder. Any dog worth its salt would have been at the door in a flash, barking its fucking head off. Silence. Gaz relaxed further. He rang the doorbell, poised for flight. No lights, no footsteps, nothing! His intelligence-gathering had paid off. Mere seconds later, Gaz had snapped the lock and entered the property.

He made his way through the house methodically, using the dim light of a pencil torch to guide him. He picked up bits and pieces en route, small things he could quickly pawn or sell on: an iPod left on a table, a couple of china figurines, some loose change. It wasn't much of a pay-off considering all the trouble he had gone to. He made his way upstairs, hoping for better luck. But that ship had already sailed. He found a few pieces of cheapo jewellery in one of the rooms, but bugger all else. He tipped them into his bag, shrugged at the kid's photograph staring at him from on top of the chest of drawers. He recognised her from her Facebook profile. Her name was Lindsey Sutton. She was a seventeen-year-old blonde with a passion for shoes, Johnny Depp in *Pirates of the Caribbean*, and chocolate. "Sorry," he said to her photograph. "Still, if you're nice to your boyfriend, he'll buy you more." He'd seen him on Facebook too, and reckoned she could do better. He was checking out some items on the window ledge when the headlights from an approaching car lit up the room. Gaz ducked quickly to one side. Through a gap at the side of the lace curtain, he saw the car draw up outside and a girl get out. She was wearing pink Playboy bunny ears and a minidress. She was slightly unsteady on her skyscraper heels. Clearly, she'd had a good night. A bloke got out of the driver's side and walked round. They groped and kissed for a moment or two before the he got back in the car and drove off. Gaz nearly had a heart attack as a streetlight fell full on the girl's face and he recognised her as Lindsey Sutton, the girl in the photograph. Gaz froze to a statue. Fuck! He hadn't bargained on anyone showing up. They were all supposed to be on holiday. He didn't want to have to hurt her. Violence wasn't his thing. At the same time he didn't plan on going back to prison any time soon. Panicking, unsure what to do, he watched her draw closer to the gate. Just as she raised her hand to open it, she seemed to recollect something. He saw her hesitate a moment, then turn and run after the car, windmilling her arms in a vain attempt to attract the driver's attention. The car sped on, its red tail lights reducing to pin pricks till eventually it disappeared around a corner and was lost from sight. She halted then, threw her hands in the air in a despairing gesture and turned back towards the house. Gaz was just about to scarper when the sound of an approaching vehicle made him look again. A white van, headlights dipped, was making its way down the street. He ducked back as it stopped beside the girl. Within seconds it was accelerating away. When Gaz looked again, all that remained of Lindsey Sutton was a pair of pink bunny ears lying on the ground.

...

At 4.15 a.m., Adam Murphy walked into Rosewood nick to report that his girlfriend, Lindsey Sutton, had gone missing. By 5.00 a.m. Jessica Wideacre was sitting opposite the anxious young man, hoping the fear in his eyes was not reflected in her own. His story was straightforward and plausible. The couple had been to a party at a friend's house in Fulham earlier that night. He'd dropped Lindsey home at about 3.30 a.m. No, he hadn't waited to see her indoors. His voice had faltered at that point. The guilt was already starting to bite. When he got home, he discovered her handbag in the passenger foot-well. In it were her mobile phone and house keys. Her parents were away on holiday – Lindsey was supposed to go too, but changed her mind. Worried that she was locked out, he lost no time in driving straight back. When he reached the house, there was no sign of her. He found the lock broken on the front door and the house ransacked. He was scared she might have disturbed a burglar and that something terrible had happened to her. He'd broken down completely then, sobbing like a baby, "Please. Please find her."

Jessica wished she could reassure him, but when he pulled out a photograph of a pretty young blonde exactly fitting The Director's spec, she thought she might actually be sick. The

SOCOs were already over at the house. For now, all they could do was wait. And pray.

...

At Dover that same evening, Gaz Brown was picked up attempting to board a ferry to Boulogne. In his haste to leave the scene of his recent crime, he had torn one of his latex gloves and left a partial fingerprint on Lindsey's bedroom window. A quick trawl of the database and the cops knew who their man was right down to his shoe size.

The news stunned Jessica. As criminals went, Gaz Brown was at the low end of the spectrum, a neighbourhood vandal who had graduated to petty theft and burglary. He had served a couple of short prison sentences, but had no record of either violence or sexual misdemeanours. Experience told Jessica he wasn't their man. Though criminals could and did escalate their crimes, those crimes generally remained within roughly the same classification. Though not completely unheard of, a petty burglar without priors for violence or sexual misdemeanours, rarely progressed to violent, sexually motivated killing sprees of the magnitude of those carried out by The Director. Her doubts were further reinforced when Gaz Brown, sandwiched between two burly PCs, was hustled into the incident room. To describe him as weedy was to big him up. A strong wind, Jessica suspected, would send him skittering down the street like a fallen leaf. His hair was thinning, the little that was left lank and greasy. His complexion was pasty-white, marred by a crazy-paving of broken veins. His upper lip had attempted to grow a moustache and surrendered halfway. Tattoos reading "Lvoe" and "Htae" adorned the knuckles of either hand, clearly all his own dyslexic work.

He held out under questioning for all of thirty seconds, before putting his hand up to the burglary, but not to abducting Lindsey Sutton.

"From the beginning," Jessica ordered. "And just so you know, I don't do bullshit!"

...

"Fucking toerag," Hennessy swore, when Gaz Brown had been handed over into the ungentle custody of their burglary squad colleagues. "That could have been our big break. If only he had phoned us, we might have caught the fucker red-handed and Lindsey Sutton—" He fell silent, leaving his colleagues to fill in the gaps for themselves. The silence spread into every corner of the room, lying heavy as a shroud as everybody contemplated the likely fate in store for the young woman. The white van, coupled with her age and physical description, left little room for supposition that she had been abducted by anyone other than The Director.

"I wouldn't like to have Brown's conscience," Jessica said, "especially since, by his own admission, he guessed she had been taken by, 'that bloke wot's been killing all dem young wimmin'. He was going to call us from France, he said. A likely story! Even if he did, it would have been far too late." Her gaze swept the room, seeing the despair in her colleagues' faces, knowing it was mirrored in her own. "Christ up a totem pole, *why* can't we get a break!"

A young WPC entered the room and sent her a speaking glance. Jessica nodded wearily. Lindsey Sutton's parents had arrived back from their holiday. "I'll be there in a minute," she told her. "In the meantime, put them in Room 2, and make them as comfortable as you can." As if tea, coffee or a ginger nut biscuit could ease the pain of losing their lovely daughter. Jessica steeled herself. Today was one of those days she hated her job; they seemed to be getting more and more frequent.

...

Ed Hatcher was buzzed. Stroke of luck, last night; he hadn't even been on the prowl. Like manna from heaven the girl just seemed to appear on the road in front of him. She was perfect too, made up for the other little slut – Stacey Wotsherface. He looked forward to acting with this one; that's what the boss called it, acting. He liked the sound of that. It made him feel special, important. He'd joked once that maybe there should be an award like an Oscar, a "Snuffer" maybe; that had cracked the boss up. He put the finishing touches to the set, checked the props and camera angles, made a last-minute adjustment to the key light, and went to fetch the star of the show from the basement room where he kept the girls prior to their starring role. She had regained consciousness and, in the dim light filtering in from the sack-covered window, he could see her peering up at him wide-eyed and tearful, her eye make-up smudged like a panda. Her blonde hair was tangled and grimy from where she'd been lying trussed up on the floor, and her mouth was working soundlessly beneath the strip of masking tape running ear to ear. Her shirt had worked its way off her shoulder revealing the top of her floral bra. Pink! Pink! To make the boys wink! He leaned over and playfully twanged the strap.

"C'mon, Goldilocks," he said, "time for your close-up." He hoisted her effortlessly over his shoulder and bore her off to the studio, singing his own version of a Katy Perry song en route, "I Killed a Girl and I Liked It".

...

That evening, Jessica took the opportunity to pop into Hammersmith Hospital. It was late, gone ten o'clock, and strictly speaking visiting hours were long over. Her father, however, was in a private room and the staff tended to be more accommodating to family turning up at all sorts of odd hours. She was dismayed to find both Carol and her mother still there. They didn't see her at first; both had their backs turned to the door. After the day from hell, she wasn't sure she was up to either Carol's histrionics or her mother's determined attempts at stoicism. She half-turned to go, then froze in her tracks. There was something strange about the tableau. On closer inspection, she could see her mother's hand stretched across the bed, her head bent low over the covers. Carol's shoulders were shaking. An icy claw of fear coiling itself around her heart, she stepped forward into the room. Her eyes flew to her father's face.

Carol caught the movement. She looked up. Triumph, hard and ugly, flashed through her tears. "You're too late," she said. "You're always too late when it comes to this family. Now, fuck off, Jessica. Just fuck off."

...

Jessica didn't smoke. Still, she cadged a cigarette from someone smoking outside the window of the Oncology department. The smoke stung her eyes, burned harsh and acrid in her throat. She welcomed the pain; it made her feel less numb. Night had thumb-printed its seal in the form of a shilling moon on the sky. She found herself staring at it, remembering that silly nursery rhyme about the man tumbling down. Why not? Everything else was.

"I hate my life," she said aloud. "It's shit."

"Yeah? Well mine's no fucking picnic!"

Jessica jumped. She'd forgotten her fellow smoker, secreted in the shadows behind her. He flicked his still-lit cigarette butt onto the ground and shuffled away. It was only then she noticed the large drip he was attached to. She grinned, despite herself; David would roar his head off at that one. She imagined herself telling him, ramping it up to make it sound funnier than it actually was. Except that, actually, it wasn't funny at all, and when she next saw David, she doubted they'd be sharing any little jokes.

Her mother and Carol emerged shortly after and Jessica stepped quickly back into the darkness. Her eyes tracked them across to the car park – Carol, unwieldy, slightly off-centre as she walked; her mother, small, little more than skin and bone, diminished by the loss of her husband. Jessica's natural instinct should have been to go to them, to close familial parenthesis around their shared grief, except that she couldn't. All her life she had felt like an outsider, a cuckoo in the Wideacre nest. Rightly or wrongly, the death of her father served only to reinforce the feeling that she was the wrong fit. She waited till they had driven off and went back up to his room.

"Give me a minute, please," she told the staff, who were preparing to remove him to the mortuary. "I'd like to sit with him a while."

When they had gone, closing the door softly behind them, she pulled a chair up to the bed. He didn't look much like her father – the powerhouse of energy, who for thirty-six years had kept her on her toes as she strove to earn his approval. In a moment of absolute clarity, Jessica realised that, actually, that was one brief she could never have fulfilled. No matter what she did, what heights she managed to scale, what glass ceiling she smashed her way through, she could never have shone in his eyes. With that knowledge came a strange sense of freedom, a lifting of a burden that had hog-tied her for many years. She rose and dropped a kiss on his already cooling forehead. The gesture felt alien; forced and unnatural. She felt sad that she couldn't remember ever kissing him before, or being kissed by him for that matter. Not even as a little girl.

"Goodbye, Dad," she said, a catch in her voice. "I'm sorry we never understood each other. Maybe in the next life, eh?"

...

There were lights on at the house when she got back from the hospital. David had returned from France, sooner than expected. Reluctant to face him, Jessica sat in her car outside. She was so not up for "the conversation", not now when there was so much else to process. Mr Singh came out to empty the rubbish, shot a frightened smile in Jessica's direction and scurried back indoors as fast as he could. Jessica rolled her eyes. His elderly, overstaying mother was the least of her worries. Immigration could do their own dirty work. She had problems enough of her own to be going on with. She stayed a while longer, fiddling with the radio, scanning through the frequencies, hitting eventually on a crackle of conversation that made her pause. Psychic Sam, whose swift rise to TV glory had come about following her accurate prediction that the Duchess of Cambridge's first child would be a boy – like there wasn't a 50/50 chance of that - was busy airing her thoughts on the serial killer known as The Director. Jessica, sceptical as shit, nevertheless twiddled the dial for a better reception.

"He's young," Psychic Sam declared confidently in a thick Liverpool accent. "Asian, or maybe Arab. Foreign, anyway. He doesn't approve of these young girls, their clothes, their behaviour. It's about sharia law. He wants to impose it on us all. Put the women in burkhas. It's his way of teaching the wicked West a lesson."

Jessica switched off the radio. "Jesus, who would have thought it? Psychic Sam working for the BNP!" She climbed out of the car, sighed when she saw Mr Singh's curtains twitch. Enough! She marched over and rapped smartly on the door. If it wasn't exactly the fear-of-God knock, it was as near as dammit. Through the glass panels she saw a flash of colour, caught the sound of panicked voices, someone shushing someone else. A moment later, the door opened and Mr Singh appeared, an obsequious smile draped across his otherwise anxious face.

"Mr Singh," Jessica said. "I know your mother is staying with you and I know she's overstayed her visa. What *you* need to know is that I don't give a flying one. Not my circus, not my fucking monkeys! Neither you nor your mother has anything to fear from me. Are we clear about that?" Mentally dusting her hands, she walked away. One irritation down. Next on the list, David!

...

He was in the kitchen, half-dozing over the kitchen table, a copy of *The Times* spread out before him.

"Jess." He leapt to his feet, arms outflung, and came to meet her. "Ted texted me about your father," he said. "I caught the first plane back." Side-stepping him, Jessica headed straight for the wine rack on the kitchen counter. His arms returned slowly to his sides. Not understanding, he frowned. "Jess? Jess, sweetheart, whatever is the matter?"

"Nothing. Nothing's the matter." Jessica twisted the cap off a bottle of Shiraz, splashed out a large glassful and, sarcastically, held it up. "Unless you count my father dying, my husband shagging another woman, and my boss thinking I'm a gross incompetent. Cheers!"

David's face collapsed. His eyes raked her in disbelief. She had to hand it to him; it was an Oscar-winning performance of innocent bewilderment, but she wasn't buying it.

"Oh, what," she said, her mouth twisting. "I've got it all wrong, have I? My eyes were playing tricks. That was *not* you in the back of the taxi. And the blonde you were kissing was what, a figment of my overwrought imagination?"

David's mouth opened and closed several times before he actually found his voice. It would have been comical, were it not for the fact that Jessica was in no mood for laughing.

"Jesus! Is that what you think?" He asked eventually. "That I – oh, Jess, don't be ridiculous. I am not cheating on you, never was, never will. Yes, there was a blonde in the taxi, but she's just a colleague, twenty years older than you and happily married. And I certainly didn't kiss her."

"I *saw* you," Jessica said in a tight, controlled voice. Her fingers gripped the stem of the glass.

David shook his head in denial. "No. No, you didn't. Perhaps you thought you saw me kiss her, but it simply didn't happen." His hand raked through his hair in exasperation. "Think about it. Seriously. Why? Why would I? Yes, things have been a bit difficult lately for both of us, but I love you, Jess. I thought you knew that. Neither am I the type of man to throw away a perfectly happy marriage for a seedy fling with a colleague." He rose and helped himself to a glass of wine, the stiffness of his body conveying both hurt and outrage. If it was a ploy, it was a good one, and Jessica began to feel the moral high ground shift beneath her feet. She thought back, replayed the image in her mind frame by frame, saw herself standing outside the house that morning, bone-weary and exhausted, disappointed at the brevity of David's parting kiss. She struggled to recall exactly what she'd seen in the taxi, freeze-framed it. There was the blonde. There was her head turning towards David's; his turning towards her, leaning slightly in, but then the picture grew fuzzy. Seen in the cold light of day, it wasn't unfeasible that David and his colleague might simply have been exchanging pleasantries. Could her depleted, exhausted mind have joined a load of imaginary dots to paint a masterpiece of her worst fears? Jessica's shoulders slumped suddenly. Her fingers trembled. Yes, was the shocking answer; it was perfectly possible. She put down the glass on the granite-topped counter, slowly, carefully, conscious that its fragility, its breakability, had become synonymous with her own. And suddenly she was in David's arms, pressed against his shirt front, breathing in his warm, familiar smell, feeling the flutter of the little pulse at his throat against the flushed skin of her cheek.

"Christ, I'm such an idiot," she said. "It's just that …oh, hell… I don't know how you've put up with me lately. It must be like living with a lunatic."

"A nice lunatic," David said, dropping a kiss on her hair.

"But it didn't help that you moved into the guest room," Jessica accused, irrationally.

"Your idea," David reminded her. "I wasn't happy about it, but I didn't object because I thought, perhaps, you needed some space." He held her away, gazed down into her teary eyes, love and sincerity shining from his own. "But, I'd like to move back into ours. Right now, if that's all right with you."

Jessica's face, as she took him by the hand and led him upstairs, said it all. Tonight, more than any other, she needed him to hold her – to hold her, that was all.

CHAPTER EIGHTEEN

Jessica went into work the following morning to find the police grapevine already buzzing with the news of her father's death.

"I might as well be at work," she said, brushing off the expressions of sympathy and the concerned mutterings about whether she should have come in. "There's plenty I can be getting on with here." Calling the team together, she got straight down to business. "Lindsey Sutton. Where are we? Hennessy?" She was painfully aware, as indeed they all were, that time was not on the young girl's side.

"Nowhere, to be exact." The sergeant looked rueful. "We've had the usual run of sightings, one as far afield as Dubai, but nothing of any substance."

"And the press is really on our case now," Connors chipped in. Yours most of all. The latter, unsaid, was very much implied.

"Do they think we're sitting around playing tiddlywinks?" Jessica asked bitterly. "But they're right. We should have caught him by now." She went and stood in front of the whiteboard and stared at the photographs of all the young girls, as if she would find the answer in their innocent, pretty faces. They looked so alive, all of them – vibrant, full of dreams and plans for a future destined never to be realised. They had been relegated to just another notch on a maniac's belt. Jessica's gorge rose at the thought of him out there roaming free, some other poor kid possibly already in his sights. Her gaze lingered on the photo of fourteen-year-old Stacey Herbert, set apart from the others, yet, her gut insisted, not apart.

She tapped the picture. "Tell me someone's in the frame for this. Fuck's sake, you lot, give me something!"

Connors shrugged. "We'd have had more response from the three wise monkeys. It'll probably go down as an unsolved."

Jessica shot her a look, saying with emphasis, "That, it won't. Stacey deserves justice and her parents whatever peace we can give them; it's up to us to make sure we deliver both." She knew what they were thinking, that her words were rhetoric, glib bullshit; the files chock-full of cold cases – victims and grieving families for whom there had never been justice – were the stark reality.

She consulted her notes. "White van/clown face. Where are we with that?"

DC Liversedge stepped forward with a list. "Not much joy there either, guv. Kiddies' party vans in the main – Koko the Clown, face-painting and such like, a couple of ice-cream vendors and one advertising a range of children's clothing." He handed her the list, shrugged. Nothing iffy about any of the owners, unless you count Koko's big feet. There's definitely something odd about them."

Connors flicked imaginary dust from her skirt. "Could be, he's given it a respray by now anyway."

"Unless it belongs to his employer," Hennessy said. "Mind you, you'd have to be one thick son of a bitch to use your boss's vehicle like that."

"Most murderers aren't MENSA types," Jessica pointed out. For the moment, though, he does appear to have the Devil and his legions on his side. But he *will* come unstuck." She spoke earnestly, trying to imbue her team with a sense of confidence lacking in herself. "And when he does, we need to make damn sure we're there to put the noose around his neck." Brave, meaningless words. Connors had almost laughed outright, while Hennessy and Liversedge were quick to park their expressions in neutral. It didn't surprise her too much as she made her way to Beckwith's office to hear Connors' voice floating down the corridor in a mocking rendition of "Send in the Clowns". Bitch didn't miss a trick!

...

DCI Beckwith's eyebrows rose, when, after a brief knock, Jessica stuck her head round the door. "DI Wideacre, you are allowed to take compassionate leave." He nodded her into the chair opposite. "I was sorry to hear about your father. He was a bit before my time, but I hear tell he was one of the good ones."

"He was an awkward sod, actually," Jessica said, settling herself into the chair. "An old-school copper, who most definitely wouldn't fit in with what he considered to be today's namby-pamby society. Everyone in their place, that was Dad's philosophy, and if they didn't go easily, he put them there with a firm fist."

Beckwith let that pass. "Seriously, aren't there things you need to be getting on with at home?"

"No. My mother and sister are seeing to the funeral arrangements; it doesn't take three people to choose a wooden overcoat. I'd prefer to go on as normal, if that's all right."

Jessica's gaze was clear and direct, although a redness about her eyes and the tip of her nose suggested she wasn't quite so – Beckwith fished for the right word – bloodless, as she appeared to be. If he knew anything about the Wideacres of this world, it was that they hid their wounds from prying eyes. He nodded. "I can't pretend it wouldn't be easier having you at the helm. I don't have time to break in someone new, and better the devil you know."

Talk about damning with faint praise. Jessica almost laughed at the backhanded compliment, another reminder of the low esteem in which he held her. And, just in case she ever needed further reminding, it was all there in black and white in the memo in her bedside drawer. She got abruptly to her feet.

"In that case, I'd better crack on." It took every ounce of her self-control not to take the door off its hinges on her way back out.

...

"All be over soon, pretty Lindsey." Ed Hatcher adjusted the bindings round the girl's wrist, so that they cut tighter into her delicate flesh. He smiled as she flinched. "Gonna make you a star, take the best selfie you've ever had." He grinned. "Though, strictly speaking, it won't be a selfie. He yanked suddenly on her hair and she screamed, gratifyingly long and loud. He glanced impatiently at the camera, waiting for the red light to come on. Seconds later, it did.

"And, action!" the boss called.

Ed didn't need a second invitation. He fell on the girl like a rabid dog.

...

Jack Kingsman was well out of sorts and acting like a twat – at home, on the set of *Killer Queen*, and especially to Venise Love-Davies. Somewhere along the line, a tiny seed had taken root in his brain, a rogue thought that had bedded in and which was sending out shoots by the day. Jack thought he might have hit on a way of saving his own skin, while making Venise the fall guy. Yes, it was unfair; she was a nice young woman who certainly didn't deserve such shabby treatment. But when flames were shooting out your arse, you didn't question whose hose you grabbed to put them out. His plan was beautifully simple; instead of being forced to pull the plug on *Killer Queen* himself, and copping for all the accompanying excrement from the investors and critics alike, he would let Venise do it for him. He just had to make her life so goddamn fucking miserable that she'd throw a strop and storm off set. No leading lady, no film. Simple. Not his fault if she was an unprofessional diva. Except, she wasn't. That was the kicker. Jack had reckoned without her Rottweiler determination, the way she gritted her teeth and hung on in there despite the escalating raft of insults and humiliations he hurled her way. Under other circumstances, he would have found her tenacity laudable. Right now, with a runaway train bearing down on him and no way to get off the track, it was a king-size pain in the arse.

His face darkened as he watched her rehearse the bloodied heart scene, possibly the biggest in the whole movie, backdrop to Marissa's famous catchphrase, "*See, I told you I'd steal your heart.*" She was word perfect. Perfect in every way. It was sacrilege to say so, but possibly even better than the original. Despite the heat of the studio, Jack felt a ring of cold sweat break out round his neck and start to trickle down his back. He imagined he heard the rumble of the train thundering down the track, drawing ever closer.

He jumped to his feet and launched a tirade, getting right up in her face. "No! No! No! What are you, Venise, a fucking block of wood? Christ, what was I thinking when I gave you this part? Why didn't I just shoot myself in the head and end my career that way? Better that than death by this slow torture." He could feel the collective disapproval of the rest of the cast and crew wafting his way; they knew he was talking utter bullshit. Fuck 'em, it was his goddamn movie and he'd do whatever was necessary to kill it.

...

Ed Hatcher, who was on set delivering some props, gloated inwardly at the exchange. A damsel in distress. Nothing he liked better, especially when the damsel in question was that jumped-up little pretender Venise Love-Davies. His eye caught Jack's, a flicker of acknowledgement, nothing anyone else would notice. Whistling silently between his teeth, he turned back to his work. Life was beautiful.

CHAPTER NINETEEN

Jessica stood outside her parents' house, working up the will to ring the doorbell. The last time she'd visited had been on the occasion of the ill-fated birthday dinner for her father. She remembered storming out, snatching back the book she'd bought him en route. She waited for the guilt to kick in. If she'd known it was the last time she'd see him alive etc. etc. Except, the guilt refused to materialise. In truth, had she known that he'd expire not five minutes later, she would have done the exact same thing. His death didn't change the fact that he had been a bully and a misogynist. Their relationship had been a trial to them both. Jessica hadn't enjoyed his company, nor he hers. True, she'd wanted to impress him and earn his approval, but only because she felt she had to. Such was the diktat of society and God. It was the fifth commandment, honour thy father and mother. She pressed the doorbell, wincing as the first notes of the theme music to *The Bill* rang out. Her father had loved it. Jessica found it naff and embarrassing. Poles apart when he was alive. Poles apart for ever. Ted opened the door. He stepped aside to allow Jessica entry, waylaid her with a hand on her arm.

"Jessica, about the other day …"

She shook him off. "Not now, Ted."

"When, then?" He flushed. "I really need to talk to you. When is a good time?"

"Umm." She screwed up her face. "Let me see. How about never?" She strode away, left him standing there like a prick. Her position as a cop had earned her many enemies over the years. She'd just earned herself another. Difference was, this one was a viper in the nest.

...

Her mother, sister and a straggle of neighbours and friends were in the kitchen. Carol, head to toe in black, was holding court, her enormous stomach taking centre stage. Her mother sat at the kitchen table, wan but dry-eyed, an untouched mug of tea cradled between her fingers.

"All right, Mum?" Jessica asked, as a neighbour moved out of the chair opposite to let her sit down.

Her mother looked up. "Aye, fine." She seemed to gather herself, squinted, bringing Jessica into clearer focus. "More than I can say for you, hen. You look done in. You always did push yourself too hard."

Jessica welled up a little, both at the endearment and unusual display of concern. She was tired, dog-tired, tired to death. Every bone, muscle and sinew was exhausted. Given the chance, she could sleep for a fortnight and only then roll over onto the other side. She blinked the tears away. "I'm okay," she said. "I can sleep long enough when I'm dead." There was an audible gasp as the words left her mouth, faces turned to her in shock, hands held over mouths in disbelief. Fuck! She'd just put her big foot in it again. "God, Mum, I'm really sorry," she stammered. "I – I didn't mean ... I wasn't thinking ... oh, shit!"

"Jessie, Jessie, Jessie," her mother waved away the apology. Actually laughed. "Dinnae fret yourself, I know very well what you meant. I know you won't thank me for saying this, but in some ways you and your father were very alike. He was always one to blurt out whatever was on his mind. The amount of times he stopped people in their tracks!" The laughter died abruptly. Shadows suffused her face. "Except, in his case, he was a hard-headed bully. There wasn't an ounce of softness in him. There were times I actually hated him. I used to pray sometimes that he wouldn't come home, that he'd catch a bullet, that someone would put a stop to his gallop one way or another. And I didn't much care how." She paused, realising that the room had fallen silent and that her voice was reverberating in the chasm. Carol half reached out as if their mother had an "off" button she could press, but no button could have held back the repressed emotions of more than thirty years.

Tea spread in a liquid octopus across the table as she pushed her mug violently away. "What!" she said, eyes darting round the room, challenging one and all. "Speak no ill of the dead, is it? Turn him into some sort of plaster saint? A lovely man, who wouldn't hurt a fly? Bollocks!" The expletive, so out of character, made her daughters flinch. "My husband, your father, was no saint. At times he was a bastard, a bugger to live with. He'd fight with his own fingernails if there was no one else to take a swing at." The strength left her voice, siphoned out of it by raw emotion. She gazed away into the middle distance, focused intently on a time and place preserved somewhere in her memory. "But, for all that I hated him, I loved the bones of him. There was passion in our marriage. It was stormy sometimes, aye. It was good, bad, a complete mess, the most exciting thing ever, and if I had my time all over again I wouldn't change a damn thing. Do you hear that, all of you? I wouldn't change a damn thing."

Carol found her voice at last. "For God's sake stop, Mum," she begged. "You're making a show of yourself!"

Her mother turned to her then, gazed at her not unkindly. "Ah Carol, poor Carol," she said. "You're always so concerned with appearances and keeping up with the Joneses. But all that glisters is not gold and a pretty face gets you by for all of five minutes. But you know that, don't you, lassie? That's why you've always been envious of your sister's intelligence and zest for life." Her gaze flipped to Jessica. "Not that Jessica isn't beautiful. She could be stunning if she wasn't always so intent on turning herself into a pig's ear." As was her wont, she was speaking about her elder daughter in the third person, talking about her as if she wasn't there. "She's got it all, really, the brains and the beauty. You were jealous, Carol. That's why you primped and preened for your father and stirred him up against her. And, hands up, I didn't stop you. Anything for a quiet life." She reached across the table and took Jessica's hand, stroked her thumb along the back. "And you, DI Jessica Wideacre, have no idea of your true worth. You're so grateful David married you, thinking yourself lucky to get him, when the exact opposite is true. Och, I don't dislike the man, but he's a cold fish, a number cruncher in a designer suit. There's no warmth to be had at a fire like that." She squeezed Jessica's hand, released it. "You could have had anyone. You should have held out for a man who deserved you."

The room had discreetly emptied while she spoke, and now only she and her daughters remained. Nothing more to say, she fell silent. The air was charged. Synapses fired, snapped with things both said and implied. Old perceptions were weighed in the balance and found wanting, old beliefs underpinning the sisters' childhoods lay shattered for ever. Jessica felt as though she was standing on quicksand. She barely recognised her mother, saw her for the first time as a person in her own right, as fallible as anyone else and, like the rest of the world, just doing her best to muddle through. The silence stretched and strained like a living thing. At last her mother stood up and reached for a dishcloth. She was wearing a white blouse and some of the spilt tea had dripped all down the front of it. Jessica watched her dabbing at the table, saw the tears begin, rolling silently down her face. She longed to rise from her seat, to put her arms around her as naturally as Carol always had, but force of habit made that impossible.

"In case you're wondering," she said at last. "I won't be staying in this house; neither will I be inflicting myself on either one of you. After the funeral, I'm selling up and going to live with your Aunt Lucy in Ramsgate. But me no buts," she said as Carol made to interrupt. "My mind is made up. I want to make a new start. You've got enough on your hands with the bairn on the way, and Jessica … well, Jessica's up to her neck in murder."

That was one way of putting it, Jessica thought, ashamed that she hadn't given her mother's future any consideration at all, and vastly relieved that now she wouldn't have to. Her mother and David were oil and water. Impossible to imagine them living together. Really, it was better this way. Though the last few minutes had shown her her mother in a different light, Jessica couldn't just shake off thirty-six years of always feeling not quite good enough. It would take more than just one soul-baring session to exorcise all that accumulated pain and insecurity.

"It sounds like a plan," she said.

Carol launched an immediate attack, snarling, "You would say that, you selfish cow. The world can go to hell so long as it doesn't interfere with your glittering career."

Drops of tea rattled in a tinny percussion as her mother wrung the dishcloth out over the stainless steel sink. "Enough, Carol," she said wearily. "Jessica is every bit as entitled as you to choose her path in life." Her glance bounced from one to the other. "And just remember that when I'm dead and gone each other is all you'll have."

Ted walked in on the tail end of the conversation. "Carol's got me," he said. Like he was some big fucking prize. Jessica suppressed a grin.

"Like I said," her mother said in a measured voice. "Each other is all you'll have. Blood is always thicker than water."

Though pleased that Ted had been cut down to size, Jessica didn't entirely agree with the sentiment, especially since Carol was still looking daggers at her.

...

Her father's funeral was well attended. Jessica noticed a smattering of police uniforms amongst the mourners. She was glad of the dark glasses shielding her eyes, hating every moment of being on show and an object of pity. She kept her focus on a gruesome painting hanging over the altar, an emaciated Jesus, his ribs protruding, his face beneath his crown of thorns stretched in a rictus of pure agony. She let the priest's words drone over her, moved on inevitably to thinking about The Director and his victims. So far, Lindsey Sutton was still officially classified as a missing person. Jessica conceded there was an outside chance the girl might yet show up alive, but somehow she doubted it. No one, having fallen into The Director's clutches, walked away with their life. Consensus amongst her colleagues was that it had to have been him. They'd bet next month's pay on it. She glared at the grotesque figure on the cross, thought irreverently, "For fuck's sake, stop just hanging around. *Do* something. Lead us to the bastard. At least, make him stop!" Yes, it was blasphemy, but really she'd long since given up on religion. It was hard to believe in a merciful and tender God, when you witnessed the kind of evil she did, day after day: babies killed by their parents; wives beaten senseless by their other halves; young lads carved up by gang members; and teenage girls butchered by a fucking maniac. Where was God for Lindsey Sutton right at that very moment? Was he listening to her prayers, preparing to work a miracle and release her to her family? Or was he busy turning a deaf ear to her howls of agony?

A nudge from Carol brought her back to the present. Her mother was out of the pew and heading up to take communion. Jessica shrugged off Carol's raised eyebrows. She didn't do bullshit and she didn't do the sacraments. Make that – she didn't do bullshit!

The uniforms stayed only long enough after the funeral mass to pay their respects. Jessica expected no less. She was grateful and, given her father's reputation as a curmudgeon, surprised at their coming at all. Several people, strangers in the main, approached with comforting platitudes. A few searched their minds for humorous little anecdotes to pass on. Most came up blank. They all received the same answer from Jessica, an evasive smile and the briefest of handshakes. All she wanted was to get the hell out of there and back to normality. But there was still the burial to get through and an endurance-testing car ride to the cemetery, wedged between her mother and Carol, who was now the size of a baby elephant.

A recent downpour had left the earth churned up and people standing ankle-deep in mud around the grave. Everyone looked miserable. Jessica felt an unreasonable flash of resentment that her father hadn't been cremated. But, oh no, he'd wanted the whole nine yards, had drawn up a long list of instructions many years before. If it were down to Jessica, she would simply have ignored them. It wasn't like he could object, come back and sue her or anything. Her lips drew together in a half-smile that was quickly erased when her eyes locked with those of DCI Beckwith standing on the opposite side of the grave. Jessica's heart flipped, then sank to her shoes. His face was drawn and serious. He gave a small, almost imperceptible nod. She guessed immediately why he was there, and it had nothing whatsoever to do with her father. She grabbed a yellow rose from the bunch of mixed flowers Carol was holding and flung it into the open grave.

"Sorry, Dad," she muttered, "duty calls."

...

"I didn't see your husband." DCI Beckwith observed, as Jessica climbed into his car, parked on nearby double yellows. Cops' privilege. "Does he know you've left?"

Jessica shook her head. "He and my father brought each other out in a rash. It would have been hypocritical for him to attend. She reached for her seatbelt. "I take it Lindsey Sutton has been found?"

Beckwith nodded. "I thought you'd want to know, before word got out. I wouldn't have dreamt of intruding otherwise. "

"Thank God you did." Jessica said, clipping the belt into place and waving away the apology. "It was getting to the point where I was considering topping myself." She shuddered. "All that ashes and dust stuff is so depressing. So, what's the score? Who found Lindsey? When and where?"

Beckwith answered her questions in the order asked. "A woman found her this morning when she was –"

Jessica cut him off. "Out walking her dog?" She'd been threatening since for ever to write a book on murders entitled *A Man Out Walking His Dog*. Volume Two: *A Woman Out Walking Her Dog*. Buster sniffing out mortal remains, while out on his constitutional, really was the commonest of scenarios.

"A particularly nasty little ankle-biter, with a face like a mashed turnip," Beckwith confirmed. He switched on the engine, threw the car into gear and nosed a little too quickly into the traffic. "All the usual creepy bells and whistles, but with an added twist. Lindsey's heart was missing. And, surprisingly, her body was dumped, not on one of the commons, as you might expect, but on a patch of waste ground over by Battersea Power Station."

Jessica raised her eyebrows. "That was sailing close to the wind. It's busy round there all times of the day and night." At this juncture, some people might have theorised that The Director had reached the stage where he *wanted* to be caught. Not Jessica. In her experience, perps kept on keeping on for as long as they could get away with it. It was their *raison d'être*, their big turn-on. It was the fix masking the reality that really they were nothing special, just another lowlife piece of shit. More likely, something had spooked him and he'd had to offload Lindsey fast. Either that or he was taunting them, swinging his dick. Mine's bigger than yours.

"I'd say something rattled him." Beckwith echoed her thoughts. "In an ideal world, that would have made him careless; he'd have shed something of himself. A hair. A fingerprint. A fibre. Anything." Frustrated, he thumped the steering wheel. "He must be made of fucking Teflon."

Jessica shot him a sideways glance. He looked tired. Grey, beneath his summer tan. Grey in his hair too. Lots of it. Like David, it gave him that silver fox look. "I'd like to see her," she said. "Before Laura Shackleton carves her up."

He nodded, and swung a right. "I phoned ahead. She's expecting us."

Jessica leaned back as he switched on the radio. *Woman's Hour*. Some woman wittering on about veganism. He flipped to the stereo. Gordon Lightfoot's honeyed tones spilled out. "If You Could read My Mind". Jessica closed her eyes, thankful to Christ no one could read her mind. If they could, they'd see that she didn't know shit from a fried egg.

...

"Bit of a turn-up for the books, that," Laura said, heading across to the table where Lindsey Sutton was being prepped for autopsy by one of the mortuary technicians. Beckwith had stayed only long enough to drop off Jessica and exchange a few words.

"What?" Jessica looked blank.

"Beckers collecting you in person, instead of sending one of the underlings." Laura cocked an eyebrow.

"Don't read anything into it," Jessica warned. "Everyone knows, the higher you climb, the more you can sit round on a branch all day scratching your backside. I daresay everyone else was actually doing what they're paid to do. Working."

Laura shrugged. "If you say so."

"I *do* say so," Jessica snapped. "Now, leave it, please. I've just come from my father's funeral, and I am *so* not in the mood."

Laura was immediately apologetic. "Stupid me, of course you have. Was it really awful?" She pulled a pair of purple latex gloves from a box and eased them on.

"No, it was a fucking laugh a minute." Jessica quipped sourly. She relented immediately. "Sorry, that was ratty. It's just that I've been to so many funerals recently, I'm reciting the requiem mass in my sleep."

They fell silent a moment, side by side, gazing down on the dead girl, Jessica's professional side assessing the bruises and contusions marring her once beautiful face, her human side sickened at the waste of it all. "Poor kid," she muttered.

Laura nodded. "Poor kid, indeed. Damn fine job he did on her. Really pushed the boat out. Even took her heart. Did you hear?"

Jessica nodded. "Evil bastard."

"Sick, or evil?" Laura picked up a Stryker saw. It was a debate Jessica didn't rate. Her stomach turned at the fuggy smell in the room – pine disinfectant, decay and the mortuary technician's too-strong aftershave. A cheap copy of a designer fragrance. "Makes no difference," she said, itching to get out of there. "The end result is the same. Lindsey's dead. They're all dead. Game over." She turned away. "I'll wait for your report."

"Coffee, some time?" The pathologist's finger hovered over the "on" button on the saw. "Better still, if you're free one evening, there's a new wine bar in Balham I've been meaning to check out."

Jessica's mouth watered. Christ, what she wouldn't do for a glass of the grape right at that very minute, except she knew she wouldn't be able to stop at just one. "Maybe coffee," she conceded. "Free evenings are a thing of the past."

"I'll call you," Laura said, switching on the Stryker. The noise rattled Jessica's fillings. She hurried out, calling a cab from her mobile en route. A heavy Indian accent informed her that all their cars were busy – could madam please wait thirty minutes?

Sure, madam could wait thirty minutes. Jessica's eyes settled on the appositely named Dead Man's Inn across the road. She hesitated, but only for a moment. Pub grub, she told herself. A cup of coffee and a ploughman's. Good wholesome fare. She ordered a glass of Shiraz. Large.

...

Venise was in tears. These days, Venise was almost always in tears, and Beckwith was losing patience.

"Why don't you tell Kingsman to stuff the part?" he urged, for the umpteenth time. "You did all right before he happened on the scene. You'll do all right again."

Her reply was to launch a pot of face cream past his ear. "You just don't get it," she screamed. "All right doesn't cut the mustard. I want to be a star, Marky. A bone fide Hollywood star. Not just some piddling little actress, doomed to soap operas for the rest of my life. Or, God forbid, playing pantomime fairies in flea-ridden provincial theatres in the arsehole of nowhere." She dabbed at her eyes with a pair of pink silk panties. "Yes, Kingsman's turned into a pig, but this is my one chance at making it big. If I storm out, there might never be another."

Beckwith returned the pot to her dressing table. Apart from a chip off the lid, it was undamaged. "Diva," he said mildly. "That could have done some real damage." He found her in his arms suddenly, all repentance, her golden head tucked below his chin, her slender body pressed to his, playing havoc with his determination to cool their relationship.

"I'm sorry, Marky. You're all that keeps me sane, really. I don't know what I'd do without you."

Great," he thought. In deeper than ever. Trapped in a web of flattery and feminine need. No place to go. No way out. Venise's lip-glossed mouth came up, searching for his. Her breasts pressed against his chest. He felt a flicker below stairs. His brain had sent a memo, but his todger couldn't read.

He stayed the night, waking in the small hours to discover her gone, her place beside him grown cold. He went in search and found her in the living room, wandering up and down, perfecting Marissa Bloom's stupid lisp. "See, I told you I'd steal your heart."

He went back to bed, but it was a while before he closed his eyes. Beckwith prided himself on being a good judge of character. He just couldn't figure out how the hell he'd got Kingsman so wrong.

...

The end is nigh!

Jack Kingsman tossed the latest note away in disgust. Talk about unoriginal. Jesus, if he'd come across that in a script, he would have shot the scriptwriter. No escaping the meaning, though. His very own apocalypse was looming ever closer. He was almost resigned. Only a fool would have discounted the possibility of fate eventually catching up. Still, as time moved on he'd allowed himself to be seduced by the possibility that the day of reckoning would never come.

Though it was only just gone ten o'clock, he poured his first scotch of the day. A double measure. Neat. His hands were shaking slightly, his breathing ragged and fast. His shaving mirror had already announced that he looked like shit. He felt it too. It had got to the point where a good day was a bottle-and-a-half day. He knocked back his drink in one and stared round his beautifully appointed den. It was modest – the most modest room in the house – but the furniture was top notch, elegant and understated the few ornaments eye-wateringly expensive, the prints limited editions by well-known artists. The wall, which had once hosted his gallery of film stars, held just Marissa now, a large studio portrait by Mario Testino, pet photographer of Princess Diana. Stark, black and white, it showed her in all her flawless beauty: perfect skin, high cheekbones, full lips, her Rapunzel-blonde hair rippling over bare shoulders.

He poured another drink and lofted it in a silent toast. His stunning wife, the love of his life, had spoiled all other women for him. Blondes, anyway. He'd looked for her equal once or twice in the early years, but it had always been a disaster. One had even kissed and told. "I was ready for my close-up, but the director couldn't perform." The gutter press had had a field day. After that, Jack confined his sexual liaisons to dusky beauties like Melis and Mahlika. Low-maintenance women who did what they were told.

"Bitch!" he said aloud. "You fucking destroyed me."

CHAPTER TWENTY

The people at *Crimewatch* had been kept even busier than usual since The Director had started his spree, but, to date, the programmes had failed to turn up any real clues as to his identity. Predictably, after each airing, the nutter brigade came out in force, resulting in hours of valuable police time being wasted as all but the most bizarre 'leads' were checked. The number of UFOs that had been spotted lurking in the vicinity of every abduction made Jessica's head spin. In the unlikely event of the prime minister asking her advice re immigration, she would strongly advise forgetting about the hordes of illegals arriving via Calais and focusing his energy on all the little green murdering bastards sneaking in via flying saucer. Nevertheless, there was always a chance that someone who was not a hundred-carat fruitcake had sneaked in under the radar and seen something of value. The chance that this one good reliable witness might actually exist made it impossible not to carry on with the re-enactments, which is why Jessica found herself standing on Burntwood Close at 3.00 a.m., watching the camera crew and cast set up shop. The conditions were similar to those on the night Lindsey Sutton had been abducted, mildish with only a slight night dew falling, the half-moon wrapped in a shawl of grey cloud throwing down a faint, diffused light. The usual crowd of gawpers were safely tucked up in their beds or in someone else's, making it easier to crack on with things. A firm but polite request had been made to the Suttons' neighbours to stay indoors, and so far, so good. Jessica felt a chill as the cameras started to roll and the carefully orchestrated series of events, as related by Gaz Brown, began to unfold. Everyone fell silent as a car's oncoming headlights appeared in the distance, the pin pricks of light getting closer and closer, pulling up a few doors away from the Suttons' house. Jessica felt her breath catch as the actors playing the roles of Lindsey and her boyfriend got out and began to kiss. The girl, who bore an uncanny resemblance to the murdered Lindsey, looked so pretty in her silly pink bunny ears, minidress and high heels. And so vulnerable. Jessica wrapped her arms tightly around herself, subconsciously wishing she could do the same for Lindsey, and all the Lindseys of the world – keep them safe from harm. So far she had proved unequal to the task. The Director's victims had all died on her watch. The thought made her queasy. Her head reeled and she staggered a little.

DC Liversedge caught her arm. "You all right, guv?"

"Fine." Jessica shrugged off his concern. Tense as iron, she watched the car drive away again and, just as their petty tea leaf had described, saw the girl begin to run after it. Next scene, cue the Transit van, headlights dipped, creeping towards them, a sinister presence in the crepuscular light. It stopped beside the young actress, shielding her from their sight. Sped away in seconds. Nothing to see here, folks, except for a pair of silly pink bunny ears lying on the ground. They had their footage. Fade to black.

Weary, Jessica rolled her shoulders to loosen the muscles which were bunched into knots. She was aching in every limb. Tired. Depressed. Missing the booze. She said goodnight and headed for her car. The programme was scheduled to air at the end of the week, opening the floodgates for another round of nutjobs to come out of the woodwork. She had to keep the faith that at some point they'd strike the mother-lode. Hope, that's what it came down to. Faint hope, growing ever fainter.

She snuck into bed beside David, just as dawn was prising the blinds open on another day. She nestled into his warm back, soothed by his rhythmic breathing. Five minutes later, she was mercifully, dreamlessly, asleep.

...

Ed Hatcher lay in bed watching the dawn come up. He was knackered, hadn't slept a wink all night, felt like shite. Felt worried too. Worried that the boss was losing the plot. Going after tiddlers was one thing. Tiddlers were easy, ten-a-penny. Netting a big fish, though – one that was in the public eye – that was just plain stupid. He'd argued the toss. Couldn't see the point. They had a recipe that worked. Perfect fuckin' results every time. The boss shouted him down.

Ed reached down and scratched his balls. He'd been sweating cobs since last evening. The smell was rank, thick on the air. It mingled with the smell of stale alcohol. Not usually a drinker, he'd stopped off at the offie on the way home, picked up enough booze to float the *Titanic*. No denying it, he was shit-scared. But, now he'd had time to digest matters, he was beginning to get that clutch in the stomach, that nervous bowel spasm he used to get as a kid just before he got on a fairground ride, that jolt of danger spiked with adrenaline. This was the biggie, the one that would cement his name for ever. He'd be media gold, the subject of acres of press coverage, crime text books, reconstructions, films too, most probably. He scratched his balls again and spent a pleasant few minutes musing on which actor should play him. He'd have liked Nicholson – *The Shining* was up there in his list of all-time favourite films. But Jack was past it now, so he settled on Hugh Jackman. Yeah, Jackman would do. Ed grinned up at the cracks on his ceiling. The name of Ed – no, Edward sounded better – Hatcher, would be on the lips of every police officer and criminal profiler in every country. He would be the bogeyman in every parent's worst nightmare. If he managed to pull this off, he'd be bigger than fucking West, Dahmer, the Yorkshire Ripper and Son of Sam all rolled together. Bollocks! He'd be bigger than fuckin' Jesus!

...

A self-confessed Luddite when it came social networking, Jessica had only recently come to accept that Facebook, Twitter et al might actually have a useful role to play in modern-day policing. Considering she didn't really do friends in reality, there was even less appeal in amassing hordes in the virtual world. The younger cops were all into it, fingers flying over iPhones and iPads at every given chance. It got on her wick. DC Liversedge, she was reliably informed, had the 5,000 maximum number of Facebook friends allowed, mostly female, and actually qualified for his own fan page. That, apparently, was something to be envied. DS Connors, who was long enough in the tooth to have known better, was also to be found on Facebook, Twitter and something called Pinterest. Jessica thought it was remarkable how much personal stuff people were prepared to divulge over the internet and how little self-censorship there was. If she lived to be a hundred, she would never understand the craze for selfies and sexting. There was a time when only degenerates and exhibitionists traded in pictures of their private parts; now fresh-faced teens thought nothing of pinging anatomically graphic pictures of themselves over cyberspace for anyone to see.

Despite her misgivings, she agreed to a Facebook memoriam page being set up for each of the dead girls. The hope was that The Director, in the digital equivalent of returning to the scene of the crime, might log on and give himself away in a comment. Serial killers often had over-inflated egos. They longed for adulation, recognition of their cleverness. The temptation to boast sometimes proved so strong, so irresistible, that more than one had given themselves away as a result. There was a lot of truth in the old adage about pride coming before a fall. Admittedly, it was a slim hope – paper thin – but Jessica was desperate and willing to try anything.

It didn't take long before the trolls with their sick-making comments came out of the woodwork. They revelled in the crimes, professing to know far more than they actually did, since Jessica kept a tight lid on the facts of each case. Unbelievably, some were even hailing The Director as a kind of hero.

"Look at this," she said to the team, reading from the computer screen. "'Dem skanky ho's got wot was kumin.' Is that even English?"

DS Connors frowned. "That's mild, compared to this. "'Blonde bitches taut dey wuz better'n everywun else. Ain't nobody laffin now. 'Cept me. ROTFLMAO!'"

Jessica didn't understand the abbreviation, asked if anyone knew what it meant.

"Rolling on the floor, laughing my arse off," DC Liversedge and DS Connors said together, while Sergeant Hennessy looked just as confused as Jessica. Today, his mountain of rollies had attained Vesuvian proportions.

Jessica shook her head. "Jesus, what is wrong with these people?

Several of the postings are apparently from other young girls; you'd think they might be able to relate just a bit." She scrolled on, then stopped in shock at a photograph of a young blonde no more than a shade over fourteen. Half naked, pouting provocatively, she had written across her throat in black marker, "Final Cut".

"It gets worse, guv," DC Liversedge beckoned her over to his machine. "Someone has set up a fan page dedicated to The Director. The 'likes' are growing by the second." He whistled through his teeth. "Some of these comments are really sick. I hope the families don't get wind of them."

Reading over his shoulder, Jessica groaned. "Gawd help us all! They're betting on where he'll strike next and actually suggesting names, even posting pictures of girls they'd like him to kill." She snapped her fingers at the team. "Right everyone, I don't know the ins and outs of any of this social networking stuff, but I want this page taken down right now and whoever set it up in the first place dragged arse-first over the coals. It's really come to something when the slaughter of innocent young girls is being touted as something to admire."

DC Liversedge, the most savvy of them all when it came to matters IT, looked dubious. "That could take a while" he said. It's never easy tracking down the head honcho of these kinds of sites, someone with real clout."

Jessica couldn't have looked less impressed if she'd tried. "Best get on the case straight away, then," she snapped. "In the meantime, I'll go and put DCI Beckwith in the picture."

He was every bit as disgusted as herself. "I know we can't stop the march of technology," he said, "but the internet has provided a platform for every weirdo on the planet to air their views. All they need is a computer and an internet connection and bam! – the world is subjected to their sick opinions and fantasies." He looked slightly bemused. "When I was a kid, trolls only featured in storybooks. 'The Billy Goats Gruff'. Not by the hair of my chinny chin chin, and all that." He looked slightly embarrassed, more so when Jessica scoffed.

"I believe the chinny chin chin bit might have been 'The Three Little Pigs', sir. Though, I can't be certain, since I was never into fairy tales myself."

DCI Beckwith reddened slightly. "Not even in your work reports?"

"Touché," Jessica said, mispronouncing it to sound like touchy.

A hard glint came into DCI Beckwith's eyes. "Leave the pages up," he said. "Yes, it's a long shot that something will come of them, but right now we're just sitting round spinning our wheels."

It was Jessica's turn to blush, quick to grasp the implication that she had come up short in the investigation; that she should go and sit on the naughty step and think about the many ways she'd failed. In the never-put-a-foot-wrong world of DCI Beckwith, she'd tested positive for gross incompetence. No antidote, as yet.

"What about the families?" she asked, damned if she was going to give him the satisfaction of seeing her rattled. "What if they read those awful things?"

DCI Beckwith shrugged. "Things can't possibly get worse for them than they already are. Even if we advise them to stay off the internet, I have no doubt some fair-weather friend will be only too happy to fill them in on what they're missing. "

There was a song about that, Jessica recalled. Something about someone not being able to wait to bring all their bad news to someone else's door. Under the guise of being a good friend, of course. It was getting so that she was losing faith in the entire human race. The life of a yogi living halfway up Kathmandu was growing in appeal. Shame she hated yoga. And was scared of heights.

"Okay," she said. "I'll tell DC Liversedge to leave the Facebook page up, but it kills me that the murdering piece of scum is being bigged up like some sort of hero. It feels like those poor girls are being violated all over again."

Rummaging in his drawer, DCI Beckwith pulled out the bottle of scotch and waved it about. "For medicinal purposes." He unscrewed the cap and splashed some into his empty coffee cup, skidding it across his desk. "Drink, DI Wideacre," he said. "That's an order."

...

Jessica met Laura Shackleton for lunch later that same day. For convenience, and also because they'd both liked it, they again chose O Sole Mio. Jessica suspected Laura's liking wasn't so much to do with the food as the young waiter upon whom she'd set her sights last time. She'd already ordered by the time Jessica, running late and slightly out of breath, arrived.

"Seriously?" she said, eying Laura's plate on which a large and very bloody steak rested. "I would have thought with your job you'd be a committed vegetarian."

Laura grinned. "If it's got a nervous system, bleats, baas, moos or clucks, I'll eat it." She cut into the steak, and the blood, purplish pink, oozed out across the plate. "I'm particularly partial to a nice bit of offal, devilled kidneys, liver and onions, even tongue." She eyed the young waiter as he arrived to take Jessica's order.

"Particularly tongue."

Jessica ordered pasta primavera and a bottle of sparkling water. She was relieved to find that Laura was also on the wagon. She told her about the earlier whisky incident with DCI Beckwith.

Laura's eyebrows rose. "He ordered you to drink it? Now those kinds of orders, I can take."

Jessica eyed her sternly. "Just don't go reading anything into it, okay?"

"My lips are sealed," Laura promised, moving the conversation swiftly on to Ted. "Any news of your brother-in-law?" she asked.

"We traded a few words recently, in which he left me in no doubt that he can't stand my guts and thinks he was robbed of the promotion." Jessica's lips twitched. "Before enlightening me as to his true feelings, though, he had the gall to ask me to put in a good word with the decision-makers to get his suspension lifted."

Laura looked astonished. "I take it you refused?"

"They'd have laughed their heads off," Jessica said. She speared a pasta bow with her fork. "On the scale of who's who in the constabulary, I'm in the 'who's she?' section."

"My policeman squeeze tells me he's not that popular with his colleagues, that there have been rumours of shadiness for some time."

Jessica swallowed her food. "Oh, Ted's all right, really. He's not intelligent enough to be involved in anything serious. To think I used to shag him."

"You what?!" Laura almost upset her drink. "You shagged your sister's husband? And you think I'm a hussy!"

"*Before* they married. David and I had had a brief parting of the ways. I met Ted on the rebound. I came to my senses before too long."

"I bet that rankles with your sister." Laura's eyes tracked the young waiter as he delivered food to a neighbouring table.

"She prefers to pretend it didn't happen," Jessica said, "as do I." Thoughtfully, she stirred her pasta. "He threatened me, you know, gave me some guff about karma and *The Wizard of Oz?*"

Laura put down her cutlery. "*The Wizard of Oz?*"

"Oh, something about over the rainbow and me getting my comeuppance. He was furious with me."

"Enough to do you mischief?"

Jessica laughed off the idea. "No. Ted's all talk. He's just worried that he's got himself in a mess and needs to vent, that's all."

"Well, you just be careful," Laura said, but her attention had already moved on. The waiter was back and hovering.

"The food?" he asked, in his heavily accented English. "Is good?"

"Good?" Laura said in an exaggerated fashion. "Darling, I thought I'd died and gone to heaven."

Jessica smiled, sat back and enjoyed watching her flirt, another skill in which she was deficient. That David had bothered pursuing her at all, let alone put a ring on her finger, was something of a miracle. In Jessica's book, all that eyelash-batting, simpering and girly stuff was just bullshit. Laura, however, was a past master. The waiter looked entranced, delighted, excited – shit-scared too. A phrase came into Jessica's head. *As the minnow to the whale.*

...

That evening, Jessica found herself in the unusual – make that unheard of – position of dining out twice in one day. David had booked a table at a brasserie close to where they lived.

"What for?" Jessica regarded him with suspicion. "Oh, Lord, I didn't forget your birthday, did I? Or our wedding anniversary?" She panicked slightly. "I didn't, did I?" Damn! She was crap at remembering important dates. More ammunition for Carol. *How come I never forget Mum and Dad's birthdays, Mother's Day, Father's Day, your fucking birthday ...* She wished she would forget her birthday. Better still; forget that she existed at all.

"Slow down, Sherlock," David said. "There's no mystery here. I want to take you out for dinner. Nothing wrong with that, is there?" Still processing the idea, Jessica shook her head. David frowned. "We've both been working so hard, I thought a little time out would be nice. Should I cancel?"

"No. Not at all," Jessica said. God, she was so rubbish at this kind of thing, hadn't a clue how to be gracious. "It's a lovely idea, really. You just surprised me. What time's the booking for?"

"Eight thirty, plenty of time for you to get titivated." David grinned. "I'll even run you a bath." Jessica passed on the offer. She preferred a shower – less chance of drifting off.

Luxuriating beneath a cascade of warm water, she reflected that it was nice that after sixteen years together David could still surprise her, or even wanted to. Sixteen good years in the main, with just the occasional blip, Ted being one of them. That was one bit of history she'd go back and rewrite in a heartbeat. She adjusted the spray to turbo jet, angling her neck and shoulders so that the water pounded against her sore muscles. It felt good to relax, to feel her tension slithering down the drain along with the soap suds.

In honour of the occasion, she put on her green wraparound

dress and left her hair loose. She dug out her court shoes and dabbed on some tinted moisturiser and a slick of peach-coloured lipstick from a tube fully five years old. She smacked her lips together, hated both taste and texture and wiped it off again. Without even looking in the mirror, she went downstairs. David whistled as she came into the kitchen.

"You look stunning, Jess. Gorgeous. You should wear your hair down more often."

"It's not practical," she said, "After five minutes I end up looking like a loo brush." She extended her foot. "No more than these damn shoes are practical. Just as well Alberico's is not far."

"I wish you'd learn to accept a compliment." David held her coat out for her. "I know, I know. Jessica Wideacre doesn't do compliments, or bullshit, or a million other things other people do to oil the wheels of civilisation."

Jessica's conscience pricked her. She slipped her arms into the sleeves and shrugged it on. He was right. She was a stroppy cow. "I do appreciate the compliment, really." She picked up her bag with its meagre contents: purse, mobile phone, tissues and roll of extra strong mints and smiled. "Lead on, Macduff."

...

Midway through their main course, Jessica wasn't smiling any more. David had dropped an atomic bomb into the conversation, leaving her feeling betrayed, hurt and angry. And a bit jaded too. It seemed that everyone, even her husband, had an agenda. No such thing as a free dinner.

"New York?" she said, repeating herself for at least the third time. "You want to move to New York? This is not an April fool's joke. This is serious, right?"

"Perfectly serious." David reached across the table for her hand, but she snatched it away. "Think about it, Jess. This is a brilliant opportunity. Not just for me, but for you too. Acting CEO of Hazeboittes NY, with a view to taking on the position full time – that's pretty heady stuff. I'm flattered to have been chosen."

"And you want me to go with you?" Jessica asked, wanting to be clear in her mind.

"Naturally," David said. "You are my wife."

Jessica bit down on her anger. "And what about *my* job, David? Do you think I can just up and leave and come swanning back after a year, tell Beckwith to suck it up?" She picked up the glass of wine she'd been carefully eking out, tossed back the contents and banged it down hard on the table. "Or doesn't my job count? Maybe, like Carol, you think I'm just marking time before popping out the obligatory sprog. Because that's never going to happen. You were clear on that from the start. I am not mother material. I do not do shitty bottoms and baby sick. Not now! Not ever!"

"Jess, stop," David pleaded, as her raised voice began to attract the attention of the other diners. "I never said your job wasn't important, but have you seen yourself lately? You're on edge constantly. Irritable as hell. You're—"

"Under intense pressure," Jessica interrupted. "Up to my neck in murder, as my mother put it recently. And, I've just lost my father. All things considered, I think I might be excused a bit of irritability, don't you?" There was also the Ted business, but it seemed wrong to mention that. Her fling with Ted meant absolutely nothing, but David didn't need his face rubbing in it. Bad enough that Carol had ensured her ex was a permanent fixture in their lives.

"Exactly," David said. "But it doesn't have to be like that. Surely a new start is just what the doctor ordered." He leaned across the table and this time succeeded in capturing her hand. "It would be really good for us."

"It would be really good for you," Jessica corrected. "I'm the one who's being asked to make all the sacrifices, to give up a career I've worked my rear end off for. And now that I'm finally getting somewhere, you just expect me to walk away." She snatched her hand away. David flinched, as if she'd physically hit him.

"It's killing you," he said. "And quite possibly our marriage too."

Jessica sat back in her seat. "You're blackmailing me," she said incredulously.

David picked up his wine glass, put it back untouched. "I'm telling it like it is. I value our marriage, Jess. I value us. But living as we are, both of us at full throttle, isn't sustainable. Something's got to give."

"That would be me," Jessica said drily. "Doing the giving, I mean."

David shrugged. "So, what's the answer?"

"Stay as we are. Things will quieten down. The UK markets will recover. You'll get a position equally good or even better than Hazeboittes are offering. The Director will get caught."

"Possibly, but irrespective of Hazeboittes and New York, one thing is certain, there will be another Director and another and another, because that's the nature of your job."

Jessica swallowed a lump in her throat. "But you've always known and accepted that," she said. "I don't understand why you want to change things now."

"I want a normal life," David said, exasperated. "I want not to have to tense every time your bloody phone rings. I want to lie beside you knowing you're home safe with me and not tearing off after some madman in the small hours of the morning. I'm tired of lying there wondering if you'll come home in one piece. It's tearing me apart."

"You never said anything before," Jessica accused.

"I'm saying it now."

"And, if I don't want to go to New York. Will you still go?"

"I don't want to get on the plane alone."

Jessica pushed the point. "But you will still go?"

David sighed. "Probably. I just can't keep doing this."

A waiter wandered over with the dessert menu, got a whiff of the poisonous atmosphere and backed off quickly.

"How long have I got?" she asked David. "To make up my mind."

"It's a big ask. Two weeks."

She would have laughed if it were funny. "You must be kidding. I'm in the middle of a major investigation. I can't just walk out and leave my colleagues in the shit. There's no way I'm going anywhere until The Director is behind bars." She shook her head, unable to believe they were actually having this conversation. To expect her to throw up her career and what was left of her family – admittedly, not as heartbreaking for her as for the average person – at two weeks' notice was not only unreasonable, but insane. The logistics of the upping sticks and moving in that time frame would be a nightmare. Damn near impossible.

"I can't do it," she said. "It's complete and utter bullshit, not to mention totally unreasonable, to expect me to turn my life upside down at the drop of a hat."

"I know. And I apologise for that," David said. "But the pressure is really on. The former CEO has had a major heart attack and there's nobody steering the ship. I need to give my answer now, or the position will go to someone else." He looked glum. "I'll have lost my chance."

"And you'll end up resenting me," Jessica said. "So, where do we go from here?"

"Let's be clear on this, Jessica," David said, his use of her full name underscoring the gravity of the situation. "I do *not* want our marriage to end because of this. I love you with all my heart. Perhaps we could come to a compromise?"

"I'm listening," Jessica said.

"How about, you follow when you're ready? Three months. Six months, even."

Jessica's heart dropped to her shoes. "And what if I'm never ready, David?"

"I'm hoping that you will change your mind."

"But what if I don't?" Jessica persisted. "What if in three months, six months, a year on, I'm still not ready? What then?"

"Then, we'll cross that bridge when we come to it." David finished the conversation by signalling for the bill.

As she pushed back her chair, Jessica couldn't help but feel that her bridges had all been burned and her husband had lit the match. Her eyes were a blur of tears as they left the restaurant, which was rather fortunate considering DCI Beckwith was seated just round the corner and had heard virtually every word of their heated exchange.

"Isn't she that scary WPC from your station?" Venise asked, catching sight of Jessica storming through the restaurant doors.

"Yes," he confirmed, amused by her description of his DI. "That's Jessica Wideacre. She's not really scary, though, just driven." He applied himself to his dessert, barely tasting the too-sweet concoction of chocolate and cream. His mind was churning with the implications of the couple's row. Were DI Wideacre to leave, it would certainly make life a whole lot easier. He would immediately lobby for a senior male officer to step into her shoes. It would be the answer to all his prayers. Venise's voice broke across his thoughts. She was looking at him curiously.

"What?" she asked, "what did you wish for?"

Beckwith looked blank.

Venise grinned. "You just said, be careful what you wish for."

"Did I?" Bemused, he shook his head. "Must just have been a random thought."

He was still having random thoughts all the way home, thoughts he wasn't entirely comfortable with, thoughts about DI Jessica Wideacre. He went back to his own place that night and sat in the conservatory for a long time drinking green tea and listening to his collection of Gordon Lightfoot vinyl LPs. He hummed along to "Early Morning Rain", wondering when he reached the part about the big 707 on runway number nine, if Wideacre would, in fact, take the plane to New York. His last thought before he fell asleep that night was that David Wideacre was an unreasonable prick.

CHAPTER TWENTY-ONE

Jack Kingsman was discovering that troubles came not as single spies, but in whole battalions. His home, the one sanctuary where he could get away from the shit-fest that was his life, had turned into a battleground of warring women. He was considering giving all three – the housekeeper and the two Turkish sisters – their walking papers. Sheila Walters, having appointed herself his moral guardian, had stepped way over the line. She had no business interfering in his private life. If she continued to stick her oar in, he'd terminate her employment on the spot. As for Melis and Mahlika, he was growing bored of them too, hadn't had much use for them, in truth, his elevated stress levels having put him on a par with a eunuch. Give the pair their due, they had tried out every trick in the Kama Sutra and then some, and still not a peep. A fourth note had utterly destroyed the little libido he had left.

tick tock, tick tock!

The message couldn't be clearer. The vice was tightening around his bollocks. His carefully constructed house of cards would soon come tumbling down. Nowhere to run. Nowhere to hide. Except in a bottle. Jack Kingsman opened a fresh bottle of scotch and, without stopping to pick up a glass, walked over to the window and stared out into the darkness that was studded with a million enchanting, twinkling lights. No fabled nightingale was singing on Berkeley Square; the only melody was the drone of passing traffic.

He drank deeply, wondering how much longer the view would be his. Tick tock, tick tock.

···

"I see DCI Beckwith's girlfriend is in the paper again." DS Connors waved the newspaper at Jessica. "That film she's in is behind schedule or something."

"And this is of interest to me, why?" Jessica asked, batting it away.

"No reason," Connors said. "I just thought you might want to read it."

"Think again," Jessica snapped. "Better still, apply your thought processes to the job in hand. It's of no relevance to me whether DCI Beckwith is dating a film star or a chimp." She clapped her hands to round up the team, who were scattered round the office. "Hennessy," she said. "What the hell is that you're smoking?"

Sergeant Hennessy looked despairing." It's an e-cigarette. The wife got it to encourage me to give up smoking."

"Is it working?" Jessica asked, as he exhaled a vapour trail big enough to have come from a Learjet.

"Tastes like shit, if I'm honest. Bubblegum flavour," he informed them all miserably. "What am I, six?"

"Then, for heaven's sake, put it away," Jessica said. The rest of the team gathered round in a semi-circle. "Right," Jessica said, "where have we got to with the investigation? Nowhere? Okay, let's all go home." There were a few timid sniggers. She glared round, her gaze bouncing from one to the other. "No, I mean it. Let's all go home, because, sure as hell, we're getting absolutely nowhere. Why? Because you're a bunch of useless incompetents, that's why." She jabbed at her own chest. "And I count myself in that. Any more deaths will be solely down to us. So here's what I propose. Connors and Sedgie, I want you two out on the street – find some more bodies to help. We're woefully understaffed. Go back over all the old ground we've covered and look for new. Knock on doors, take a leaf out of the charity-muggers' books and accost passers-by. Do whatever you have to, only don't come back here without something concrete. I repeat, no one, barring the invisible man, passes through this world without leaving a trace. Luck has been with The Director so far, but she'll kick his arse sooner or later. Maybe she already has, but we've been too busy picking the fluff out of our navels to read the signs." She scowled at Connors and Liversedge. "Are you two still here? Go on, move it!" She turned to Hennessy.

"Sergeant, grab the case files. Yes, I know you've gone over them before, as has everyone else – but do it again. Right from the top. Scrutinise every last word of every report. Put yourself in the killer's shoes. Think outside the box. What is it that drives him? Is it anger? Is it sex? Is it anger driven by sex? We know he's probably impotent or got some sort of erectile dysfunction disorder. Is he striking out because he's unable to perform in a normal fashion? Is his hatred directed at women in general, specifically young blondes, or is he killing the same woman over and over again? Is power his head-rush? Is he the abused turned abuser? What's his next move? Where does he go from here?" There was the tinny noise of Hennessy dropping his e-cig in the metallic waste bin beneath his desk. Slightly breathless, Jessica raised an eyebrow.

"I'm going to need a proper fag," he said sheepishly. "Maybe several."

Jessica shrugged. To each their own. She could murder a drink. But it would have to wait. "If anyone's looking for me," she said, "I'm meeting with Dr Shackleton.

...

DCI Beckwith watched Jessica stride across the car park and commandeer a pool car from a nervous-looking young policeman. Her walk was purposeful, distinctive, yet strangely graceful. In another life she might have been a ballerina. He thought briefly about that, but his imagination didn't quite stretch to DI Wideacre as the Sugar Plum Fairy.

He'd been expecting her to hand in her notice any day, but so far she appeared to be carrying on as normal, yelling at her team and at him too on occasion. An email received from his own superior officer, Superintendent Green, was sure to put the cat amongst the pigeons. Her brother-in-law was under investigation for the misappropriation of a large quantity of Class A substances seized during a major drugs bust and Beckwith had been tasked with *leaning* on Wideacre to find out if she, herself, was somehow implicated in the whole sorry business. It wasn't a task he relished. His gut instinct was that she was straight as a die. Whatever his misgivings, he'd never doubted her honesty. That said, Ted Carling had been his number one choice for the position of DI – so, if Carling came up dirty, what did that say about his judgement?

He turned back to his desk as Wideacre's car shot through the exit gates. Days like today, he wished he was out on a boat somewhere, fishing, lost in the vastness of the ocean. A blip, off everybody's radar. It was a favourite fantasy, despite the fact that boats made him sick and he hated fishing. He glared at the email

from his superior, still open on screen. *Lean on her.* He closed it
down, consigned it to the recycle bin and deleted it from there. On
the plus side, it might be the catalyst Wideacre needed to decide
about her future with the force. It was a thought that didn't give
him quite as much satisfaction as he might have wished. Feeling
the need to shout at somebody, he picked up the phone.

...

There were layers of smells in the mortuary: the iron smell of
blood; the meaty smell of newly removed organs; the cloying,
sickly-sweet smell of death and decay; the pungent smell of the
pine disinfectant designed to, but not succeeding in, masking the
other smells. They clung to Jessica's skin and hair and clothes, got
inside her nostrils, so thick she could almost taste them.

"You become immune," Laura said airily, snapping off a blood-
soaked pair of latex gloves and gesturing for a technician to sew
back up the cadaver she'd been working on. "High as a kite," she
said, gesturing towards the body. "Thought he could fly out the
twenty-fourth floor of a tower block. He was wrong. Tea?"

"Yes, please," Jessica said, thrown slightly by the seamless
switch from the tragic to the mundane. "I'd prefer coffee, though."

"I think I can drum up some instant," Laura said, leading the
way into the kitchen. "The percolator's bust and there's no money
in the kitty to repair it. The way it's going round here, I'll soon be
taking a leaf out of Burke and Hare's book and selling body parts
to raise some cash."

Jessica grinned. "Instant's fine." She leaned against the work
surface as Laura filled the kettle and took a couple of mugs from
a cupboard over the sink. She held one up for Jessica's inspection,
pointing to the tea-stained insides. "That's what passes for clean

in this joint. Men! Fuckers. All of 'em." She exchanged it for a slightly cleaner one, opened a roll of digestive biscuits and tipped them onto a plate. "So, what's on your mind?" she asked, nibbling on one as they waited for the kettle to come to the boil. "I mean what's *really* on your mind? You have all my case notes; there's nothing further I can add."

Jessica felt wrong-footed. In her own mind, that was the only reason for her visit, but in the light of Laura's shrewdness, she had to admit she'd been fooling herself. The truth was she needed to talk. "Are you some kind of a witch?" she asked, snatching a biscuit from the plate and dunking it in her coffee.

"Only on a good day," Laura quipped. "So, what's up?"

"David," Jessica said, and told her about the proposed move to the States. "I'm so torn, I don't know what to do."

"Wow, that's a tough one," Laura said, when she had finished. "I wouldn't want to be in your shoes." She grinned. "Not least because they're ugly."

Jessica smiled. She was pleased the other woman hadn't tried to play down the enormity of the decision or rush into offering band-aid solutions. Her clear head and willingness to listen was just what Jessica needed to bring clarity to her own brain. "I don't want to be in them either," she confessed. "The problem is, I love David. I don't want this to be the death knell for our marriage. Still, it feels unfair that I should have to give up my own life's dream so that he can follow his. Is that selfish?"

"If you do chuck it all in, resentment may well kill your marriage anyway."

"That's what I'm afraid of," Jessica said honestly. "My resentment if I go to the States. David's, if I don't. Oh, bugger!

What to do! What to do!" She glared into her coffee. There were no answers there.

Laura said nothing further, just stood watching Jessica's face work as she wrestled with the problem. At last she put her cup down and threw up her hands. "One thing's for certain, I can't just turn my back on my team right now. They've been putting in all the hours God sends – I can't just jack it all in and leave them to it. What kind of person would that make me?" She frowned. "And the girls, The Director's victims, I swore I'd get vengeance for each and every one of them, that I wouldn't rest till such time as we'd banged him up and thrown away the key."

Laura looked her straight in the eye. "I think you've found your answer," she said.

Jessica gathered her things together: handbag, jacket and car keys. She smiled. "I didn't like you much when we first met, Shackleton," she said, "but you've kind of grown on me."

"Great," Laura said. "Perhaps one day you'll even lend me your shoes." She chuckled. "That, let's be clear, was a joke."

···

Jessica was grinning as she left the mortuary, probably one of the few people who ever did. Back at the nick, less than an hour later, she was laughing on the other side of her face. Her good humour first started to dissipate with the news that Beckwith wanted to see her in his office. When the reason why became clear, the last vestiges fled, to be replaced by a thunderous frown.

"Why," she demanded, "would you think I have any involvement in Ted Carling's affairs? Simply because of our tenuous family connection?"

"Hardly tenuous," DCI Beckwith said. "He is, is he not, married to your sister?"

"But not to me," Jessica snapped. "Besides, I wasn't aware that he had actually been found guilty of anything."

"He hasn't, as yet, but it's not looking good for him." DCI Beckwith cleared his throat. "Some of his connections are looking decidedly unsavoury. You've heard of Nub Hollingbroke?"

Jessica nodded. "You'd have to have been living under a rock not to. Everyone in London knows that name. Like the Krays."

"And almost as notorious," Beckwith continued. "Not the kind of person you would expect a serving member of the police force to play nice with." He quirked an eyebrow. Jessica made no response. Let him say what he had to and be done with it. She disliked her brother-in-law intensely, but she was damned if she was going to put him in the frame for anything. Beckwith tried the direct approach. "Are you aware of Ted's connection with Hollingbroke?"

Jessica locked her arms behind her head and leaned back in her chair, deliberately casual. "Am I my brother-in-law's keeper?" she asked, neatly avoiding directly answering the question. She could tell by the pulse zigzagging crazily at Beckwith's temple that she was frustrating the hell out of him.

He flicked to nice-cop mode. "Look, I'm sorry to have to make these enquires, DI Wideacre, but you must understand it's a delicate situation. Should it transpire that DS Carling is, indeed, guilty of the charges laid against him, it is only natural that close attention will be paid to all those in his orbit."

Jessica unwound her arms and stretched in an exaggerated fashion. She yawned widely, fanning her hand over her mouth. "A

–", she said, "as yet, Ted has not been found guilty of anything. And, B – I am not in his orbit." She stood up, effectively dismissing him. "If that's all, I really would like to press on with those matters that do concern me."

"What's wrong with this picture?" DCI Beckwith asked himself wryly, as Jessica slammed the door behind her.

...

Jessica's day continued on a downward trajectory. Carol was waiting outside her house when she got home.

"Here," she said, thrusting a pot plant into Jessica's arms. "Your weirdo neighbour said to give you this."

Jessica sighed. Mr Singh's gratitude apparently knew no bounds. She was forever coming home to find pot plants, Indian knick-knacks and once, bizarrely, a large hairy coconut left on her doorstep. She hated to think what construction Immigration might put on such behaviour.

"I wish he wouldn't," she said, looking across at his house and seeing him wave from the window. Hands full, she searched awkwardly for her key and inserted it in the lock. "So, to what do I owe the pleasure?" As if she couldn't guess.

"Ted," Carol confirmed her suspicions. She lowered her bulk onto one of Jessica's kitchen chairs and glared at her. "He's told me how they're trying to stitch him up at work and how you won't do anything to help him. Why, Jessica? Why are you such a mean, spiteful cow? I would have thought you'd have got over the fact that Ted and I are together by now. You're married, for God's sake, move on."

Jessica's feet were aching. She kicked off her shoes, flexing her toes to relax them, and rotating her ankles. "Get this into your head, Carol," she said, wanting to limit the potential for any argument. "I am not in any position to help Ted. I have neither the rank nor the clout. Besides, if Ted is in shit, it's no more than he deserves. As a police officer, he should know better than to rub shoulders with a scumbag like Nub Hollingbroke. When drugs go missing on your watch, fingers are going to point when an acquaintance like that shows up on the radar."

"Ted had nothing to do with those drugs going missing," Carol said, red-faced and angry. She jabbed her finger at Jessica. "This is personal, isn't it? You'll never forgive him for dumping you. You want to destroy him – first by taking his job, then by refusing to stick up for him. Of course that's going to make him look guilty, his own family sitting on the sidelines and keeping shtumm."

Jessica was tired. The needle on her patience meter had dipped below zero. She padded over to the counter, opened a bottle of wine and splashed out a glass. "Ted Carling is not my family," she said. "He's nothing to me. If he was on fire, I wouldn't piss on him."

"Oh, hark at you," Carol sneered. "Lady-fucking-Muck. You think you're something special. But you're not. You can't even catch the madman that's murdering all those poor girls."

Jessica flinched at her sister's unerring ability to kick her right where it hurt. Two could play at that game. "Know what, Carol?" she said. "Ted didn't dump me. It was the other way round. I lied about it to spare your feelings about being second choice." She snapped her fingers together. "Know something else? I could have him back, just like that. God knows, he's made it plain often enough." She banged down her glass. "Lucky for you, I wouldn't touch him with a barge pole. Now get out of my house or, pregnant or not, I'll boot your fat bum out the door."

"Was there any need for that?" David asked, finding himself almost bowled over by a furious Carol as he came into the room.

Jessica grinned. "Yes, and I'd have done it too."

...

She and David made love that night. There was a kind of desperation in the act. For a long time after, Jessica lay in the crook of his arm, tuning in to the deep, even pattern of his breathing. She couldn't help but wonder if this was the last night they'd ever lie like this again. In the morning he was leaving for the States. She wasn't going with him. They'd left the door open. Three months. Six months. A year. David told her he would wait for her for ever. Desperate to savour every last moment of this, their last few hours before he jetted away, Jessica fought off sleep. Her mobile rang just as dawn punched a hole in the sky. She knew before answering that The Director had struck again. When she clicked off, David was propped up on one arm watching her.

"So, this is it," he said.

Her throat almost closed up. "This is it. I'm sorry, I can't stay to see you off."

"Perhaps, it's just as well," he said. "I hate airports. I hate the idea of leaving you."

Your choice, Jessica thought, but they'd been up and down that road so many times their soles had worn thin. So all she said was, "I know," and headed for the shower.

"I meant what I said," David said, when she emerged. "I'll wait for you for ever."

Driving away, Jessica saw that the moon had left its ghost behind in a perfect, nebulous ring; symbol of infinity. Symbol of for ever.

CHAPTER TWENTY-TWO

Ed was stoked. The final rehearsal – he liked to call it an undress rehearsal – was over and, like all the others, had gone without a hitch. The little Aussie bitch had put up a helluva fight, though. She'd clawed and scratched at him like a wildcat, tried to bite him too. He'd enjoyed showing her why that wasn't such a smart idea, knocked a couple of her teeth out and made her pick them up off the floor. The boss hadn't been too happy at missing out on the foreplay, so he'd made sure to rev up the rest of the show. Best movie yet, he reckoned. He'd even suggested a soundtrack, cracked the boss up, the pair of them singing "Tie Me Kangaroo Down", the kid wailing like a banshee. Times like that, he felt like God, fucking invincible. He was on the international stage now, going for global domination. No one was going to piss on his bonfire, specially not the plods. Thick bastards couldn't find their dicks in the dark, not even if they were Day-Glo. All sorts of talking heads had started to get in on the act, from priests – shower of fucking kiddie-fiddlers – to have-a-go politicians. Ed swelled with pride. He couldn't wait for the grand finale, after which he would step out of the shadows and be crowned the greatest serial killer of all time. There'd be books and films and interviews, the world's greatest brains trying to psychoanalyse him. Jack the Ripper could fuck off. Harold Shipman could do one. What none of them knew was that he was nursing a delicious secret, one he would take to his grave. Would the real Director please stand up?

...

"We're pretty sure the body is that of Eva Castle, a seventeen-year-old Australian backpacker," DS Connors told Jessica. "Her parents filed a misspers report just hours before her body was found here on the common."

"A man out walking his dog?" Jessica asked.

Connors looked at her oddly. "Refuse men, emptying the doggy bins. One nipped off to make a call on his mobile and almost fell over her. She was just a few metres away from the roadside. No attempt made to hide the body."

"And this was at what time?"

"Six thirty, I believe. They start work early to avoid the rush hour."

"Not round my way, they don't," Jessica snarled. "Get caught behind one of those big bin lorries and not only do they stink you out of it, but you're trapped for an eternity." She walked over to where Laura Shackleton was hunkered down, making her preliminary examination. She nodded in greeting and rose slowly to her feet, groaning in an exaggerated fashion. "I'm past all this bending down malarkey. Past everything, really. These nights when I go to bed, it's with the sole purpose of going to sleep."

Jessica begged to differ, but it wasn't the time or the place to argue the toss. "So, what have we got?" she asked.

"Female, fourteen to eighteen, blonde, white, appears to have been strangled. I'll know for certain when I get back and check the hyoid. She's been dead a while – at a rough guess five, maybe six hours." She frowned. "What's with this stupid hair and make-up ritual?"

"I wish I knew," Jessica said, gazing down upon the victim's battered face, her hair arced round her, weighted down by stones, a scene that had become horribly familiar.

"Laura gave voice to her thoughts. "Your killer is blessed with a limited imagination. It's a carbon copy of the other killings." She winced and put her hand to the small of her back. "When he finds a formula, he sticks to it." She handed a plastic evidence bag to Jessica. "Another calling card for your ever-growing collection."

She gave the signal to remove the body, and both women, by silent mutual consent, walked to a nearby park bench and sat down. It was fully light now, but the sky was the grey of a window splashed with dirty water. A breeze, not cold, rippled through the surrounding trees. Rain scented the air.

Laura sniffed. "Petrichor," she announced. "A pleasant smell that accompanies the first rain, after a long period of dry weather." She smiled, self-mockingly. "That's one from my glory days as a Scrabble champion."

Jessica looked at her askance. "More petrol fumes than petrichor, if you ask me. This is London, after all, And rush hour is upon us."

Laura rummaged in her pocket and produced a roll of mints. She offered one to Jessica, who shook her head. "You look as miserable as sin," she remarked, popping a sweet in her mouth. "I take it David has gone?"

Jessica sighed. "Not quite. He leaves this afternoon at four o'clock."

"Regrets?" Laura eyed her keenly.

"Several," Jessica admitted. "And fears. And doubts. But, right at this moment, I can't see how I could have made it work. How can you just down tools and walk away from something like that?" She nodded across to the activity surrounding the body –

the police, the forensics team, the usual bunch of ghouls straining to see beyond the police cordon, camera phones at the ready. The press too were already in evidence. Jessica caught sight of a couple of journalists, whose sole *raison d'être* seemed to be to trash the police. She had a theory that after the apocalypse the only thing left, apart from the cockroaches, would be the scumbag journos.

"Plenty would walk away and not think twice about it," Laura said. "But not you, and that's what makes you a good cop."

"But a rotten wife."

Laura shrugged. "Some jobs are just not conducive to relationships, unless you have a selfless saint for a partner. I speak from experience."

Jessica looked at her curiously. "Which is why you never married?"

"Not at all," Laura said. "No one ever asked me."

Jessica grinned and stood up. "I doubt that, somehow," she said.

"It's the truth. There wasn't a man of my acquaintance who could handle the fact that there would always be somebody else in my life." She nudged Jessica. "See what I did there? Some *body!*"

Jessica laughed despite herself. "Fancy getting together for lunch or a drink soon?" she asked, and this time if felt natural to make the suggestion.

Laura turned towards her vehicle. "Sure," she said breezily. "Why not?"

...

Eva Castle's parents flew over from Australia to make the formal identification. Jessica's heart bled for them.

"We begged her not to go," the mother kept saying over and

over again. "But she wouldn't listen. She wouldn't listen."

"Eva was very independent." This, from her father. "She kept saying she wanted to see a bit of the world before settling down to her studies." His face worked in an effort to keep from breaking down. "She wanted to be a neurologist. She could have been, too. She was highly intelligent and a good girl. Everybody's friend."

He had broken down then, and Jessica knew she would never forget the sight of Eva's parents standing in the draughty mortuary corridor, arms around each other, trying both to give and receive comfort. Eva's father was a big man. Yet, in the space of a few minutes, he seemed to have lost both height and bulk, and by the time they left the building, he was actually stooping.

...

Back at Rosewood, the team were piecing together what little they knew of Eva Castle's last movements. Pinned to the whiteboard was a photograph given to them by her parents. It showed a pretty, blonde girl cuddling a cat and smiling for the camera. Next to it was a photograph of her body on Wandsworth Common, her face so badly battered as to be virtually unrecognisable.

"So, here we have Eva Castle," Jessica said pointing from one to the other. "A seventeen-year-old backpacker from Melbourne, travelling alone against the advice of her parents." She consulted her notes. "However, knowing how worried they were, she checked in with them every couple of days without fail. The red flag went up when they didn't hear from her for five days straight, and all attempts at making contact came up blank. Calls to her mobile went straight to voicemail. Then, the battery either died or the phone was switched off. They checked her Facebook and Twitter accounts; she was a prolific poster of selfies. Again, no activity for five days. The last posting was a picture taken at the London Eye. Apart from one text message sent to a friend, also on that same day, there was no further contact." DS Connors made to interrupt, but Jessica stayed her with an upheld up her hand. "The text said she was going to stay with an old friend in Tooting. Neither her parents nor the friend she texted have any idea who that person might be." She nodded thanks, as DC Liversedge handed her a mug of coffee, wrinkled her nose as she took a sip. "Jesus! What did you put in this? Piddle?" She put the mug down and pushed it away. "Obviously, we need to find the friend in question and determine if Eva actually got to Tooting."

Sergeant Hennessy came into the room waving a piece of paper. "She did, guv. This is a CCTV image showing her withdrawing cash from an ATM machine on Mitcham Road. It's a bit grainy, but it's her all right. That was Thursday night, at 7.30 p.m. Five nights ago. The withdrawal was for thirty quid. There's been no movement on the account since then."

The phone shrilled at the far end of the room. Everyone fell quiet as Liversedge picked it up. Jessica watched him scribbling furiously in his notebook. He'd been angling for an office iPad for ages. Given the departmental budget, he was more likely to be issued with a slate and a piece of chalk. She raised an eyebrow as he put down the receiver.

"That was a John and Marian Green," he said, "a couple who say they met Eva Castle in a pub in Tooting last Thursday night. They recognised her from her picture in the papers."

"Which pub was that?" Jessica asked. She was familiar with several of the pubs in Tooting, having spent much of her misspent youth getting off her face in one or other of them.

"The Cock-a-Hoop. It's on the corner of Vant Road."

"I know it," Jessica said. "And they're sure it was Eva?"

"Definite. They were chatting to her for quite a while. They'd been on honeymoon to Melbourne and had only recently come home. They heard her Aussie accent at the bar and struck up a conversation."

"Did she mention anything about where she was staying?" Jessica asked.

"Yes. She told them she'd intended to surprise a friend in Tooting, but they'd apparently moved out months before. Gone travelling, according to the next-door neighbour."

"Didn't she have the friend's phone number?" Connors asked.

Her colleague shook his head. "It was one of those loose arrangements you make on holiday. You know the kind of thing – if ever you're in my neck of the woods, come and stay. Of course, you never expect them to take you up on the offer."

"Daft," Connors said, shaking her head.

"Kids of that age *are* daft, "Jessica said. "Did she say what she planned to do instead?"

DC Liversedge made a big performance of rattling the pages in his notebook. "The Greens said they told her about a youth hostel in Tooting Bec and gave her directions on how to get there. They all left the pub together at around eleven thirty. Eva turned up Church Lane and that was the last they saw of her. And they don't half feel bad now. Mrs Green was crying her heart out."

"Ah, the benefit of hindsight," Jessica said. "All the sad 'if onlys'." She picked up her mug of coffee, remembered at the last second how foul it was and put it down quickly. She nodded to Liversedge. "Send someone out to get a written statement from them, Sedgie. Also to the pub. If they have security footage taken on that night, we'll need that too."

Liversedge nodded. "Already on it," he said, heading for the door.

Jessica looked around the remaining team members. They looked worn down and dispirited. By the time the case was over and The Director banged up for the rest of his natural, every man jack of them would benefit from counselling. Herself included. But, for now, it was every nose to the grindstone. The briefing over, she dismissed them about their various duties and psyched herself up for what she intended to be her last meeting with DCI Beckwith. Eva's death was the final nail in her own coffin. Beckwith was right. She was incapable of handling an investigation of this magnitude. Pride and bloody-mindedness could not be allowed to stop her from doing the right thing.

...

"I'm not accepting this." DCI Beckwith pushed Jessica's resignation letter back across the desk. The pulse in his temple was registering furious. "What?" he asked. "Surprised I'm not letting you off the hook that easily?" He leapt to his feet and leaned across the desk, glaring down upon her. Your new toy no fun anymore, is that it? You've smashed it up and now you want some other poor sod to glue it back together again?"

Jessica reddened. "No, that's not it at all. I just felt ... I just thought ..."

"What?" DCI Beckwith escalated to shouting. Anger made the cords of his neck stand out like ropes. "That you'd just turn tail and piss off into the wide blue yonder? That you'd turn your back on your colleagues? Never mind that they've worked their bollocks off on this case, given their all, and then some, to solving it. I have never seen a harder-working bunch of people in my life."

Slowly, he sank back down in his seat. "Jesus. Was it all a game to you, DI Wideacre? A way to prove that you could swim upstream with the big fish?"

Jessica shook her head. "No!" she yelled, finding her voice at last. "That's not how it is at all. I thought you'd *want* me to resign." Goaded into retaliating, her eyes shot darts. "You never fucking wanted me in the post to begin with." She turned up the heat, forgot David's advice to keep her powder dry and let rip with the pent-up resentment of months. "After all, who'd want someone who's *volatile* and *hasty* and *prone to the kind of excesses of emotion that lead to poor judgement and rash decision-making*?"

"Quite finished?" DCI Beckwith snapped, when she finally ran out of steam. "That memo was never meant for your eyes; I'm sorry you ever read it. And, frankly, I was the one guilty of poor judgement. You've proved your abilities beyond a shadow of a doubt, which is why I find it difficult to believe you're throwing in the towel now."

"How can I go on?" Jessica asked, struggling to hold back tears. "Christ's sake, there are nine dead girls now. *Nine*! That's nine sets of grieving families, parents, brothers and sisters. And the impact on the wider community is colossal. Yet, so far, our investigations have led absolutely nowhere. All we have is a job lot of lunatics phoning up with sightings and theories, each more outlandish than the one before." She jabbed her chest. "Someone needs to be held accountable, and the buck stops with me."

DCI Beckwith leaned back in his chair. His gaze swept over her flushed face. "No one needs a martyr," he said. "What is needed, however, is someone who can hold things together, someone who can inspire confidence in their team and get the best out of them, even when they're dragging themselves on their bellies with exhaustion." He leaned over and picked up the letter of resignation, ripped it up and let the pieces flutter into his waste bin. "Your team needs you, DI Wideacre." Worried that he was beginning to sound like Lord Kitchener, he backed off. He could see Jessica's mind working overtime, the struggle going on behind her eyes. He waited, as if they had all the time in the world till, finally, she nodded.

"Okay," she said, the merest twinkle coming into her eye. "I've climbed down off the cross. What now?"

DCI Beckwith smiled. "Chop it down," he said. "We need the wood."

...

How the mighty are fallen, Jack Kingsman thought, sitting amongst a nest of empty scotch bottles. To the outside world he was still functioning, still sane. He got up in the morning, showered, shaved, dressed, went to work at the film studios, carried on tickety-boo. No one realised it took half a bottle of whisky and an awful lot of mouthwash to get him to that stage. A year, six months ago, he was still riding the crest of the wave. Hailed as an inspiration – the East End boy done good – he featured frequently in the press and the media and had a ticket to all the best events in town. Every hostess for miles around clamoured to have him at her table. His presence at a soirée was the mark of success. His unfortunate past lent him an air of tragic glamour, making him irresistible to pretty, sad-eyed women with a saviour complex. They queued up to offer respite from his sorrowful past, opening their arms wide and their legs even wider. He'd lost track of the number of romanticised articles written about his private life, purple-prose works of fiction in the main, in which he had supposedly declared his intention never to marry again. He steered clear of such romantic entanglements, preferring to pay for his pleasure – that way he got to stay in control. Except, he didn't feel in control any more. At some point, when he wasn't looking, someone had yanked the chain and his life had gone right down the toilet.

The house was Tumbleweed City, almost eerily quiet since he'd sacked Sheila Walters for meddling in his affairs once too often. She'd tried, and failed, to pull at his heartstrings, bleating on about Marissa, family ties and loyalty. It might have had more impact had she, like her arch enemies, the Turkish sisters, been thirty years younger and fair of face. It hadn't taken long for her to shape-shift into a foul-mouthed, screeching harpy, shaking her bony fist and vowing revenge like something out of a comic book. He'd laughed sourly, told her to fuck off and get in the queue.

...

Back in her office, Jessica was trying to figure out how she had emerged from Beckwith's office with a smile on her face. It was a mystery how he always managed to turn the tables on her. Went in like a lion, came out neatly butchered, she thought. Five minutes more and she'd have been oiling herself ready for the oven; inviting him to come dine on me.

She looked through the glass-panelled door into the office beyond, where everyone had their heads down, united in the common aim of nailing The Director. They were family, she realised suddenly, feeling slightly embarrassed by the mawkishness of the thought. The bullshit, which, as a rule, she didn't do. She was glad not to have to say goodbye.

She was settling down to work when the door burst open and DC Liversedge burst in.

"Guv, I've just taken a call from a guy who says he saw a girl struggling with a bloke on Church Lane a few nights ago. They drove off in a white van."

Jessica felt the ground shift beneath her feet. "I take it he's coming in," she said, trying not to let hope overwhelm her.

Liversedge, showing no such restraint and beaming like a lighthouse, nodded. "He'll be here in thirty."

CHAPTER TWENTY-THREE

Jessica was sending up prayers of thanks to a benevolent God for finally providing them with a coherent and credible witness. No talk of aliens or spaceships or things going bump in the night.

She ran an approving eye over his sober appearance – clean and neat, but not flashy. He was that comforting type, Mr Middle-Class Average. Without him saying a word, she could glean that he lived in a pretty little semi with a pretty, biddable little wife and one or two pretty little children. He worked in middle management and drove a Ford Focus, Toyota Yaris, or something equally uninspiring. Nominally, he would be C of E. Politically, he would lean towards the right.

His name was Toby Phillips – Tobes to his friends. He was thirty-nine, a loss adjuster, married with two children. He lived in a semi in the nicer part of Colliers Wood and he drove a second-hand Peugeot 208. He didn't divulge either his religion or his politics, but, so far, Jessica was more than pleased with her powers of deduction. Suck on that, Holmes!

She waited till he was settled with a mug of Rosewood's cheapo coffee and smiled across the desk to put him at ease. Most upright citizens never saw the inside of a police station and, when they did, it tended to have a loosening effect on their bladders. Hennessy, whose default facial expression was bulldog-licking-piss-off-thistle, generally did nothing to allay their anxiety. This time, though, Sedgie, an altogether more benign presence, was also sitting in on the interview.

"So, Mr Phillips," she said. "I understand from my colleague, Detective Constable Liversedge here, that you witnessed an incident three nights ago. A dispute between a man and a woman?"

Mr Average was cursed with the kind of skin that blushed easily. "That's right," he said leaning forward, so eager to please she guessed he must have been bullied at school. "I was coming home from a works do, nothing fancy, just curry and a beer with the lads. Just the one beer," he added hastily, "I was driving."

"And this would have been at what time?" Jessica asked, not giving a hoot if he'd necked an entire brewery.

"Eleven thirty or thereabouts." He flushed to beetroot. "I … er … curry doesn't always agree with me. Touch of IBS, you see. Anyway—"

"You were caught short?" Jessica guessed, discreetly elbowing Hennessy, who couldn't be trusted not to laugh.

"Yes. Exactly. So, time being of the essence, I pulled in at the side of the road and hopped over a wall into a graveyard on Church Lane. That's off Mitcham Road. I think it's called St Nicholas'."

Jessica nodded. "I know it. What happened then?"

"I was climbing back over when I heard a couple arguing in the street."

"How do you know they were arguing?" Jessica asked. "Perhaps they were just horsing around?"

He shook his head. "Admittedly, they were too far up the street for me to hear clearly, but the woman screamed a few times. It didn't sound like a fun scream, if you know what I mean." He examined his fingernails, not really seeing them. "I guess I should have gone and checked it out, but I'd promised the wife I'd be home early, and," he smiled a little self-consciously, "I'd already exceeded my late pass."

Jessica marked herself down – not such a biddable little wife after all. "But you didn't actually see anything, Mr Phillips, did you? As I recall, Church Lane isn't very well lit."

"You're right, it was pretty dark." He knitted his brow, clearly doing his best to bring the detail of the evening to mind. There was a fair gap between the street lights, but at one point the woman broke free and some light fell on her. She was blonde, long hair, I'm sure of that. A second later, she disappeared back into the darkness – hustled, I assume, by him. Next thing I know the van's lights go on. And that's pretty much it. Sorry."

He looked stricken. "I feel bad now that I didn't pay more attention. "If I'd known it might be important …" His voice trailed off.

Jessica's heart sank. It wasn't a lot to go on. A bloke and his bird having a bust-up in the street was de rigueur in most of south London, especially after the pubs had let out. The cells in the nick were full every single weekend for the exact same reason. And oftentimes it was the women, fired up on a potent mixture of vodka and Red Bull, who instigated the whole thing.

She was beginning to gather her papers together when he dropped a game-changer into the conversation.

"I did catch a glimpse of the van as it sped off, though. It was a white Ford Transit with a logo on the side."

Jessica looked up, suddenly transfixed. "A clown face?" she asked hopefully. She could feel Hennessy tensing beside her. Mr Average shook his head.

"Not a clown, no." He appeared to think about it. "Well, not strictly speaking. It was a pair of those theatrical masks. Tragedy and Comedy." He smiled shyly. "I'm into amateur dramatics."

Jessica's heart began a slow thud against her ribs. "Tragedy and Comedy," she repeated. She'd seen that same symbol somewhere recently. She called time on the interview, rose and shook his hand. "Thank you for coming in, Mr Phillips," she said. "We'll certainly be following this up." She smiled, taking him into her confidence. "Do you think we could just keep this information between ourselves for the moment? It really would be very helpful."

Mr Average's chest expanded. "Of course," he said importantly. "You have my word."

"He actually tapped his nose," Jessica said to Hennessy as DC Liversedge showed their witness out. "I thought people only did that on the telly."

"At least he didn't do that zipping his lips thing," Hennessy grunted. "Fucking drives me mad, that does. Fucking morons."

Jessica flapped her hand. "Go," she commanded. "Outside and have a fag." It was a great relief to all of them that he'd dispensed entirely with the e-cigarettes and was back to sucking on rollies. Without his daily dose of nicotine, the sergeant was like a bear with a boil on the bum. Jessica sat for a while racking her brains. Theatrical masks. Theatrical masks. Where the hell had she seen them? It came to her in a flash. Erupting into the incident room, she yelled at Connors. "Quick! Where's that article you were shoving in my face earlier?"

Connors gave fifty per cent of an eye roll. "Sedgie took it for the crossword."

Jessica opened her mouth to roar, but the police constable, who had just returned to the room, was already on his way over with the paper. Flicking furiously through it, she stopped at page six. "There, she said, stabbing at the photograph of Venise Love-Davies. "Can anybody tell me what that big white thing standing behind our heroine is? Hint – it has four wheels and drinks petrol like DS Connors drinks gin?"

Connors' eye roll reached a hundred per cent "A van?"

"Correct. And, what's that on the door of the van?" Jessica asked, stabbing harder. "A clown face, that's what." Her voice rose. "Only it's not Bozo the friggin' clown. It's a pair of theatrical masks. Tragedy and Comedy, easily mistaken for clowns, by clowns. Listen up, people – our witness, one Mr Toby Phillips, who witnessed a bit of argy-bargy between a man and woman last Thursday night, has them driving away in a vehicle exactly like that." She paused. "The location – Church Lane, Tooting, where Eva Castle was last sighted." She paused to let the import of her words sink in. There was a collective intake of breath, the faintest glimmer of hope in the air. "That van," Jessica continued, "belongs to Kingsman Film Productions."

"Films and directors," Connors said, awed. "That certainly puts a certain slant on matters. Up till now, that title could have had one of several different meanings. It's certainly feasible that our man could have such a background." They exchanged horrified glances. Hennessy put their fear it into words.

"Christ," he said, paling noticeably. "Snuff movies?"

"Could be," Jessica said quietly. "Someone working in a film production company would have access to all the right equipment. That might also go some way to explaining the garish make-up and hair extensions."

Connors bit her lip. "The bastard wanted them camera-ready."

"It's a theory," Jessica said. "Bear in mind that that's all it is at present. It's just one line of enquiry." One more line than they'd had. She knew by their sombre faces that their imaginations were firing on all cylinders. "Look," she said emphatically. "Let's not jump the gun here. Kingsman Film Productions is a bone fide film company, not a dirty mac outfit churning out blue movies. Briskly, she clapped her hands. "So, who fancies a trip to the flicks?" She chose Sarah Connors. Give her her due, the woman had a way of coaxing information out of people fooled by her pretty face into thinking she was a soft touch. In the way piranhas were a soft touch. First, though, she dropped by Beckwith's office with the glad tidings that his significant other might unwittingly have been rubbing shoulders with a serial killer.

...

"We're not suspecting Jack Kingsman, himself, are we?" DCI Beckwith said, looking shocked. "The man is a legend in the film industry."

Jessica squinted. He was in deeper with the luvvies than she'd thought. "We're suspecting anyone and everyone," she said tartly. "If Jesus owned the van, we'd be nailing his arse to the cross too. We're also running a check to find out if any other vehicles have the same logo. Neither are we discounting the original clown logo. In the meantime, it's something to go on. We can't afford not to, *just because your girlfriend's boss might be in the frame*." She finished the sentence in her head. He divined it anyway, shot her a chilling look and reached for his jacket.

"I'm coming with you. Something as high profile as this requires delicate handling."

Jessica had no objection. Kingsman might be more amenable

to them crawling all over his film studios and grilling him and his staff if his leading lady's boyfriend was in tow.

Again, Beckwith seemed to guess her thoughts. "Don't editorialise, DI Wideacre. Jack Kingsman and I are acquaintances, no more than that."

Jessica shrugged. "No skin off mine."

As they made their way out of the building, the desk sergeant waved a note at Jessica. "Might be just a looney," he said. "She sounded hysterical. Wouldn't leave her name or number. Just kept saying the same thing over and over like a broken record."

Jessica read it, passed it to DCI Beckwith. She could sense the shock go through him as he read the six little words written there. "Ask Jack Kingsman about the girls."

...

"Could just be a coincidence," he said, as they drove to the film studios. Connors had taken a separate car and DC Liversedge along for the ride. Hennessy was co-ordinating a forensics team in the event that they decided on a full search of Kingsman's studio lot.

"Sure," Jessica said carelessly. "You know him better than I do. I don't get invited to red carpet events." It was a below the belt dig. He refused to take the bait.

"Certainly, I met him on a few occasions," he said calmly. "I've even dined at his house once. But, do I know the man? Not really. Do I think he's our killer?" He shrugged. "Potentially everyone's a killer, including you and me, DI Wideacre. So, let's keep an open mind, eh?"

There were four white Transit vans as they drove onto the studio forecourt, all bearing the same livery – the theatrical masks on the doors and "Kingsman Film Productions" written in a striking font on the sides and back. The studios were alive with activity. Actors and extras, many in costume, strolled in groups of two and three about the lot, some pulling on cigarettes. One group was animatedly playing a card game – snap, by the looks of it. Workmen in navy overalls, KFP embroidered on the back, were ferrying props to and from some of the vans.

Beckwith made an involuntary noise and Jessica followed the direction of his look to where Venise Love-Davies, resplendent in Tudor garb, sat hunched on some steps, her head buried in a script. There was an air of fragility about her, a sense of aloneness. Too far away to see clearly, Jessica got the distinct impression that she might have been crying. As they pulled over to the side, Jack Kingsman emerged from the building and spoke to her. They could see his arms waving about, the angle of his head and stiffness of his back suggesting this was no friendly chat.

DCI Beckwith's eyes narrowed. "He's been giving her a hard time recently, getting on her case about every little thing."

"Isn't that what directors are supposed to do?" Jessica remarked. "Play God, give everyone hell?"

"Venise says he's changed lately, turned into a right bastard. Seems she can't do right for doing wrong."

Jessica put on the handbrake, pulled the key from the ignition. "Well, let's go see Mr Bastard, then, and see what he has to say for himself."

···

Jack Kingsman presented a very different sight to the man DCI Beckwith had dined with in Berkeley Square. He was badly shaven, the skin of his face nicked in several places. His eyes were bloodshot, his hands shook and even a heavy application of aftershave couldn't disguise the stink of booze emanating from him. Although he tried to project his former air of bonhomie, pumping Beckwith's hand vigorously and clapping him round the shoulders, he convinced no one. He led them both into his inner sanctum, waved them into the seats opposite his desk, and reached for a bottle of whisky. It was barely past lunch.

"Drink? No? You don't mind if I? … They watched him splash a large measure into his glass and knock it back. "Pressures of the job," he said, making light of it. "Now, what can I do for Her Majesty's finest?

Beckwith left it to Jessica to explain, carefully watching Kingsman for any giveaway reaction. There was none. He propped his elbows on the table and rested his chin on his hands, patiently waiting till Jessica was finished.

"Sounds highly unlikely," he said. "I can't imagine any of my people being involved in something of that nature."

Beckwith gave a reassuring smile. "I'm sure you're right, but as you'll appreciate, it's something we have to follow up."

"So, you want to interview my van drivers?" Kingsman said.

"We want to interview *everybody* who might have had access to the vehicles, including you, Mr Kingsman," Jessica returned coolly. There was something about the film director that got her goat. He was too slick, too oily. Too pleased with himself by half. Connors had mentioned something about him being the proverbial East End boy who, despite making it big, had managed to keep his feet firmly on the ground. Not from where Jessica was sitting. His desk was the size of the Atlantic Ocean and he'd employed the old tactic of sitting in a higher chair to enable him to look down on his visitors. Everything in his office was oversized – from the furniture to the paintings and, most definitely, his head.

He smiled down on them. At least, she thought he did, but his lips barely quirked. "And you genuinely think that I could be" – he did jazz hands – "*that* Director?" He grated out a laugh. "That, instead of going home knackered after a day's shoot, I get my rocks off by killing young girls?" He paused to let his words sink in, then slammed his hands down on his desk. "That is fucking preposterous."

DCI Beckwith kept his voice neutral. "We have to consider all possibilities, Mr Kingsman, no matter how unlikely. I'm sure you understand and will cooperate fully."

Kingsman's belligerent side, of which Venise had spoken, came hurtling to the fore. His mouth twisted. "What happened to Jack, *Mark*? Oh, I get it, no Christian names when you're playing hardball, is that it?" And what if I don't want to play, what then? What if I just tell you and your ginger sidekick here to fuck off?"

"Then we'll just have to haul you down the station for questioning," Jessica snapped. She sent Beckwith a "what?" look.

"I'm hoping that won't be necessary," Beckwith said. He could tell by the way Wideacre was fidgeting that she was hoping for quite the opposite.

"Have you any idea how disruptive it would be to have your plods crawling all over my set?" Kingsman asked. "We've already been beset by delays on *Killer Queen* – thanks, in no small part, to your girlfriend, DCI Beckwith – any more and we might as well throw in the towel." He was being deliberately provocative. It was working. Jessica itched to wipe the smug look off his face. Beckwith could pussyfoot round him as much as he liked. She decided to take matters into her own hands.

"We can do it the easy way, or we can do it the hard way," she said. "But one way or another we're here to find some answers. Now, are you going to cooperate, or am I going to have to arrest you?"

Kingsman stood up. "Hadn't you better read me my rights first?" he said.

Jessica had no difficulty in acceding to his request. She read him his rights and unclipped a set of handcuffs from her belt. "Pick a hand," she said. "Any hand."

...

Sitting in the back of the police car, Jack Kingsman wasn't at all upset by the turn of events. On the contrary, he had manipulated them to his advantage. Negative publicity would do what he had so far failed to do; it would kill the film stone dead. The investors, fearful of any breath of scandal, especially one of this magnitude, would jump headlong off the sinking ship. That Jack Kingsman might feasibly turn out to be The Director, Britain's worst-ever serial killer was a film script in itself. Ultimately, of course, he'd emerge bloody but unbowed, the victim of a gigantic police cock-up, free to resume his career with no stain upon his character. More importantly, the secret he had striven to keep buried for so long would stay that way.

He turned his face towards the car window and smiled for the many camera phones clicking away. No prizes for guessing what today's news headlines would be.

...

Kingsman was proved correct. His arrest was all over the press and internet in a matter of hours, screaming speculative black headlines "IS OSCAR-WINNING FILM-MAKER, JACK KINGSMAN, *THE DIRECTOR?*" "JACK KINGSMAN ARRESTED IN CONNECTION WITH DIRECTOR MURDERS." One perceptive hack drew attention to the similarities between The Director's victims and Kingsman's late wife, asking the question, "Can it be coincidence that all the victims bear an uncanny resemblance to the late, great Marissa Bloom?"

"It's a theory," Jessica admitted. She'd pinned a picture of Marissa Bloom on the whiteboard next to photographs of The Director's victims. "Although it's a generic resemblance. They're all blonde, pretty girls. Could just be coincidence – the press trying to make something out of nothing.

"But the hair extensions," Connors said. "The make-up. Seen in this context it might well be relevant. If you look closely at the victim photographs, you can see that little cat eye flick at the corners of their eyes, which was Marissa Bloom's trademark. Venise Love-Davis has adopted it recently too."

Jessica looked at her scathingly. "Jesus, Connors, don't you have a life? Did your mum never tell you all those trashy celeb magazines will fry your brain?"

Connors hit back. "A life? What's that? Since all this started. I have to find some way to relax."

Jessica conceded the point. Hennessy had his rollies. Sedgie, his legion of girlfriends. She had her wine. Rather too much of it. DCI Beckwith had her – as a punch bag to relieve his stress. And Venise Love-Davies to soothe his fevered brow. Why shouldn't Connors have her trash-mags.

"Fair enough," she said. "So, running with that scenario,

outlandish though it is, what's Kingsman's motive?"

Hennessy took an unlit rollie from his mouth. It acted almost as a comfort blanket. "He's bitter because his wife died and he's taking it out on girls who remind him of her?"

"She died several years ago, so why now? What's the trigger? Something must have changed."

"Something to do with that movie Kingsman's making," DC Liversedge speculated. "Maybe it's stirred up all sorts of emotions in him."

"On the contrary," DCI Beckwith said, entering the room. "He was very gung-ho about it. I was there the night he offered Venise the role of Lorelei Turner. He mentioned something about it being twenty-five years since his wife died and made the point that one shouldn't wallow for ever."

"Did you get anything out of him, sir?" Jessica asked. "She'd left him interviewing Kingsman while she briefed the rest of the team.

"No. He's got his no-comment cap on. The strange thing is, he seems to be enjoying himself. He's not at all fazed. When I mentioned the fact that forensics were crawling all over his studios and home he just laughed and said he hoped they didn't damage the china."

"Either he's all front or he's not our man," Jessica said. She nodded to Hennessy. "How are the interviews with the actors and staff at Kingsman Studios proceeding, Sergeant?"

"Slowly," he said. "Not everyone is accounted for yet. Some are out and about picking up props and the likes, others are on leave. The luvvies, predictably, are hamming it up. I've never seen such hysteria and drama outside of a nuthouse." Recalling too late

DCI Beckwith's connection with the acting fraternity, he huffed a bit. "Er, sorry, sir, I didn't mean—"

Mark waved away the apology. "What about the vans?" he asked. "And Kingsman's Jag?"

"Already impounded," Hennessy said. "Forensics are gearing up to start their examination."

"And the domestic staff?" Jessica asked, looking around. "Have they been brought in for questioning? No? Connors, you go. Take Sedgie with you." A sudden commotion from outside brought their heads spinning towards the door. A moment later, red-faced and panting, the desk sergeant appeared in the opening.

"Got a live one out here, guv. A real gobby piece. Says she's got evidence that Jack Kingsman is innocent."

"Put her in Room 3," Jessica said. She glanced at DCI Beckwith. "You want in on this, sir?"

"Most definitely," he said. "We'll give Kingsman some more time to cool his heels and have a second go later."

They were met in Room 3 by an angry middle-aged woman pacing up and down. "Why?" she demanded, before they had even exchanged greetings, "are you lot so thick? Jack Kingsman is no murderer."

Jessica waved her into a seat, and she and DCI Beckwith took the chairs opposite. She spoke calmly and made the introductions. "I'm DI Jessica Wideacre and this is my colleague, DCI Mark Beckwith. And you are?"

The woman sat down grumpily. "Sheila. Sheila Walters. I was housekeeper to Jack Kingsman for more than thirty years. Till he sacked me a few days ago." She glowered across the table. "Booted me unceremoniously out the door. After all my loyalty." Her lips thinned. Her voice quavered slightly. She was fighting for control. "I gave that man the best years of my life. Threw up my own chance of happiness, at having a family, a husband and children. For what? So that I could watch him fuck a succession of trollops and never even look my way."

The expletive falling from the mouth of the otherwise demure-looking, middle-aged woman gave it back the rather shocking impact lost through years of casual use.

"So, you were in love with him," Jessica said.

The woman nodded. "You could say that, though much good it did me. The last pair, the Turkish *maids*, were a straw too far, though. Talk about brazen. After a couple of days, they didn't even bother disguising the true nature of their role in the house. The two of them together, sometimes. Sisters too! It didn't half make my blood boil."

"Threesomes?" Jessica exchanged a quick look with Beckwith. It didn't much sound like the behaviour of a still-grieving widower.

"Foursomes, for all I know. They might even have dragged in the butcher, baker and the candlestick maker. Maybe even the cook, Mansour. He's foreign, like them. I'd put nothing past that disgusting pair of little madams."

"Why did he ... let you go?" Jessica asked diplomatically, pouring a cup of water from a pitcher and passing it across the table, along with a box of tissues.

"Because I finally flipped and told him what I thought of his behaviour. I hoped it might wake him up to himself, but no. There was a bit of unpleasantness," she broke off a moment, looking a little guilty. "I ... I told him I'd make him sorry. He told me to fuck off and get in the queue." She looked astonished, as if she still couldn't quite believe it. "That's when I decided to phone you lot and spill the beans about Melis and Mahlika." She spat the names like vinegar from her mouth. "Only you shower of cretins clearly thought I was referring to those other girls, the murdered ones."

A piece of the jigsaw slid into place. *Ask Jack Kingsman about the girls.* "You're the woman who rang in," Jessica said, recalling the note passed to her by the desk sergeant.

Sheila Walters nodded vehemently. "Yes! Yes! Yes! But all I meant was that he was harbouring illegals. Not that he was a murderer. So, you'll have to let him go now, won't you?"

"I'm afraid it's not quite that simple," Jessica began, only to be howled down.

"Of course it's that bloody simple. How many times do I have to tell you? – Jack Kingsman is not a murderer. Do you think my cousin would have married someone capable of that kind of thing? Marissa could have had anyone. *Anyone!* But she chose Jack."

"Marissa Bloom was your cousin?" Jessica asked, awed by the lottery that was genetics. By anyone's standards, Marissa Bloom had been a very beautiful woman. Sheila Walters had fallen out of the proverbial ugly tree, hitting every branch on the way down.

"I know exactly what you're thinking," the woman snapped, seeing the quickly masked look of surprise on both their faces. "But it's true. Marissa's mother and mine were sisters." Her lip curled with resentment. "Not that she acted like we were blood. Flamin' Madame Pompadour. Fetch me this! Fetch me that! Like I was her personal servant. But I didn't stay for her. I stayed for him! He was always nice to me. That's why I *know* this is all trumped up nonsense."

"Jack Kingsman hasn't actually been charged with anything," Jessica pointed out. "We're simply making enquiries."

Sheila Walters rummaged in her handbag. "I've got a diary." She flushed. "It ... it's a record of Jack's movements – times, dates, where he was going, who he was meeting."

Again, Jessica exchanged looks with DCI Beckwith. The word "stalker" vibrated on the air between them.

Jessica took it from her. "I'm sure that will be very helpful," she said. Assuming it wasn't a work of fiction.

The woman took one of the tissues and dabbed briefly at her eyes. "I owe him. I'm afraid I behaved rather badly of late. I – I did things I'm not proud of, destroyed his picture gallery. All those smug film stars." She stole a look at Beckwith. "You'll recall the pictures from your visit to the house with your fancy piece. Hers was one of them. I was so angry, I wanted to hurt him the way I was hurting." She paused for a sip of water. "I sent him cryptic messages too, threatening to expose his sordid secret. Taking revenge, I suppose you'd call it."

She grabbed a tissue and scrunched it into a ball. "I could see it was getting to him, turning him into a nervous wreck. He was drinking like a fish." She addressed Jessica. "I suppose you think that's awful? Maybe, but have you any idea how it feels to have someone look through you day after day, never noticing that you've made a special effort with your appearance, that you're wearing a new dress or had your hair done?" She began to fold the tissue, over and over again, into minute squares. "It saps your soul, grinds away at your confidence and ultimately destroys your self-respect." She smiled fleetingly, no humour in it. "The worm turned. What more can I say? I led him a merry dance. It was pure *Schadenfreude*. I was clever too. I learned how to manipulate the CCTV footage so he wouldn't see me leaving the notes. It's amazing the kind of hobbies one can take up to fill the long lonely evenings." Impressed with herself, she nodded, "I do believe I could teach your IT department a thing or two. Could be, even Scotland Yard."

She tossed the tissue onto the table, where it began to unfold into some semblance of its former self, and eyed them defiantly. "You're thinking I'm that pitiful thing, a woman scorned. And I'll own up to it. But, I swear, I never meant to get him into this kind of trouble."

...

"Woman scorned?" Jessica remarked when she had left. "More like a psycho." She made a stabbing motion, hummed the theme music to *Psycho*, the part where Janet Leigh gets done in. "Yet she looks like she's come fresh from a Mary Berry cookery lesson."

"We all know how looks can be deceiving," DCI Beckwith remarked. "Remember the Angel of Death?" he said, referring to Beverley Allitt, a young nurse turned notorious child-killer. "Looked like butter wouldn't melt. She killed four children and tried to murder a further nine. By that yardstick, Sheila Walters is still in kindergarten."

"She didn't take much to your *fancy piece*, did she?" Jessica said.

DCI Beckwith ignored the barb. "Time for another bash at Kingsman?"

Jessica nodded. "Yes, let's go and tell him what his erstwhile housekeeper has been up to."

...

"Jesus!" Jack Kingsman was incandescent with rage. "You mean to tell me those notes, those fucking notes, were from my housekeeper?" He leapt to his feet and began pacing up and down the interview room.

Jessica gestured him into his seat. "Sit down, Mr Kingsman, please."

He threw her a dirty look, but flung himself into the chair. "The bitch!" he raged, dropping his head into his hands. "Of all people, I never would have guessed—"

"Sheila was a classic case of a woman scorned," Beckwith said. "She was in love with you, apparently, for years."

Kingsman's head came up. "Really? I guessed she had a bit of a thing for me, but not … Fucccck!" He hammered his fist on the table. "I don't get it. How the hell did she do it? There was nothing on the CCTV."

"She learned how to doctor the film," Jessica said, unable to keep an admiring note from sneaking into her voice. Anyone who could wrestle technology into submission had her deepest respect. "But what I don't understand, Mr Kingsman, is why you didn't contact us about the notes." The question threw him a little.

"Oh, well, because … I suppose I thought it was all a bit of a joke," he said, with the sideways eye-shift of a liar. "The world is full of weirdos. In my world, if you don't have a stalker you're nobody." He grew more confident in the lie. "Besides, it wasn't as though it kept me awake at night."

"That's not quite how your housekeeper tells it," Jessica said. She looked to DCI Beckwith for back-up.

He took his cue. "No, indeed. The way she told it the whole episode turned you into a nervous wreck and had you drinking rather more than was, perhaps, advisable. She was quite unapologetic. If I'm honest, she seemed rather to enjoy the fact."

Jessica's turn for another bash at him. 'We've also discovered that the actors and crew at your studios have been remarking on your recent change in behaviour. And not for the better, I might add." She had no clue where they were headed with the line of questioning, but she had an instinct that Kingsman wasn't quite as sanguine as he let on. Beckwith's body language – he had that watching air of a cat just before it pounces – obviously thought likewise.

"Hardly surprising," Kingsman said waspishly. "Work. Pressure. Nothing whatever to do with the notes. A movie is a many-headed thing. I don't expect either of you to understand since you're not in the business, but it takes tremendous stamina to pull it all together." He glowered at Jessica. "So, I get a little pissed off at times. Throw my weight around some. Drink a little too much. So what?"

Jessica tried to look as if she was buying his explanation. She reached for a folder and opened it. "We recovered the notes during the search of your house." She read them out in a deliberately flat voice. "I know. Soon everyone will know. The end is nigh. Tick tock, tick tock." She pushed the papers across to him. "As a matter of interest, what did you think these meant, Mr Kingsman?"

He held her look a fraction too long. "Like I said already, I assumed it was some kind of a joke. Someone with too little up top and too much time on their hands."

Jessica played dumb. "Oh, really? I would have read them as a threat of some sort. The sender implies that they have something over you, something you'd rather keep under the seal of the confessional." She threw him an insincere buddies-in-it-together smile. "Personally, I'd have been on to our lot like the clappers." She paused a second, then slyly turned up the heat. "Or, could it be that you actually do have something to hide, Mr Kingsman, something you'd rather not bring to the notice of the police?"

Kingsman started to fidget. The line of questioning was getting to him. He appealed directly to DCI Beckwith. "Mark, please, you must believe me. I thought it was a joke – in rather poor taste, but a joke nevertheless. That makes me guilty of nothing more than poor judgement."

DCI Beckwith said nothing. Instead, he let Jessica pile on the coals, something she was very good at.

"Sheila Walters phoned the station after you sacked her," she said, pausing to let that bit of news sink in. She rifled in the folder again and extracted another piece of paper. "This is the note from the policeman who took the call." She read it to him. "Ask Jack Kingsman about the girls." She waited a beat, then repeated it, squint-eyed. "Ask Jack Kingsman about the girls. What do you suppose she meant by that?"

Kingsman rapped his temples with his knuckles. His face turned turkey-cock red. He looked as though he was working himself up into a stroke.

"Jesus! What is she implying? That I'm that Director bloke; that I'm the one going around murdering those young girls? That bitch! That nasty boot-faced cow. I wish I'd fired her years ago. But I'm too nice," he raged. "That's always been my problem." He rocketed upright in his seat. "On my life, I had absolutely nothing to do with any of those murders. And if you have one shred of evidence to the contrary, go right ahead and charge me." He directed his gaze from one to the other of them, bitter, challenging. "Otherwise, I'm walking out of here right now." Again, he rose to his feet.

Jessica shrugged carelessly. "You're free to go, Mr Kingsman. Expect a call from immigration, though. The girls Sheila Webster was referring are actually your Turkish *maids*. Something about them being illegal immigrants?"

Kingsman came to an abrupt halt. He turned back, his face clearing. "That's it? That's what those notes were about? Melis and Mahlika? Their fucking visas? Oh man!"

"Did you hear that?" Jessica asked DCI Beckwith, once the reverberation from the door slamming behind Jack Kingsman had died down. "If that wasn't relief in his voice, I'm the Queen of Sheba. He may not be The Director, but at the very least Kingsman is being economical with the truth."

CHAPTER TWENTY-FOUR

Ed had seen the frenzy of police activity as he drove back to the studios with a delivery. Luckily, they hadn't seen him. It had been the work of a moment to throw the van into reverse, spin his wheels and get the hell out of there. He was shitting a brick by the time he pulled up behind a disused warehouse in the armpit of Mitcham. It looked like they were on to him. "Fuck! Fuck! Fuck!" he yelled aloud, hammering with both hands on his steering wheel. "He couldn't let them take him. Not yet. Not till the fat lady sang, or the skinny blonde bitch groaned her last." He turned on his radio, swore as his eardrums were assaulted by a crackling burst of static. Fucking building was blocking the signal. He tried again, inching the dial by degrees, impeded by his fat fingers. At last he got the BBC, some stuck-up newsreader poncing on as usual about stuff no one gave a toss about, war in the poxy Middle East, disease in some shithole country in shithole Africa. Then, the weather. Some other cunt with a Scottish accent wittering on about fucking low pressure and isobars. "C'mon! C'mon! C'mon!" Ed raged, desperate for a reprise of the main headlines. Sweat beaded on his forehead. A drop rolled into his eye, stinging and partially blinding him. His fucking pulse was all over the shop. Added to which, he was dying for a piss. Just when he thought he might actually wet himself, the poncey newscaster returned and gave him just what he'd been waiting for.

"In a startling turn of events, the award-winning film director and producer, Jack Kingsman, was today believed to have been helping police with their enquiries into the murders that have struck terror into an entire city. To date, a total of nine young women have met their deaths at the hands of the serial killer known as The Director. We understand, however, that Mr Kingsman has not been formally charged with anything, but will keep you informed as the story unfolds. More of that later, but for now here's the rest of the day's headlines—"

Startled, Ed flopped back against his seat. He hadn't seen that one coming. The plods had gone straight to the top of the tree, but it wouldn't be long before they started ferreting around at the roots. Ed blew out a breath. His hands strangled the steering wheel. He'd been given a reprieve. No more fannying around. He had to act now. When the next one showed up dead, they'd have to let Jack go. Not even DI Thick-as-a-bottled-turd Wideacre could believe that he could be in two places at once.

Ed jumped out of the van, unzipped his flies and relieved himself all over a snail clinging to a dandelion stalk. He got back in and fired up the engine. He switched on his satnav, took a slip of paper from his pocket, and began painstakingly to type in an address. Grinning, he did his favourite Jack Nicholson in *The Shining* impersonation in the rear-view mirror. "Ready or not. Here comes Eddie."

...

To avoid a clash of the personal and professional, DCI Beckwith tasked Jessica with the job of interviewing Venise Love-Davies. Though still as attractive as ever, Jessica noticed the actress looked strained, a little jumpy and nervous. Under the circumstances, it was hardly surprising. One moment she's riding high, feted as the new Marissa Bloom, the next she's sitting in the dingy confines of Rosewood nick, being grilled as part of a murder enquiry. Jessica offered her the usual coffee/tea/water and stale biscuits refreshments but, wisely, she waved them away.

"Do you really think Jack is guilty?" she asked. "I mean, he could be, like, a bit mean at times, but I … I would never have thought he could, like, do something like that."

Three "likes" in one sentence, two of them unnecessary. Jessica wondered if that was, like, a record of some kind. She put her inner bitch on the back burner to answer the question.

"Despite the rumours and scandal-mongering in the press, Miss Love-Davies, Jack Kingsman isn't in the frame for anything. At the moment, all we're doing is making some general enquiries."

"Oh?" Venise sat back in her chair. "Well that's a relief. And you can call me Venise," she said with a tight little smile. "Miss Love-Davies makes me sound, like, ancient."

About as ancient as Jessica felt listening to her. Christ, why couldn't Beckwith have given the job to Connors, who might actually have enjoyed the experience. She forced an unwilling smile and said, "And I'm DI Wideacre."

"Oh, I know that," Venise said, brightly. "I saw you a few times when Mark was mentoring me for my role in *Raining in My Heart*. And more recently in Alberico's." She grinned impishly. "You and your husband were having a bit of a domestic." The hair on the back of Jessica's neck began to prickle. Her stomach roiled; she thought she might actually be sick. *Please, please, God, let her have been with friends.* "Mark and I were sat just round the corner."

"Were you, indeed?" *Fuck you, God!* Jessica shook a mental fist. The one time she rowed in public and Beckwith's big ears just happened to be flapping just round the corner. How disappointed he must have been when she'd failed to hand in her notice and jet off out of his life.

"Don't worry," the actress continued breezily. "We row all the time. And he doesn't think any less of you. What was that word he used? Oh, that's right, 'driven'." She looked pleased at her recall. "He thinks you're very driven." Venise Love-Davies chewed off another piece of nail varnish, oblivious to the fact that every word was driving a stake through Jessica's heart. She leaned forward, impishly. "Personally, I just thought you were scary. Sorry. I don't think that now. It might be just your hairstyle. It's, like, so all over the place."

Jesus wept! Jessica gritted her teeth. The woman was as shallow as a pool of puke, inane and completely clueless. She fought to keep her smile from turning into a grimace. "Well, thank you for that," she said drily. With a huge effort, she addressed herself to the task in hand. There would be time enough later to beat herself to death with a large claw hammer. Before she could ask a question, however, Venise did that confiding thing again, leaning across the desk, dimpling cutely.

"I suppose you wonder what Marky sees in me," she said.

Marky! Jesus wept double! "Not at all," Jessica said politely. She could have given her at least two good reasons, both of them straining against her too-tight T-shirt.

...

"I expect Venise had nothing of any significance to say?" DCI Beckwith accosted Jessica as she returned to her office.

Her eyes sought the heavens. "Par for the course, I would have thought." She imagined the most significant thing Venise Love-Davies ever had to say would be along the lines of, "Does my bum look big in this" and "How's this for a twerk?"

"Unnecessary, DI Wideacre, and completely unworthy."

"Speaking of which," Jessica said with a scowl, "you obviously deemed it unnecessary to tell me you'd been eavesdropping on my *private* conversation with my husband in Alberico's recently?'

Though surprised at the attack, Beckwith came back at her snapping. "Hardly private. The whole of the restaurant and probably half the street were privy to your histrionics. I thought the gentlemanly thing to do was to sit on my hands."

Jessica's own hands fisted into knots to stop herself from screaming hysterically. "I was *not* hysterical. Things got a bit heated, no more than that."

Beckwith backed off. "Fine. Fine. Not my business anyway." He began to walk in the opposite direction, stopped and turned on his heel. "As a matter of interest, why didn't you go to the States with your husband?" Jessica's answer was the stare of a gorgon. He shrugged. "Okay. But, for what it's worth, I'm glad." He left her at the door of the Incident Room, leaving her the one that was turned to stone.

Jessica glared after him. Wanker! Playing mind games. She fucking hated him. Yet, when the blood flowed back into her body and she could move again, her step felt strangely lighter.

She was just about to open the door when Hennessy yanked it open from the other side. "One of the vans," he said breathlessly. "The luminol lit it up like a fucking Christmas tree. Someone made a good fist of trying to clean it up, but not good enough. There are numerous spots of blood in several areas. Samples are with the lab now."

"I assume they know there's a rush on," Jessica said, trying not to let her excitement show. Mentally, she was doing the hokey-cokey. They'd waited so long to catch a break.

"They've called in extra staff," Hennessy said. "Another thing – that particular van is primarily used by one Ed Hatcher, referred to by his workmates as 'a weird son of a bitch', 'seriously offline', 'an antisocial retard' and 'Lurch's younger brother'." He grinned. "Those were just the compliments."

"And where is this Ed Hatcher now?" DCI Beckwith asked, having doubled back upon hearing the commotion.

"He went out to pick up some props from a warehouse, which he did," Hennessy said. "We checked and the company's records show him arriving on site at 10.00 a.m. this morning and leaving an hour later. The journey back to Kingsman's Studios, even allowing for traffic, would have taken him no more than an hour, possibly an hour and a half."

"He saw us," Jessica said with certainty. "Turned round and hightailed it out of there. What kind of vehicle is he driving?"

"Another Ford Transit, exactly the same model as the others on site. There was a problem with the steering on his usual vehicle."

"Stroke of luck for us," Jessica said.

"Anything showing up in any of the other vehicles, Sergeant?" DCI Beckwith asked.

"Not so far, but they're still being checked."

"Kingsman's Jag?" Jessica asked, half-hopefully.

"Clean as a whistle. Nothing of any account at his home, either. Apart from a few illegals: couple of Turkish sisters and a Moroccan chef."

Beckwith shot her a regretful grin. "Sorry, Wideacre, looks like Kingsman's off the hook."

"For the moment," Jessica agreed. "Still, we'll have Sheila Walter's diary checked out anyway. Do we have a picture of Hatcher, Sergeant?"

"We pulled one from his employment file. It's being circulated now, along with his address, a description of the vehicle and registration number."

"But not to the press," Jessica warned. "Not yet. I don't want it getting into the hands of the public and some have-a-go twit ending up dead. What about an address?"

"Got it! It's over Sutton way, the crap end." Hennessy told them.

"AFOs?" DCI Beckwith asked, referring to the authorised firearms officers who attended any scene where a firearm might be used. "If Hatcher is our man, heaven knows what kind of reception we'll receive."

"On notice." Hennessy said.

Though Jessica's faith had long since lapsed, she made a mental sign of the cross and sent up a silent prayer. She rubbed her hands together. "Right, so what are we waiting for? Hennessy, go fetch the rest of the team. They deserve to be in on this. Coming, sir?"

Mark nodded. "Right with you. I'll just call Superintendent Green and make sure we've got the green light. We'll take your car, Wideacre."

Jessica was so eager to get going, she'd have agreed to Satan coming along for the ride. Her head was spinning. The day had started like any other, the police wading through treacle, making absolutely no headway. And now, in the space of a couple of hours, they had a possible face, name and address for The Director, and soon, hopefully, hard evidence. "Make sure to call me if any of the blood tests come back," she instructed the desk sergeant, before heading out the door to where a convoy of police vehicles was waiting. DCI Beckwith followed a moment later.

"Good luck, everybody," Jessica called to her team, who were piling into the various vehicles. "Remember, don't take any stupid risks and come back safe."

CHAPTER TWENTY-FIVE

Ed knew it was only a matter of time before the Old Bill caught up with him. The important thing was that it was in *his* time, not theirs. He had it all planned out, the grand reveal. He'd call a news conference, with the press, the TV networks, promise them the scoop of the decade – the century, even. Fuck Jack the Ripper – he was old news. It was time to give London a brand new legend, only Ed wasn't going to go slinking off in the dark somewhere. He was coming out loud and proud into the spotlight. Wasn't no fuckwit detective going to steal his thunder. It was his intention to personally exhibit his latest piece of handiwork. But, before that, he was going to treat them to a film show the likes of which they had never seen before. The boss had spent ages editing it. All the best scenes. They'd had a laugh about bits ending up on the cutting-room floor. That was witty, that was. He'd shouted out, "Stop, you're killing me," and laughed so hard he thought he'd burst a blood vessel.

Smooth as clockwork, all the pieces were moving slowly, inexorably into place. The cops had let Jack go. The secret was still safe. A well spring of happiness washed over him as he sat in a stolen car, staking out the building where Venise Love-Davies had her home. He cracked his knuckles. The only possible fly in the ointment was her copper boyfriend showing up too. That would mean a postponement. But so far the gods had been with him, and when, only moments later, a taxi pulled up and Venise Love-Davies got out alone, he was confident they still were.

Ed was well aware he unnerved her; he'd made it his business to. But now, in order to get her to trust him, he was playing down his scary. He was actually wearing a suit for the first time ever – he'd nicked it from the costume department. Made him look like a bleedin' undertaker; which, in a way, he was. He watched her pay the fare and the cabbie drive off immediately. Not one of those PC cab drivers who hung around waiting till their fare was safely indoors, then. Good.

"Miss Love-Davies," he called out through the car window, putting on the respect. If he'd a cap, he would've doffed it.

"Ye-es?" she said, starting to walk tentatively towards him.

"Mr Kingsman's been released. He asked me to come and collect you."

"Now?" she said, looking puzzled and slightly anxious.

"Something about being way behind on the shoot and wanting to get a scene in the can tonight. He sends apologies. Said he knows a professional like you will understand."

"Oh, of course," she said taking the bait, a little flustered, yet clearly flattered.

Women, they were too easy! Sprinkle a bit of sugar on their egos and they'd follow you all the way to hell. Thrilled at how bloody stupid she was, he leant across and opened the door for her and – come into my parlour –in she stepped. In a matter of seconds she was out for the count, the faint acetone tang of chloroform wreathing round her. Ed pushed her down low in the seat and threw his suit jacket over her head. Friggin' thing came in useful for something.

...

Ed Hatcher's house was a two-up, two-down, 1930s end of terrace in a forgotten part of Sutton. It had the scruffy look of a down-at-heel tramp. The rendering on the walls was cracked and flaking off in places, the windows hidden under years of grime. The front door hadn't seen a fresh coat of paint since God was in short trousers. The garden was a nightmare of weeds and detritus, with ragwort reaching high up above the ground-floor windows. On the wall, the drainpipe had come adrift from its moorings and the bottom section had broken off altogether and lay rusting now among the weeds. The rest of the houses on the street were no better, so it wasn't like Hatcher was bringing down the tone of the neighbourhood.

"Scuzz Alley," Jessica remarked, noting the absence of any onlookers. Normally, a crowd would have gathered by now to see what all the commotion was about, anxious to record it for Facebook and YouTube. "You can almost hear the tumbleweeds starting to roll this way."

"I've nicked several lowlifes in this neighbourhood," Connors said, coming up behind her. "There's not a one of them that hasn't something to hide. It's a perfect place for a slimeball like Hatcher to hide out."

Hennessy performed the FOG knock with relish, but predictably, no one was at home, a fact confirmed by a pimply, ferret-faced youth, who eventually emerged from the neighbouring house to tell them how he'd seen "the bloke wot lives there drivin' off that morning. Is 'e a nonce or wot?"

Only when they were absolutely certain that the greater spotted youth was right did DCI Beckwith take the decision to stand down the firearms unit.

Hennessy kicked the door in like matchwood. Inside, the decor matched the outside. A bare, low-wattage bulb showed paint peeling off the mould-infested walls. The floor was littered two-foot deep in junk mail that had been mulched and trodden into the floor. Spiders had been busy turning the corners of the ceiling into web city. The whole place reeked of damp. "Jesus," Jessica exclaimed kicking her way through, "remember to wipe your feet on the way out!" She halted at the door to the only reception room, put her latex-gloved hand round the door jamb and felt for the light switch. "Jesus!" she said again, as light trickled slowly from an energy-saving bulb, illuminating by degrees the room inside. Coming to an abrupt stop behind her, Hennessy peered over her shoulder. He echoed her surprise.

"Holy moley, I've heard of fan clubs, but ..." There were similar exclamations of surprise from the rest of the team as they all crowded into what was in effect a shrine to Marissa Bloom. The walls, every inch of them, were a *découpage* of pictures of the late actress. Every ledge, every surface, was strewn with film memorabilia and cuttings from old newspapers. Stacks of ancient movie magazines towered in mini-skyscrapers on the floor. A couple had toppled over, and spilt magazines lay higgledy-piggledy at their base.

Jessica ploughed forward into the centre of the room, looking round in awe. "This takes obsession to a whole different level."

"It's downright weird," DS Connors said, picking up a Marissa Bloom doll, whose blonde curls were grey with dust and whose once resplendent ball gown was now little more than a tattered rag. "I can understand someone having a fixation on, say, Julia Roberts or Nicole Kidman, but a movie star who's been dead for yonks? I can't get my head around that at all."

"Unless, you knew them personally," DCI Beckwith said, holding up a photograph of Marissa Bloom in her heyday. He turned it over and read the back.

To Edward. As surely as the tides ebb and flow. As surely as the seasons change, I know you will always be there for me. And I thank you with all my heart. Marissa X.

He held it up for them to see the flowing female hand, the signature particularly flowery and underscored. "More than a passing acquaintance, by the sound of it."

"A love affair?" Jessica said. "Kind of unlikely, I would have thought. Beauty and the beast. Let's talk to Kingsman again, see if he can put it into perspective for us. He'll know what the score was there. A bit of heroine worship, or something more intense." Her attention was claimed by DC Liversedge shouting from a corner of the room.

"Hey, guv, look what I found." He angled a cardboard box to display the contents. "Blonde hair extensions." He kicked at a box on the floor. "And this one's full of make-up."

The label on the box containing the hair extensions had been posted from some obscure supplier in China, which probably went some way towards explaining the difficulty in forensics finding a match. The make-up was a collection of odds and sods that could have come from anywhere. Jumble sales. Discount stores. Jessica picked up a tube of lipstick, squinting her eyes to read the label on the bottom. "Candy Pink," she said, twisting the cap off. "Or, as I like to call it, Zombie on Crack."

"Marissa Bloom's signature colour," Connors contributed,

then defensively. "Look, I don't know how I know that. I just do, all right?"

Jessica shrugged, put the lid back on and returned it to the box. "Ever think about reading a real book, Connors?' she asked. 'One without pictures?" She put the cap back on the lipstick and returned it to the box. "Unless Hatcher is a transvestite, I'm guessing we'll find both the hair extensions and the make-up match those found on our victims." A moment later, when Hennessy discovered a stack of business cards and a fully operational inkjet printer, they hit the mother-lode.

"Bingo!" he said, holding one up like a trophy. There were two words printed on it: The Director.

A sigh seemed to echo round the room. After all these fruitless, frustrating, exhausting, traumatic months, they finally had a name, a face and some hard evidence. Ed Hatcher was The Director.

"They never quite look like you imagined, do they?" Connors said, pulling a photo-flyer out of her pocket and examining Hatcher's picture. "He's innocuous, isn't he? He's the guy that packs your bags in the supermarket, or sells you an ice cream on the street. You see them, but you don't, if you get what I mean."

Jessica was reminded of her recent conversation with DCI Beckwith regarding the angelic-faced child killer, Beverley Allitt. Fred and Rosemary West, the husband and wife serial killers, were another case in point. Both were average looking, middle aged and wouldn't have looked out of place at a church meeting. Yet, between them, they tortured and raped several young women, killing at least eleven, including their own daughter. It was a common feeling among decent people that murderers ought somehow to stand out in some way that would make them instantly identifiable

– the mark of Cain, a hunchback, a cloven hoof – something ugly on the outside to match the ugliness within. It didn't work that way. Bogeymen came in all shapes and sizes, everything from cuddly, grey-haired grandmothers to raving, psychotic monsters

"He knows we're on to him," Jessica said. "The fact that he didn't return to the studios says as much. My guess is that he's holed up at the kill site, wherever that is." She gestured round the room. "Okay, let's leave forensics to do their stuff in here. I hope you've all brought your jammies, because no one is going home tonight. I don't care whose birthday it is, whose wedding anniversary, which of your rellies is about to shuffle off their mortal coil. Keep in mind that it's for the greater good." She grinned sarkily. "There'll be unlimited amounts of Rosewood's finest coffee to help keep you all primed." As she spoke, she was vaguely aware of DCI Beckwith finishing up a call on his mobile. She noticed him stagger slightly, the colour of his skin tone change to a sickly grey. "Sir?" she asked. "Is something wrong?"

It took him a moment to find his voice and, when he did, there was a crack in it. "That was the station. It … it's Venise," he said. "She's been abducted." The room stilled with shock as he swiped droplets of sudden sweat from his. "A neighbour, one of the nosey types who spy on everyone coming in and out of the building, saw her get into a car with a man he didn't recognise. He got out his binoculars for a closer look and saw the man press a cloth of some sort over her face."

"Chloroform?" Jessica guessed.

"Could be. There was a brief struggle, then the car took off at speed." DCI Beckwith was trying hard to keep it together, but couldn't quite still the trembling in his hands. He spoke quietly, almost as though he was trying to reason it out.

"Did he get a clear look at the man?" Jessica asked.

"No. But Venise wouldn't have got into a car with a stranger. Whoever he was, she knew him. I'm thinking Hatcher."

The thought had crossed Jessica's mind. "It's possible," she said. "He works at the studios."

"Not just possible. Probable. Venise has gone all out recently to turn herself into an identikit of Marissa Bloom." He looked sick with misery. "She wasn't to know we had him in our sights."

"How old is Venise?" Jessica asked.

Beckwith balked at the leading question. He knew immediately where she was going and it wasn't a route he wanted to go down. He gritted his teeth.

"Twenty-four, the age Marissa Bloom was when she played the part of Lorelei Turner. Could just be coincidence, but ..." He left it hanging. The air was thick with dread as everyone wrestled with the possibility that Venise Love-Davies might well be on the cusp of becoming The Director's tenth victim.

"Try phoning her?" Jessica said, assailed by a feeling of inadequacy. Bad enough when the victims were strangers, but now the killer had trespassed onto their own turf. He'd struck at the heart of one of their own. She watched Beckwith get out his phone and his fingers falter over the dial pad as he keyed in Venise's telephone number. Nobody moved. They could scarcely draw breath. They could all hear it ringing until, eventually, Venise's voicemail picked up on the other end.

"It's going straight to voicemail," DI Beckwith said, unnecessarily.

"What about the car?" Jessica asked at last. "Have we any leads on that?"

"A black BMW. High-end model, an M5. The neighbour is a bit of a car buff. The registration plate was muddied up, no doubt deliberately."

"I doubt it's his own," Jessica said. "Come on," she said to the team. "Let's go question the neighbours." She took the lead herself, found Spotty still hanging about, puffing on a spliff. Cocky as hell, he took one last puff before grinding it underfoot.

"Nice onesie," he smirked, looking her protective boiler suit up and down. "Must be a bugger when you're in a hurry for a whizz, though."

Jessica ignored the vulgarity and the weed – she'd bigger things on her mind – and questioned him about Hatcher's vehicle.

"He never drove nuffink," he told her scornfully, "'cept for that van wiv the clowns on the door. I don't like clowns, me. Fuckin' creepy paedos."

"So, definitely not a BMW?" Jessica asked.

"No one drives shit like that round 'ere," he said, telling it like it was. "Five minutes 'n' it would be on its way to flamin' Nigeria."

Probably because he would have been instrumental in sending it on its way. She left him picking his spots and returned indoors. The rest of the team received similar replies from those few neighbours not too stoned or too scared to answer the door. "Yes, more than likely stolen," she confirmed to the others assembled in the house. "We're bound to get a call when the owner discovers it's missing. In the meantime, let's get the word out there. Make sure Hatcher's photo is circulated to all units across the city. Make that nationwide." She nodded to DS Connors. "Take care of it,

Connors, will you? The rest of you, back to the nick too and let the tech team get on with bagging and tagging this lot."

On the face of it, Hatcher's house didn't appear to be the kill site, though only a thorough examination by forensics could rule that out completely. Of the two upstairs rooms, only one, Hatcher's bedroom, was occupied. The other contained further evidence of his obsession with Marissa Bloom – more newspaper cuttings, magazines, posters and a stack of videos, including several copies of *Killer Queen*. The mess continued into the bedroom, which was so untidy it resembled an Oxfam reject skip. Piles of clothing and towels littered the unmade bed and spilled onto the floor. A chest, minus half its drawers showed a further lack of housekeeping skills. A wardrobe in one corner, the door hanging drunkenly on one hinge, contained a motley assortment of women's clothing. Closer inspection showed them all to be of an age, probably 1970s, and not the 'good Seventies' that were selling for eye-watering prices in the vintage stores. An old print of Constable's *Hay Wain* hung lopsidedly on the wall, and the wallpaper, though yellowed and peeling, had once been a pretty floral. Jessica didn't do floral. Anything flowery had an adverse effect on her gag reflex. She wondered if the house had previously belonged to Hatcher's parents, which would explain the homely touches.

Her gag reflex was further tested in the bathroom. The bath had acquired a trail of slimy green moss beneath one tap, and the toilet bowl was so hellish only a hefty dose of Semtex and a detonator would shift the stains. A small shelf held the few toiletries – everything from Poundland – Hatcher needed to make himself vaguely presentable to the world. It was the first time Jessica had ever seen dust on a tube of toothpaste.

She was diplomatically silent on the drive back to Rosewood, having no wish to intrude on DCI Beckwith's thoughts. She guessed he'd be torturing himself, his mind going round in circles, cursing himself for failing to put Venise on her guard. It would do no good to rationalise, to remind him that until the visit to the house, Hatcher had been nothing more than a person of interest. There had been no concrete evidence to prove that he was their man. Short of having a crystal ball, there was no way anyone could have foreseen Hatcher going after Venise.

CHAPTER TWENTY-SIX

When they arrived at the nick, it was buzzing like a hive of bees, every one of them with full-blown ADHD. Hatcher's burned-out van had been found at the back of a disused warehouse in Mitcham. He'd used a mixture of petrol and diesel both on the interior and exterior, ensuring it burned quickly, and so ferociously there was bugger all chance of forensics recovering anything of value from the remains.

As instructed, Connors had put out an APW. Every airport and port in the country, as well as the Channel Tunnel, was on alert just in case Hatcher tried to flee abroad.

"No competition for Brad Pitt," Jessica observed, picking up the photo-flyer of Hatcher from a stack on Connor's desk. Again, the words that sprang to mind were: ordinary, unremarkable, forgettable. "Did you pull his record on the PNC?" she asked.

Connors nodded. "Yes, but there's not a lot of interest. It's petty stuff in the main. Vandalising a car. An allegation, never proved, of breaking and entering. To be honest, these should have been scrubbed from his record years ago."

Shoulda, woulda, coulda, Jessica thought. Spent convictions of a petty nature were meant to be erased from the computer after seven years. In theory. "No hint of violence?" she asked, surprised.

"An allegation once that he poisoned some blind woman's guide dog. Again, insufficient evidence to charge."

Jessica pitied the poor copper who'd been sent out to follow that one up. Her brain went off on a tangent. '*Er … so you didn't*

actually see the offence take place? Well ... er, how do you know Mr
Hatcher poisoned? ... I mean to say, you're ... er ... um ...'

Connors brought her back to the here and now. "Since then, he
seems to have smartened up his act. From the point of view of the
law, he's been clean as a whistle for donkey's years."

Jessica edged her bottom onto the corner of Connors' desk.
She screwed up her face. "I don't buy it. He'll have been up to
something. Scrotes don't suddenly sprout wings and a halo."

"Could be," Connors agreed. "But whatever he was doing, it
was off-piste and under the radar." Pointedly, she moved her mug
away from Jessica's bottom.

"Any more addresses for him, apart from the dump in Scuzz
Alley?" Jessica asked.

"No. That was the family home. Mother long dead. Father
unknown. He's worked as a van driver/props man/gofer for
Kingsman Productions for thirty-five years."

Jessica's eyebrows rose. "Really. And he's how old?"

"Fifty-two."

Jessica did the maths. "So, he was working there for ten years
before Marissa Bloom's death. More than enough time for his
obsession to take root."

Connors took a sip of her coffee. She was canny enough to
bring her own and keep it locked in her desk drawer. Jessica and
half the station had a duplicate key. "We're definitely going with
the theory that the murders are related to his fixation on Marissa
Bloom?" she said.

Jessica nodded. "Mad though it is, it's the only one that makes
sense." She used her fingers to enumerate why, and also to clarify
matters in her own mind. "One – motive. His obsession with
Marissa. Two – catalyst. Jack Kingsman's intention to remake

Killer Queen, which sends him into a towering rage and triggers the killing spree. Three and four: means and opportunity. His job as a van driver allowed him the freedom to prowl the streets on the lookout for prospective victims." She tapped her thumb. Five: now we get to Venise Love-Davies, who was, perhaps, the real target all along."

Connors joined the rest of the dots. "She's been given the role of Lorelei Turner, Bloom's seminal role. She's pretty much cloned herself, right down to the cat flicks at the corner of her eyes. He sees her as a usurper, a pretender to the throne."

Jessica feigned admiration. "A pretender to the throne? That's very good, Connors. I bet you were good at history."

Connors ignored the sarcasm. "There's one major flaw in the theory, though. The killings commenced before news leaked out that Kingsman was remaking *Killer Queen*."

"To the public," Jessica clarified. "Bear in mind, Hatcher works at the studios. He'd have his ear to the ground." She stood up, rolled her aching shoulders and made a mental note to see a chiropractor. Her body felt like it might be falling apart. "Let's have Kingsman in for another chat, she said, "Get on to him, would you?" In the meantime, she intended to grab a much needed forty winks in her own office. She was just dozing off when her mobile vibrated on the desk, shocking her awake again. Carol's number. Her drowsy eyes sought the ceiling. Jesus, what now? "Hello," she said, trying not to sound cranky and failing dismally.

There was a pause before Carol came on the line. "Hello … *Aunty* Jessica."

In no mood for stupid games, Jessica was about to snap when she grasped the significance. "The baby? You've had it?"

"*Her!*" Carol said. "I've had *her*! All seven pounds, ten ounces. And if any bastard tries to kid you childbirth is easy, don't listen. Believe me when I say it's like pushing a one hundred pound boulder out your nostril. Plus, I've been left with more stitches than a patchwork quilt." She uttered a sound of disgust. "And as if that weren't enough, I'm having to park my arse on a rubber ring. God knows what will happen when I need to do a number two."

"Oh," Jessica said limply, wishing to be spared the detail. A potential tour around Carol's reproductive organs and bowels left her feeling distinctly nauseous. "Are you still in hospital?"

"Yes," Carol said. "But I'll be coming home tomorrow, so you can drop around and meet your niece whenever it's *convenient*."

"It's a bit difficult at the moment," Jessica explained, not missing the emphasis. "It's all going down at work. It'll be in the papers soon enough. But I'll be there as soon as I can."

Carol gave a world-weary sigh. "No more than I expected," she said. "You're a crap sister and a crap daughter. Why wouldn't you be anything but a crap aunty too?" Jessica heard the baby gruntle on the other end of the phone. She sounded just like a little pig. Carol, in full flow, continued. "Still, never mind, Mum's coming up from Ramsgate for a few days to give me a hand." There was a slight pause while she sipped from her goblet of sarcasm. "You remember our mother, don't you? The woman who gave birth to you?"

Jessica's eyes again sought the ceiling. Their mother! Another big guilt-stick for Carol to beat her with. She hadn't been around the day her newly widowed mother took off to start a new life by the Thanet coast. Not her fault. But she still felt guilty. Not that she'd give Carol the satisfaction of hearing her say so.

"What are you calling her?" she asked, neatly deflecting the bile.

"Beyoncé," Carol said proudly. "Beyoncé Rihanna Carling." Jessica was only surprised she hadn't managed to fit Lady Gaga in too. "And that's not my only bit of good news," Carol continued. "The investigation against Ted has been dropped. He's taking a couple of weeks' paternity leave and then he'll be back to work. Personally, I think he should sue the bastards for defamation of character."

There was a kind of slurping noise from the baby. Jessica dreaded to think what it might be up to. "Let it go, Carol," she advised. "You're going to have your hands full with ..." She hesitated, gritted her teeth. "... Beyoncé. Better by far just to let things get back to normal."

"You're probably right," Carol said, but there was a reserve in her tone which made Jessica suspect she hadn't entirely given up on the idea. Fortunately – or not, as it turned out – her mind was already flip-flopping in another direction. "Another thing – you might want to consider getting us the Bugaboo pram on my John Lewis nursery list." The baby started to wail, slurp and snort and Carol rang off. Jessica slammed her phone down and glared at the desk. "I am *never* ..." she said aloud, "... repeat – *never* having a baby!" She was uncharacteristically pleased when Connors stuck her head round the door.

"Jack Kingsman's here," she said. "Room 2. He doesn't look happy."

"He's in good company," she said, delighted to be given the excuse to shut down her computer screen. "I'll be there in five."

She was just shrugging her jacket on when DCI Beckwith, looking tired and strained, came into her office. Alarmed, Jessica's eyes flew to his face.

"No news," he said, anticipating her question. "Not on that front, but some of the results have come in on the blood and hair samples recovered from Hatcher's van, the one we took from the studio lot."

Half in, half out of her jacket, Jessica froze. Her eyes never left his face.

"We have matches to hair, blood and tissue for Susan Kelly, Shania Lewis and Kerrie Gray, and hair matches to Jordan Flynn and Monika Jakubowska. Nothing on Tara James, Melanie Potts, Lindsey Sutton or Eva Castle; I think it's safe to assume that he abducted them in a different vehicle, possibly the burnt out one recovered from Mitcham. The other vans are still being examined, though, so they could yet turn up something. One more thing," he said, pretending not to notice the sudden sheen of tears in Wideacre's eyes. "We've also got a hair sample for Stacey Herbert."

The fourteen-year-old strangled to death on Streatham Common. Jessica found herself overcome by a sudden bout of weakness. She groped for her chair and sat down. "Poor little Stacey," she said. "I suppose the only mercy is that he killed her quickly, that she didn't suffer the same fate as the other poor girls."

"I only hope Venise is as lucky," DCI Beckwith said quietly.

"God, I'm so sorry," Jessica said quickly, enraged by her thoughtlessness. "I ... I didn't mean ... Oh, fuck it! Look, that's not going to let happen." She spoke with certainty, willing him to believe her. Somehow that was important, though she wasn't quite sure why. Perhaps because when one of their own was in trouble, it was time to let go of old grievances and circle the wagons. "There's a full-scale search on. We know who he is now. We'll get him." If The Director – it was difficult to think of him as Hatcher – followed his usual pattern, they probably had a couple of days left before he killed Venise. Stacey Herbert, for whatever reason, had been the exception. "I think you should go home and try to get your head down for a few hours," she told him now. He was radiating exhaustion and looking as though he had aged a full ten years. "She's going to need you fighting fit when we find her."

DCI Beckwith nodded. "I will. But … Wideacre – you'll be here, won't you? Just … just in case anything turns up."

"I'll be here," she told him, aware that she, herself, was only running on pure adrenaline. There would be time enough for sleeping when Venise Love-Davies was safely returned to the fold and the bastard who took her locked up for the rest of his natural. Besides, with David away in the States, there was little incentive to go home.

CHAPTER TWENTY-SEVEN

Only when DCI Beckwith had left did she recall that Jack Kingsman was waiting for her in Room 2. If he wasn't happy to begin with, he was positively livid by the time she arrived.

"Haven't you wasted enough of my time?" he began, without so much as a greeting. Jessica took her time answering. She poured herself a glass of water, rearranged her notebook and pen on the desk and adjusted the position of her chair. Only then did she respond.

"Yes, I'm sorry about that, Mr Kingsman. Only, as you can appreciate, it's been something of a hectic day.

Kingsman checked his watch. "And now it's night when, *normally*, by this time, I'd be safely snuggled up indoors with a generous glass of something agreeable."

"I appreciate that," Jessica said crisply. "However, there's been a rather serious development." She slid a clear evidence bag across the table containing the inscribed photograph of Marissa Bloom taken from Ed Hatcher's house. "Do you recognise this?"

He picked it up, pursed his lips in surprise. "It's one of Marissa's private collection of photographs. Not for the eyes of the great unwashed. Where did you get it?"

"From the house of your employee, Ed Hatcher. There's an inscription on the back." She waited till he read it. "It sounds rather intimate, doesn't it? Were they having an affair?" She probably could have couched it more tactfully, but she was too tired for diplomacy, time was getting on and Kingsman didn't improve upon acquaintance.

"Affair?" Kingsman gave a humourless laugh. "Don't be absurd, there was no affair. This is the kind of thing Marissa did all the time. She was needy like that. She wanted everyone to love her, a trait both endearing and annoying. Especially if you were her husband."

"So there was nothing more to it? He wasn't a friend or a confidante?" Jessica reclaimed the photograph, read the inscription aloud. "'*I know you will always be there for me*.' That suggests a closeness, an intimacy, Mr Kingsman. It's not the kind of thing you would say to someone with whom you were purely on nodding terms." She leaned across the table. "So, I ask you once again, what was your wife's involvement with Ed Hatcher?"

Jack Kingsman rubbed his eyes. He barely managed to suppress a yawn. It was catching. Jessica almost yawned in sympathy. "Look," he said. "I don't really understand what this is about. Hatcher is just a props man. A driver. He does a bit of this and a bit of that. He's worked for me for years."

"And he knew your wife," Jessica said.

"Yes, he knew Marissa. He might even have run the odd errand for her, which might explain the photograph. OTT, I grant you, but that was Marissa, always on stage, twenty-four-seven."

"Hatcher. What's he like?" Jessica asked.

"A good worker. Dependable. Does what he's paid for. I've had no cause for complaint."

"He's not popular with his workmates," Jessica said. She referred to her notes. "They refer to him variously as socially inadequate, a bit of an odd bod, a weirdo. *And* downright creepy."

"I don't concern myself with such pettiness," Kingsman

snapped. "Hatcher is employed to do a job, not to win any popularity contests. By that measure, I'd have to sack fifty per cent of my employees and every single one of the actors."

"Do you think he's capable of murder?" Jessica asked, watching him keenly.

Kingsman sighed. "Oh, please, DI Wideacre, where is this going? Are you trying to fit up an innocent man simply because some people think he's a bit odd?"

"Not at all," Jessica said calmly. "But there's odd. There's obsessional. And there's murderous." She rifled through her papers, pulled out several photographs and spread them out facing him. "These are photographs taken in Hatcher's house today. Spot the running theme." She observed him carefully as he worked his way through the bundle. At last, his face impassive, he passed them back.

"He was a fan of my wife's. So what? She had hundreds of fans, thousands. It's not a crime."

Jessica took a photograph of Marissa Bloom and put it on the table. Beneath it, she placed a photograph of each of Hatcher's nine victims. "Now, spot the running theme," she said. "Everyone who hasn't been living under a bush these past several months will recognise these young girls as victims of the killer calling himself The Director. Very like your late wife to look at, aren't they?"

Kingsman shrugged. "Not really. There are millions of pretty young blondes out there."

"What if I was to tell you that when we found the bodies they had been made up to resemble her even more? Blonde hair extensions. Same make-up palette – mauve eyeshadow, frosted candy-pink lipstick, cat flicks at the corners of the eyes. You really think that's all coincidence?"

"I think you're desperate," Kingsman said coolly. "So desperate to have someone in the frame that your imagination is working overtime." He put his hands, palms up, on the table before him, a body language cue normally indicating openness, honesty, even submission. Not in this case. "Hatcher is a win-win candidate, isn't he? He's unpopular with his colleagues, has a face like a bag of spanners and all the charm of a basket of pissed-off rattle snakes." He flipped his hands over, drummed them on the table. "All of which makes him easy meat, the perfect sacrificial lamb." He smiled unpleasantly. "The blood lust of Joe Public is assuaged and you and your buddies get to play hail the conquering hero comes."

Jessica almost leapt across the desk. "Blood lust!" she blurted. "You want to talk about blood lust!" She scrabbled among her papers, extracted photographs of the bodies of dead girls, tossed them across the divide. "Here!" She stabbed at them with her finger. "Have a good look. Here's bloodlust in all its sadistic, Technicolor glory." It was the kind of conduct that caused DCI Beckwith to single her out as a loose cannon; that made him label her prone to 'rash decision-making' and 'poor judgement'. Right at that moment she didn't give a damn. They could shoot her backside out the loose cannon. Her gut instinct was that Kingsman knew more than he was letting on, and she was going to rattle him any way she could. "We found blood, tissue and hair matches in Hatcher's van. It lit up like the Olympics opening ceremony when the luminol was sprayed." With a lightning-quick transition from bad cop to good cop, she sat back down. "Mr Kingsman, you and

Ed Hatcher go back a long way. We know he was close to your wife. If you have any information concerning his whereabouts, I beg you to tell me, please." Her shoulders slumped. "Otherwise it may well be too late for Venise Love-Davies."

Jack Kingsman's head came up at that. He actually started to smile.

"Good heavens," he said at last. "That's quite the most preposterous thing I've heard yet. I can assure you that Venise Love-Davies was alive and well on set this morning. The only murder taking place was her butchering her lines, something at which she is most adept." He smirked at her across the table. "Please look me up, DI Wideacre, if ever you decide on a change of career. Good comedy writers are like gold dust."

Jessica bit her lip. Any minute now … She mastered the impulse to deck him by literally sitting on her hands. "This is not one of your film productions, Mr Kingsman" she said icily, waiting for the urge to pass. "I can only assume that you didn't quite hear me. So, let me do a quick recap. Several young women have been brutally murdered, all bearing a striking resemblance to your late wife. Crucially, Ed Hatcher not only knew her, he was obsessed with her. Blood, hair and tissue samples taken from Hatcher's van match those of several of the victims." She watched him carefully for his reaction, before pressing on. "Hatcher has gone AWOL. And now, so has Venise Love-Davies. An eyewitness has her being abducted from outside her apartment block earlier today." She steepled her fingers and glared at him, no longer bothered about hiding her dislike. "Venise Love-Davies, who looks so much like your late wife with whom we all know Hatcher was completely obsessed. Still convinced of his innocence?"

"Still not convinced you're right," Kingsman said. He flicked his tongue over his lips. Nerves? "Just supposing I go along with you for a moment. Tell me, why would Hatcher kill those girls? Why now, all these years after Marissa's death?"

"A very good question," Jessica admitted. "One we asked ourselves. There had to be a catalyst and we think we found it – your plans to remake *Killer Queen*. It kick-started a killing spree; he set out to destroy any young woman resembling her." Jessica slid a final picture from amongst her papers and placed it next to the photograph of Marissa Bloom. "Or, perhaps, those were practice runs leading up to the main event." She tapped the picture with her finger. "The murder of Venise Love-Davis, your new leading lady. So, I ask you again, if you have any knowledge where Ed Hatcher might be hiding out, I advise you to tell me now. Before it's too late." There were a few seconds of silence, during which Jessica watched a whole array of emotions cross Kingsman's face. Contempt won.

"DI Wideacre," he said at last, his mouth twisting. "Do you seriously expect me to give any credence to this B-horror movie bullshit theory of yours? *Killer Queen* has nothing to do with the deaths of those young girls, and I resent you hitching your wagon to it." He got to his feet. "If it wasn't so preposterous, it would be downright laughable. I assume I'm free to go? Or, should I call my lawyer, since that's probably what I should have done right at the top of these outrageous inquisitions."

Jessica waved him away. She'd done her best, but if he knew anything about Hatcher's whereabouts he wasn't letting on. Kingsman left, once more slamming the door behind him. Jessica sat a few moments waiting for him to get clear, then popped outside for a fresh-air break as her non-smoking colleagues called it. To wake herself up, really. It had been a fairly warm day, but night had ushered in a chill breeze. She wrapped her arms around herself and slumped back against the wall of the station. The harsh sound of vomiting nearby brought her immediately to attention again. She went to take a look and saw Jack Kingsman spewing his guts out round the corner. He didn't see her and she backed off quietly.

Back indoors, she found the team suffering from various degrees of exhaustion. Hennessy, in particular, looked worn out and haggard. Jessica had to remind herself that the sergeant was knocking on sixty's door and not as young as he used to be. Connors had been to the loo for various tarting-up sessions. Nevertheless, she too looked like she could do with her bed – alone, what's more. Even the infant of the team, Sedgie, looked shagged out and not for the usual reasons. Jessica dreaded to think what kind of picture she herself presented. She couldn't remember the last time she'd looked in a mirror or run a comb through her hair. She decided to send them all home. Thanks to the public hue and cry over the lack of progress in catching The Director, Jessica had finally been granted more resources. She could afford to be generous to the worn out 'old hands'. First, though, she gathered everyone together and told them about Kingsman.

"Could be misplaced loyalty," Jessica said. She lifted her mug, found that it was empty. Probably just as well. She brought the cup down like a mini gavel. "But, something smells bad. I don't know what, but I have a feeling our Mr Kingsman knows more than he's letting on." She checked her watch. "Connors, it's almost the witching hour. Get your broom and fly home. Hennessy, Sedgie, you too. See you back here bright and early tomorrow with all the answers."

As they began to get their things together, Sergeant Hennessy approached her. He tapped her lightly on the arm. "Guv. Can I have a brief word with you? By the look on his face, Jessica gathered it wasn't for public consumption.

"Sure," she said, leading the way into her office and closing the door behind them.

"So," she asked, sitting down at her desk, "what's on your mind?"

Hennessy came straight to the point. "DS Connors."

"What about her?" Jessica asked. "Not been trying to get you into bed, has she?"

The sergeant sat down heavily in the chair opposite. "That. What you've just said. That's what's on my mind." He dug in his pocket and produced a rollie, playing with it between his fingers like a set of worry beads. "It's got to stop, guv, before you find yourself in the thick of a harassment case."

Uncomfortable suddenly, Jessica blocked him. "Harassment? What on earth are you talking about?"

"Connors," Hennessy said, spelling it out. "That 'get your broom' remark tonight was a perfect example. All that digging at DS Connors has to stop."

Jessica rolled her eyes. "Don't be such an old fuddy-duddy, Hennessy. That was a joke. She didn't seem to mind, so I've no idea why you're suddenly waving your moral compass in the air."

"It wasn't funny," Hennessy said, standing his ground. "You drip-feed snide little remarks to her on a daily basis." He tamped the rollie on the desk.

"It was a *wind*-up," Jessica insisted, beginning to feel slightly irritated, more so because she knew he was right. "Like I wind Sedgie up about his harem. Like I wind you up about Mary."

"It's not the same thing," Hennessy said. "With her, it's always personal – a putdown aimed to make her feel small or look stupid. You're laughing at her, not with her, and encouraging others to do the same. She'd be perfectly within her rights to bring a complaint. And there's several who'd back her up."

Jessica felt herself go red. "Including you?"

Hennessy didn't reply. He stood up and nodded goodnight, leaving her sitting like an angry child on the naughty step.

Jessica liked Hennessy, saw him as something of a father figure, the kind she would like to have had. Unlike many of the older male officers, whose mission was to give grief to every woman promoted above them, he had shown her nothing but kindness and consideration. She had come to think of him as a bit of a rock, someone she could depend on to always have her back. It unnerved her to find herself in his bad books. She wandered over to the window and gazed out. The brick wall opposite acted as a kind of background to the glass, giving a mirrored effect, so that she found herself looking at her own reflection. It wasn't a pretty sight; it never was. Warily, she began to examine her conscience. Was there really merit in the accusation that she was too hard on Connors? They were certainly poles apart in terms of personality. Jessica disapproved of Connors using her feminine wiles to get ahead; all that hair-tossing and eyelash-fluttering reminded her too much of Carol. Yet, she had to admit that the other woman had her shoulder to the wheel just as much as anyone. Under the microscope, she was no worse than anyone else Jessica had worked with. She was ambitious. She wanted to go all the way to the top. Who didn't? Jessica felt a creeping sense of unease, the niggling sense that she'd repeatedly thrown a sister suffragette under the bus. It had been an abuse of power. She'd used her position to undermine a more junior colleague. Not smart. Not nice. The bugger was that in her heart she'd known what she was doing all along, that she'd justified it to herself as banter. It wasn't. It was bullying. Hennessy was dead right. Connors would have been well within her rights to have made a complaint. That she hadn't gone whining to Jessica's superiors, but took whatever was dished out, was to her credit. It had been a shock and unpalatable to hear the truth from Hennessy. Now Jessica was grateful he'd had the balls to wake her up to herself.

She left her post by the window and headed off to make a fresh pot of coffee. She was so completely drained it was only the caffeine running through her veins that was keeping her awake. Normally, that would have meant stopping off en route at Connors' desk to help herself to the DS's personal supply. In the spirit of change, she walked on, had second thoughts and turned back again. Rome wasn't built in a day.

...

Beckwith didn't go home. Instead he went to Venise's apartment and let himself in with the spare keys she'd given him and which he'd never before used. He hadn't wanted to take them, probably because it had seemed too much like a commitment. Too cosy, too his 'n' hers. They'd gone to her favourite restaurant that evening. She'd been so happy, sparklingly pretty, a magnet for every eye, both male and female. Another man would have revelled in the attention. Not him. He'd found it embarrassing and insisted they be shown to a quiet corner. Selfishly, he'd hidden her away, like a flower from sunlight. Beckwith caught himself; he didn't usually think in such Mills & Boon terms. Midway through the meal, she'd produced the key inside a beautifully wrapped gift box, presenting it to him shyly. To his shame, he'd reacted like she'd given him poison, insisting he'd no need of it. He'd behaved like a boor, hurt her with his ungraciousness. He should have manned up, let her go to someone who deserved her. It just never seemed to be the right time to tell her.

He sat down in the cosy leather armchair she'd bought specially for him, after he'd complained about her uncomfortable modernist doll furniture, and thought about that. Her presence was everywhere in the apartment, the scent of her perfume layered lightly on the air. It was a gentle presence, soothing. He looked around the living room, *really* looked around, noticing for probably the first time that while it was undoubtedly feminine, it was also tranquil, chock-full of clues to Venise's real character, the one he'd somehow failed to appreciate. He, like everyone else, was guilty of judging her on a purely superficial level, failing to see beyond her physical attraction to the core of the woman inside. At last, just when it looked like he was about to lose her, he was discovering her true worth. He wandered across to look at her bookshelf and found an eclectic mix, everything from Shakespeare to Harry Potter, as well as a large selection of self-help books. He ran his finger over the spines: Deepak Chopra, Florence Scovel Shinn, Louise L. Hay. He pulled the last one out. *You Can Heal Your Life*. And the one next to it. *Feel the Fear and Do It Anyway*. What had Venise needed to heal? What had she feared? He felt sick at the realisation that now he might never know.

He moved on to her impressive CD collection, suddenly anxious to know more, to somehow connect with her. Again, it was an eclectic collection: pop, rock, bluegrass – that stunned him a little – a whole section dedicated to the classics. She was also a big Vangelis fan. There was a section on meditation, tying in with a little altar on one side of the room where a smug-looking Buddha sat next to an incense burner. He smiled to see that she'd put lipstick on him. On the wall opposite was a picture of Pope Francis – seemed like Venise was hedging her bets. He walked over for a closer look, found she was in the picture too, smiling up at the Holy Father. How come he didn't know she'd been to Rome and met the Pope? How come he didn't know she liked bluegrass and Vangelis, or that she felt in need of help from spiritual gurus? It came as something as a shock to realise that, really, he didn't know her at all. An even bigger shock to realise that, actually, he loved her.

Stunned by the realisation, Beckwith wandered into her bedroom, remembering her habit of sitting cross-legged on the bed while she practised her lines. She'd taken to videoing herself, determined to get everything just right. He picked up the TV remote control and switched it on. When it had warmed up, he selected the video channel and pressed play. In seconds she was before him, pouting wickedly from the screen, her voice a perfect imitation of Marissa Bloom's.

"See, I told you I'd steal your heart."

CHAPTER TWENTY-EIGHT

Careful not to damage the merchandise, Ed Hatcher laid Venise on a silk-covered bed. Film star treatment for the leading lady. Unconscious still, she didn't stir. He gazed down on her, his eyes slewing over every inch of her perfect face and body. His own body, from the top of his head to the soles of his feet, tingled with excitement and pride. Power surged through him like a rip tide. At that moment, he was God. He was the Devil. He was invincible. Untouchable. Creator. Destroyer. He had the whole of the country in his grip. Him! Ed fucking Hatcher, shit-for-brains Hatcher – loser, toerag, the butt of everyone's jokes. He would have creamed himself had he been able.

...

Having left the station in the small hours of the morning, Jessica was back again at seven thirty on the dot. She'd had a maximum of three hours' sleep, much of it disturbed by restless dreams, the product of an overactive brain. It was a relief when the alarm went off. After a quick shower and half a cup of tea, she left the house, almost breaking her neck over yet another gift left on the doorstep by Mr Singh. This time, it was a mosaic elephant. Sighing, she dumped it indoors. Her house was beginning to resemble a bazaar in Calcutta. When she had time, she fully intended taking him to task, not least because everything he left fell into the category of dust-collector, and Jessica did not do dusting. Ever!

She was pleased to find the team already assembled in the incident room, each looking marginally more human since the last time she'd seen them. Before the morning briefing, she decided to set things straight with DS Connors and beckoned her into her office.

"Here," she said, producing a large jar of Nescafé Gold Blend. "I believe I owe you this." She humphed a bit. "I ... er ... might have borrowed some from time to time from your supply."

Connors took it from her. "Thank you," she said. "I had noticed, which is why I took to filling the jar with shit from the pound shop." She winked. "Seems fancy packaging really does work."

Jessica laughed despite herself. "Well, don't go doing the same with this – I might have need of it at some point."

"Was there anything else?" The other woman got ready to go.

"Yes," Jessica said, having decided to follow Hennessy's advice and eat chalk. "An apology. I believe I might have been out of order in my conduct towards you on a number of occasions. I'm sorry about that, Connors. It was both thoughtless and ill-judged. I want you to know it won't happen again." She paused, not wanting to make a production of it, but not wanting to make too little of it either. "You're a good officer and a valued member of the team. And ... well ... that's all."

Connors clutched the jar of coffee to her chest. "Thank you," she said. "Apology accepted."

After she'd left, Jessica's nose felt strangely out of joint, although she was at a complete loss to understand why. She'd made the apology. Connors had accepted it. End of story. So, what had she expected? Something along the lines of, "Oh, no need for an apology, guv. I know I'm a pain in the arse. And you're perfectly right, I would trample over your dead body to get to your job." Bugger! It was no good. She'd never like the woman. Only consolation was, she too had filled the coffee jar with cheap shit from the pound shop and made an excellent job of both removing and gluing back the seal. Connors could stick that on her needles and knit it!

...

The incident room was like an explosion in Santa's grotto, piled high with stuff taken from Hatcher's house, which the team was busy examining and recording. Forensics had already confirmed the hair extensions and the business cards as a match to those found on the bodies of the victims. A thorough sweep of the house also confirmed that it was not the kill site, and no evidence had been recovered placing any of the girls at the property.

"Christ, look at this!" DC Liversedge called out. "It's Tutankhamun's underpants. Hatcher obviously wasn't big on his smalls." Jessica joined the team in laughing. Sedgie had a real knack for cheering them up. Factor in his good looks and was it any wonder he had women throwing themselves at his feet? He topped his own joke, bringing a fresh round of laughter. "I bet he had a Phaorah'll time in these."

The smile was abruptly knocked off all their faces as DCI Beckwith appeared at the door.

"Come into my office, sir," Jessica said, hastily pushing a large cardboard box out of the way. She nodded to the team. "Can someone fetch us some coffee, please? Hot and strong." As her office was a glass goldfish bowl, she pulled down the privacy blinds on all sides. She waited till Beckwith sat down and took the chair opposite. Close up, he looked like death. There was desperation in his eyes. He was tense as a tightly coiled spring. Jessica had the sense that if he knew where to go, he'd have bolted already. An old saying of Churchill's, much quoted by her father, popped into her head. *If you're going through hell, keep going.* Thank God, she'd more sense than to say it out loud.

"Where is she?" he asked at last. "Where has the bastard taken her?"

Jessica was about to trot out the 'we're doing everything in our power' spiel, but checked herself.

"I wish we knew," she said. She nodded thanks as DC Liversedge came in with the coffee, waited till he'd left again. "As yet, we've had no feedback from any of our units."

"What about the press? The TV?" He gripped his mug tightly. Even so, Jessica detected a tremor in his fingers, barely perceptible, but there nonetheless.

"All notified now," Jessica said. "His photograph and description has been circulated all over. Someone is bound to know where he is." She checked her watch. "I'm holding a press conference at Scotland Yard in an hour."

Both of them knew it was a gamble going high-profile. There was always a chance that it might spur Hatcher into killing Venise sooner than he'd intended. He put his mug down, the pulse beating so hard in his temple it looked like it might explode.

"I want her back, Wideacre," he said simply.

It had long been a dream of Jessica's to see her old adversary brought to his knees, knocked off his perch and humbled; there was a time when she would have taken pleasure in the sight. Today wasn't that day. She nodded. "Stay here and finish your coffee. I'd better get back to the team."

...

For once, the journos put aside any grievances with the police and united in the common cause of tracking down Ed Hatcher. Jessica hadn't realised how popular the young actress was. Normally, the great British public liked nothing better than to build someone up to monumental proportions, before whisking the rug from beneath their feet. Surprisingly, the social media trolls, normally out in force, kept a low profile too. As Jessica left the podium, she'd even spotted a hardened hack, a woman who made Janet Street-Porter look like Mother Teresa, dab away a tear. And not a crocodile in sight.

As she pulled into the car park after the press conference, she was surprised to see Laura Shackleton emerge from a swish-looking Mazda MX5 convertible.

"Nice motor," Jessica said, walking round it admiringly. Secretly, she thought it a bit of a shame she'd no longer get a laugh seeing the petite woman Tarzan it out of her gigantic 4 x 4.

"Mid-life crisis," Laura said. "It's supposed to be a babe magnet. No one told me Babe was a pig," she chuckled. "You couldn't fit a condom in the boot. I must be crazy."

"I like it," Jessica said. "It's a munchkin car."

"Fuck off," Laura said, good naturedly punching her on the arm. "Got time for a coffee? I've got a meeting with Bilious later. I need fortification." Bilious was Superintendent Green's nickname.

"Got to be a quick one," she said. "And if you've a couple of matchsticks I could prop my eyelids open with, I'd like to borrow those too."

Her companion shot her an old-fashioned look. "Are you playing the sympathy card, DI Wideacre? If so, you should know that, just as you don't do bullshit, I don't do hand-holding, unless it's with Brad Pitt. Wise up, you dozy mare. You knew what you were signing up for, now get on with it."

Curiously enough, it was the shot in the arm Jessica needed. She'd begun to flag, to feel a bit sorry for herself. There would be time enough for that when Venise Love-Davies was found, hopefully alive and kicking.

Jessica grabbed a couple of plastic trays and slid them along the cafeteria rails. "Just a coffee," she said to the woman behind the counter. "Strong, black, thick enough to pave the drive with."

...

She was just gulping back the last of her drink when she saw Sergeant Hennessy come in and cast around. He caught her eye and hurried over.

"Been a bit of a breakthrough, guv. Businessman just arrived back from abroad to find his car missing from Gatwick Airport. It's a black BMW. Same model as the one our witness saw outside Venise Love-Davies' place." He could hardly contain his own excitement. "And, guess what, it's fitted with a tracker."

Jessica's heart leapt with hope. "Jesus God," she exclaimed, "Does DCI Beckwith know?"

Hennessy shook his head. "He seems to have disappeared, guv. We've tried phoning him. Nothing."

Jessica banged her cup down and leapt to her feet. "Well, come on, then. Now's not the time to stand around scratching your balls. We need all hands to the deck, chopper in the air, firearms officers, everyone who's anyone."

Laura finished her own coffee hastily, grabbed a half-eaten doughnut in one hand and her jacket in the other. "God forbid you'll have need of my services, but I'm coming too. And, Bilious can go fuck himself."

Jessica hesitated briefly. Laura's services were only ever required when the worst had come to the worst and the urgency was past. "Sorry," she said. "Procedure and all that. Keep 'em crossed we don't have to call you." Within seconds she and Hennessy, despite his sixtieth birthday now being only days away, were sprinting for the car park.

...

The noise of a car drawing up outside brought Ed to the window. He ducked to one side and peered cautiously round the edge. It wouldn't do for the plods to come storming in at the eleventh hour. He relaxed when he saw Jack Kingsman get out. A fresh wave of adrenaline coursed through him. He was alive like never before, felt like he could walk on fuckin' water, jump from the top of the fuckin' Shard and soar like fuckin' Superman high above London. Him *and* the boss. They were a dream team. A match made in heaven. He grinned. Or hell. Nothing they couldn't do. No one they couldn't sort. Absolutely *no one*!

He heard the door slam downstairs and Jack's footsteps begin to ascend the stairs. He walked back to Venise, put his hand down her top and squeezed her breast. "Now, remember," he said. "Big smile for the camera." Oblivious, she slept on.

...

DCI Beckwith was in a store room going through boxes of Hatcher's possessions, on the off-chance that someone might have missed something. He owed it to Venise to check and double-check. So far there'd been nothing to get his hopes up; most of it was old tat, the sort the local tip would turn its nose up at. He pushed one box away and pulled out another, this one full of odds and sods of electrical equipment, most of it antiquated. Nevertheless, he couldn't rest until he examined each and every piece. He had no idea what he was looking for. He was merely going by the usual copper's instinct that if there was something worth finding, he'd know it when he saw it. At the very bottom of the box, he found a BT answering machine. It was a fairly new model, the buttons ingrained with dirt. Beckwith wondered if anyone on the team had bothered to check it for messages. Probably not, since it was missing its phone jack. He put it to one side and continued searching. None of the other boxes yielded anything remotely interesting. His thoughts returned to the answering machine. Assuming it wasn't smashed, all it needed to make it work was a bog-standard ADSL cable. He picked it up and took it back to his office.

···

Venise surfaced slowly. Her head was pounding, her eyes sticky and her tongue felt three sizes too big for her mouth. For a moment she thought she was back in her own apartment, but when she tried to move, she found she couldn't. She thrashed her head to and fro, trying to discover her whereabouts, and found herself gazing straight into the lens of a film camera that had been positioned close to her feet. She had a brief moment of confusion, wondering if her mind was playing tricks on her – if she was, after all, on set at the studios. But there were no scenes where her wrists and ankles were bound, and her surroundings were unfamiliar. She forced herself to take a deep breath and discovered she was lying on a dimly-lit four-poster bed. Her head began to clear slightly, panic taking the place of her muddled thoughts, as the events of the previous day came flashing back in a series of cameos:

the police invading the studios and carting Kingsman away; her interview with DI Wideacre; getting into the car with Kingsman's props man. Jesus! What had possessed her? The man scared the crap out of her. She'd seen him several times on set, glaring at her like he hated her. She'd complained once to Jack, told him he gave her the willies. He'd told her not to be so fucking precious, that the world didn't revolve around her. She remembered the clamminess of the cloth, the stink of it pressed against her face, how she couldn't breathe, and found herself struggling for breath again as the enormity of her situation sank in. Her eyes flew to the camera. The red light had come on. Someone was watching her, but, deep in shadow, she couldn't see who. It freaked her out.

"Fuck you," she screamed into the lens. "Let me go. I didn't do anything."

Behind the camera, Hatcher was enjoying the spectacle of the Love-Davies bint rolling around, flapping like a wet fish. He liked the analogy, thought how clever he was to have *hooked* her, landed her in hot *water*. He thought he might share them with the boss. They enjoyed a bit of witty banter. He'd *batter*, *fillet* and *gut* her. They'd have a *whale* of a time. For someone who hadn't gone past primary school level, he prided himself on his way with words. It just came natural. Like killing. Although, if it hadn't been for the boss, he might never have realised his potential. He grinned. Imagine if poisoning that blind woman's dog had been the highlight of his career? How fucking pathetic would that have been?

Before the real fun could begin, however, there was one last bit of business the boss needed taking care of. Reluctantly, he rose and stepped away from the camera. As his mother, the selfish bitch, used to say, you couldn't have all play and no work. Not that she'd have known work if it had jumped up and bit her on her fat arse. He opened a drawer and gazed admiringly at his collection of neatly lined-up playthings. First in the queue was a hunting knife with a sawback blade. He'd wanted one of those ever since he saw Rambo use it in *First Blood*. Next in line was a stylish stiletto; in *Chinatown*, someone used one to give Jack Nicholson a third nostril. Third one in was a nifty little German lockback with a wicked blade. He'd had some fun with that. He settled on the Bowie; he'd bought it off eBay from some scammer pretending that it was the same one used by Crocodile Dundee. Like he believed that bullshit. He bought it anyway. He returned for one last look at Venise Love-Davies – aw, she was crying – and switched off the camera. Later, he'd decide which to use on her. Maybe a selection. He'd recently added a cattle prod to his collection. He might even premiere it at the premiere of her movie – the one she hadn't intended to make. He left, humming "Blurred Lines". Fucking great lyrics. They summed up perfectly how he thought of "his" girls – animals in need of domestication. Hey! Hey! Hey!

...

Beckwith swore loudly when he realised his mobile battery had died and that no one could find him. He should have been with Wideacre. *She* should have looked harder. He cursed again, this time at his own unreasonableness. Time was of the essence. He'd never forgive himself if they got there too late to save Venise and he had been the cause of the delay. He called for a squad car and was told it would take a while; most were in Wideacre's convoy. His own was in for a service and there wasn't even a poxy cab to be had for more than half an hour. Short of throwing a tantrum and jumping up and down, there was nothing he could do but wait. Deciding to use the time profitably, he took the answering machine to the IT department. In no time they'd fitted an ADSL cable and plugged it in. In another five, they'd recovered several messages, but they were too garbled to be able to make out much of anything. Beckwith was on tenterhooks, his nose twitching like a bloodhound. He watched impatiently as the IT guy did some jiggery-pokery with a voice enhancement programme. Using a series of digital controls, he faded out the background noise and enhanced the speech. The result wasn't perfect, not crystal clear, but it was good enough for Mark to make out the messages. The same message every time. The same voice speaking. *"Please pick up and deliver another parcel"* The messages might have come from Kingsman's studios. They might have related to his work there. Beckwith had a strong feeling they didn't. He asked the techie to replay them. He closed his eyes, concentrating on every syllable of every word.

...

The GPS signal had tracked the BMW to an address on the borders of Sutton and Carshalton. Further enquiries revealed it to be a property belonging to Jack Kingsman, bought years before and registered in the name of Lorelei Turner. Jessica was kicking herself. The slimy toad! Her instincts had told her he was hiding something; she should have leaned on him harder.

"Don't blame yourself, guv," Hennessy said, deftly manoeuvring the car, siren blaring, lights flashing, through a red light. "You couldn't have known Hatcher and he were in it together. Especially when Hatcher fitted the bill so perfectly."

"No. No, he didn't," Jessica said. "Hatcher is a thug. You could easily imagine him jumping up and down on somebody's head. But the finesse aspect – the business cards, the make-up, the hair extensions, the careful posing of the bodies – that all points to a different kind of character. I messed up, Hennessy. We had him and we let him go. Jesus wept, he even told us who he was. Short of drawing a map and handcuffing himself, he couldn't have made it clearer." She drummed her fist on the dashboard. "The Director. It was exactly what it said on the tin!"

Perhaps sensing it would do no good, Hennessy said no more. Instead, he concentrated on negotiating the heavy London traffic as quickly as possible, never hesitating to give the finger when someone didn't move out of the way quickly enough. They were at the head of a long convoy of police vehicles, marked and unmarked police cars, vans, armed response vehicles, even motorbikes. The chopper was already hovering overhead. Jessica was vaguely aware of astonished faces flashing by, camera phones held up recording the motorcade. Only a deaf, blind and dumb hermit living up a mountain in Nepal wouldn't have known that something big was going down. Chances were, they thought it was something to do with terrorists. When in doubt, conjure up an Islamic terrorist plot.

The house, a sprawling Victorian mansion that had known better days, stood at the end of a long, overgrown, twisty drive, well away from any neighbours. All sirens were turned off on the approach. Everyone was wearing body armour, no knowing what they'd find. The AFOs, naturally, were armed to the teeth. The convoy of vehicles stopped out of sight of the house and the occupants proceeded on foot. A scout, who had been sent on ahead, returned to report the absence of any CCTV cameras. He also reported the presence of both the black BMW and Kingsman's Jag parked outside the house.

The chopper hovered a discreet distance away as, quietly, the officers threw a ring of steel around the building. The plan was to take Kingsman and Hatcher by surprise. Jessica prayed to God it wasn't all too late for Venise Love-Davies. Insisting on being at the forefront of the operation, she led the way to the front door, zigzagging deftly between bushes and trees and dashing madly across the expanse of gravelled driveway and up a short flight of steps to the front door. Her nerves were stretched as she tried the knob. Her heart pounded. She could hear the blood whizzing through her veins, was aware of every muscle, every pulse, every sinew. She was also achingly aware that these could be her last few seconds on earth; that she might never again see David, feel his arms around her or get to tell him she loved him and that she had made up her mind to chuck the job in and follow him to the States. To the moon, if need be. The knob turned. She pushed lightly. Nothing. She tried again, harder this time, meeting resistance till with an audible groan that sent her heart into overdrive, the door gave way opening into a dark, dank-smelling hallway. Jessica turned quickly and gave the thumbs up to the team. They were in!

...

Hatcher congratulated himself that the stage was all set and the arc lights positioned so as to get the best view of Venise Love-Davies, looking more like Marissa Bloom than ever, albeit a terrified version, lying on the four-poster bed. Her wrists and ankles were bound with silver ropes – a nice twist that, he thought. Her blonde hair was fanned out across a lace-edged pillow, her beautiful eyes wide with fear. Her creamy bosom peeked over the top of her low-cut dress. No replica this, but the exact dress Marissa Bloom had worn to the premiere of *Killer Queen*. A Dior number, which, he was reliably informed, cost as much as a brand new family car. He wondered if she was aware just how privileged she was. He examined the array of instruments he'd laid out with surgical precision on a small table. Shame he was going to have to spoil the dress, to tear it off her. To bloody it all up. Very hard to get out, bloodstains. Blood was a protein. It cooked in hot water. He didn't know how he knew that. He just did. Still, orders was orders.

His gaze went to a pile of CDs, each one labelled with a girl's name. He had another flash of wit, a song in his head. "To All the Girls I've Killed Before". He might sing it as a prelude to the film show he'd planned for the Old Bill later. Every hour, on the hour, he would upload a film to YouTube, starting with Melanie Potts and ending ten hours later, *ta-dah*, with Venise Love-Davies. The final frame would show him, Hitchcock cameo style, inviting the cops to come and get him. His audacity would go down in history. Let the fucking games begin!

He heard a noise as the boss came to stand behind him and almost pissed himself when he saw Venise's eyes fly to the spot over his shoulder. How was it possible for anyone's eyeballs to bulge so much and not drop out? She looked like she'd seen a fucking ghost. He could see her mouth moving under the masking tape, trying to working up to a scream, but nothing was coming out. It was downright comical. Mockingly, he tipped his head to one side. "You wasn't expecting the boss, was you? You thought it was just you and me. Sorry about that, but this is a joint operation." He sniggered. "That's to say *you* are a joint operation." He ran his fingers along the array of knives. "Eeny, meeny, miny, moe ... This one, I think." He picked up the wicked-bladed stiletto. "Let's start with a third nostril, see how that improves your looks." He turned briefly and grinned at the boss, who was now holding up a clapperboard. Lights, camera, action. And get ready, get set, go! Ed Hatcher took a deep breath and moved to the head of the bed. He was about to give the performance of his life.

CHAPTER TWENTY-NINE

Silent as a panther, Jessica, followed by several armed policemen, crept inside the door of the makeshift film studio. The room was dark, except for an area at the far end where a four-poster bed stood, ringed about by arc lights. In a fraction of a second she saw all she needed to: Venise Love-Davies gagged and tied to the bed, and two figures, one, recognisably Ed Hatcher, the other deep in shadow, positioned behind an old-fashioned film camera. There was music playing. A haunting instrumental. The theme music from *Killer Queen*. Almost in slow-mo, she watched Hatcher's arm angle upwards, a knife in his hand flashing silver, the blade glinting wickedly in the light. She froze, but only for a split second, then surrounded by her armed colleagues, she was hurtling across the room.

"Police! Stop where you are, both of you!" she yelled, as someone swiftly disarmed Hatcher, knocking him to the ground, and someone else threw on the main lights. "This film is in the fucking can." Her eyes flew to the figure behind the camera. It was dressed in the Tudor costume she'd last seen Venise Love-Davies wearing on the set of *Killer Queen* and, bizarrely, a Snow White mask. She took a step forward. "Bit tight around the bosom, Kingsman," she said mockingly. "The mask is a nice touch, though. But then you're an expert at hiding your true self from the world."

"Cuff him," she ordered, but, before the order could be carried out she found herself knocked to one side as DCI Beckwith barrelled past her. Jessica didn't blame him one bit. He could have beaten seven shades out of the murdering bastard and no one would have *seen* a damn thing. Instead, he ripped off the figure's Snow White mask revealing a face so hideous, so deformed that Jessica jumped back involuntarily."

"Christ," she said, when she could finally speak. "Is that ... is that who I think ..."

"Marissa Bloom," DCI Beckwith confirmed. "Alive and kicking."

Jessica was so shocked she could barely speak. She could hear her own shock echoed and amplified around the room, followed by a great outburst of excited voices.

"Marissa Bloom," Jessica repeated, awestruck by the turn of events. "*You're* The Director?"

"I am," the woman admitted, her wonderfully distinctive voice all too recognisable. Not so her face, which was a stomach-churning mass of burnt and scarred tissue. One eye socket was completely empty. Her lips had burned away completely on one side, leaving her mouth twisted into a permanent snarl. Of her remaining teeth, several were broken and blackened. Her scalp was a corrugated, lumpy mess with just a few strands of wispy grey hair strewn randomly about, some of which trailed almost to her waist. Defiant, imperious, she fixed her good eye on Jessica who, despite herself, felt a fleeting moment of pity for the once beautiful, now grotesque, actress. Very fleeting.

The woman appeared to gather herself then, to ready herself for one final performance. Her head came up, queenly. She smiled her awful rictus smile, bowed to the room, and reprised her most famous line, altering it to suit the occasion.

"See, I told you I'd steal their hearts!"

...

"How did you know?" she asked DCI Beckwith when he returned to Rosewood later, having left his shocked, but otherwise unharmed, girlfriend safely in the care of her family. He told her about the answering machine and the messages left on it.

"I'd heard that voice a million times," he said. "Grew sick of it, to tell you the truth. Venise played Marissa Bloom's videos over and over again, struggling to get the intonation exactly right. Since the answering machine wasn't that old, I reckoned she must still be alive and that the packages referred to was very likely code for the victims."

"I really thought it was Kingsman," Jessica said. "I was convinced he was hiding something."

"He was," Beckwith said. "He was hiding the fact that Marissa was still alive. The only person he could trust to keep the secret was Marissa's loyal and faithful admirer, Ed Hatcher. He paid Hatcher to look after her, keep her company, fetch and carry and be general dogsbody to her, which he was only too happy to do." They were silent for a moment, both digesting the events of the day and turning them over in their minds. "We'll know more later, when we can talk to him," Beckwith said, eventually.

"*If* he lives," Jessica said, referring to the fact that Kingsman had been found in a pool of blood in the trunk of his car. He had been stabbed several times.

"If he lives," Beckwith agreed.

...

Against all odds, Jack Kingsman survived Hatcher's violent knife attack. He was weak, but conscious and willing to talk when

Jessica, accompanied by DCI Beckwith showed up at the hospital with a whole raft of questions.

"Start from the beginning," Jessica said, getting straight to the point. She had no intention of indulging in the niceties. "Tell us about Marissa. Why keep up the pretence that she had died?"

"She did," Kingsman said quietly. "To all intents and purposes. My wife was a very beautiful woman, DI Wideacre, and hugely vain with it. She couldn't bear that anyone should see her reduced to a monster. So she hit on the plan of faking her funeral and going into hiding. I acquiesced, as I did to all her wishes. I bought her a property and entrusted her care to Ed Hatcher. I visited her occasionally, but probably not as often as I should have. It was … it was upsetting."

"Did you know about the killings?" DCI Beckwith asked. Now that Venise was safe and recuperating at home, he had begun to look more like his old self. Jessica wasn't quite sure if that was a good or a bad thing.

"Christ, no!" he said. "I realised all too late that I had made a serious error when I decided to remake *Killer Queen*, but I'd no idea what I'd sparked." His eyes slid away. "Marissa had started threatening me. She could have ruined me."

"Threatening you, how?" Jessica asked.

"She wanted me to bin the movie. She threatened to come out of hiding and reveal to the world that she hadn't died." Again, his eyes slewed away. "I couldn't let her do that."

"Because you'd collected on her life policy," Jessica said. "We checked already. Fifteen million. I'm guessing when you started receiving the anonymous notes, you thought someone else had discovered your secret. No wonder you were relieved to find they were the work of your lovesick housekeeper."

"I tried to kill the movie," Jack Kingsman said, "like she wanted, but it wasn't that easy. A lot of people had invested heavily in it." He shot an apologetic look at DCI Beckwith. "I'm afraid I gave Venise rather a hard time. She didn't deserve it. But I somehow thought if I could force the leading lady out, the rest would simply crumble."

"And she'd take the rap," Beckwith said. "Not very chivalrous."

"Not my finest hour," Kingsman admitted.

"Get to the killings," Jessica snapped. Even his close brush with death didn't make her dislike him any less. "When did you become aware Marissa was involved?"

"Not till after I'd seen you. All that evidence you put on the table, the photographs of those young girls and the case against Hatcher." He shrugged. "At first, I didn't want to believe it. Then, when you told me Venise had been taken—"

"You still didn't say anything," DCI Kingsman accused. "Venise could have died."

Kingsman looked genuinely upset. Nervously, his fingers pleated the sheet over his chest. "I … I had some idea that if I just saw Marissa, that I could stop her and Hatcher. That I could rescue Venise. That's why I went to the house." His voice dropped almost to a whisper. They had to strain to hear him. "I'm afraid I had no idea that Marissa had become so completely deranged." He pointed to his bandages. "She ordered Hatcher to do this. Imagine that. She ordered him to kill me. Take care of business, is how she put it. Sweet God in Heaven, it's a miracle I survived."

Jessica pushed her chair back. She'd heard enough. "You

might wish he had killed you, Mr Kingsman," she said. "By the time the police, the press, the insurance companies, your movie luvvies and the world and his wife have done with you." She threw a last glance of contempt at Kingsman and turned away. "If you're ready, sir," she said to DCI Beckwith, "Let's get out of here before I kill him myself."

In the incident room, Jessica was fitting the last pieces of the jigsaw together. The team, and several others totally unconnected with the investigation, listened, riveted. Amongst them, sitting almost humbly was the profiler, Robert Edwards. Presumably he was there to listen and learn and, maybe next time, get it right. As for the rest, this was likely the biggest case most of them would come up against in the whole of their lives. And what a case; it had all the elements of a Shakespearian play.

"Basically, it all comes down to jealousy – the green-eyed monster hooking up with a psychopath." Jessica said. "Kingsman's plan to remake *Killer Queen* was the trigger. Her starring role as Lorelei Turner was the only thing that Marissa Bloom had left. The thought of another beautiful, unblemished young woman – Venise Love-Davies – 'stealing' that role and winning *her* accolades flipped her into full-on insanity. Every beautiful young woman bearing a resemblance to herself became a target. She, herself, was first 'discovered' at age fifteen, hence the age range. She wanted to take from them what had been taken from her – their beauty, their hopes, their dreams, and ultimately their lives. She wanted to destroy them, just as she had been destroyed. In her sick, twisted mind, they came to represent her; hence the hair extensions and make-up.

"To aid her in her sick fantasies, she recruited Hatcher, an easy task considering he was already her willing slave and came fully equipped with a psychopath button. She needed only to switch it on. She was The Director, but he had artistic licence and, as we know, he exercised his creativity to the max." Everyone was silent a moment, thinking of the nine young victims – ten, including Stacey Herbert – who had met their death at the hands of the evil pair. Their photographs were on the whiteboard still, gazing down, young and innocent, captured for ever at their very best.

"Venise Love-Davies was to be the final target," Jessica said. "Once she was removed from the scene, Marissa's crown as Lorelei Turner would remain intact and her place in movie history would be forever assured."

"But wouldn't Hatcher have just gone on killing?" DS Connors asked. "Most psychopaths are like vampires. Once they get a taste for blood …"

"True," Jessica said. "But Hatcher is also a fame junkie. His ambition was to be the most famous serial killer in the world. Ever! He and Marissa Bloom had made a pact. Once they'd killed Venise Love-Davies, she would simply fade back into the ether and he would come out as The Director."

"He got part of his wish," DCI Beckwith said sourly. "No one is ever likely to forget who he is."

"He'll get life in prison," Jessica said. "No chance of ever getting out. If she's found insane, as I suspect will happen, Marissa Bloom is looking at spending the rest of her life in a nut house – Broadmoor, or some such. I'm sure she'll be horrified to know that her role as Lorelei Turner will not be the one for which she's best remembered after all."

"I wonder when we'll see the Hollywood movie version," Sergeant Hennessy said, playing with a rollie, twiddling it between his fingers. "I wonder who'll play you, guv."

Connors batted her eyelashes. "Jennifer Lawrence can play me."

Everyone grinned, even Jessica. "If you say so, Connors." She gestured round the room at the boxes of files and papers. "We'll make a start on clearing all this tomorrow and sorting out the stuff for the CPS." She walked over to the whiteboard and began to take down the photos of the girls. Gently, she laid them to one side, thankful that she had fulfilled the promise she had made to find their killer. They and their families would get justice and know peace. Finally.

"Who's for the pub?" DC Liversedge asked.

DCI Beckwith excused himself. They understood he wanted to get back to Venise as soon as possible. Rumours were already rife of a possible engagement. Jessica wished them well. Though she hadn't entirely forgiven him for trying to scupper her promotion, kicking his head in was no longer at the top of her bucket list.

Jessica also excused herself, despite the team pleading with her to change her mind. More than anything she wanted to get home to phone David. She was longing to hear his voice, longing to tell him that she had made her decision and that he'd better start house-hunting in New York.

...

Mr Singh had left yet another gift on her doorstep. This time, it was a bottle of champagne. Good stuff, too. At last, something she could actually use. She looked over and saw his living-room curtains twitch. Jessica grinned and raised the bottle in a toast. "Cheers," she mouthed. "And tell your mother, I said, welcome to England."